The *Storm* over Paris

A Novel by
William Ian Grubman

The *Storm* over Paris

Dupapier Press

Publisher's Note: This is a work of fiction. Names, characters, places, and incidents are a product of the author's imagination. Locales and public names are sometimes used for atmospheric purposes. Any resemblance to actual people, living or dead, or to businesses, companies, events, institutions, or locales is completely coincidental.

ISBN: 978-1-7326100-0-2

For Mathew and Emily

Although The *Storm* over Paris is a work of fiction, the majority of the artwork referenced is real as are many of the minor characters who interact with well-known historical figures.

PROLOGUE

January 22, 2000, New York City

I tie the bow tightly at my collar. Its grip reminds me of a hangman's noose. I should be sweating for what I'm about to do, but I feel surprisingly calm.

I stand facing the mirror in my dressing room. The four small diamond studs that dot the front of my starched tux shirt glint in the light, as do their larger brothers adorning my cuffs. I comb back my hair, then touch the grey at my temples, which seems to have appeared overnight. Although my smile lines have deepened and crow's feet are etched at the corners of my eyes from years of looking closely at paintings, one might call my look rugged, perhaps even dashing. The face still looks good for a man in his late fifties. My father always said, "Life is like a painting. The depth of the image is made on the surface, so pay attention to your image and what you show the world."

I hear Claire in the next room, fielding another congratulatory call about this evening's celebration. In New York society, museum openings are attended by the city's rich, the powerful, and, of course, the media—the last a smattering of social reporters who hang on every word uttered by the first two groups. Tonight will be yet another fundraising opportunity for the museum; we've been to many such events. This one, however, will be special for us because Claire and I are the honorees.

Claire calls to me through the open door of her dressing room which is adjacent to mine. "Porter, I need some help."

This is part of what makes the two of us close, needing each other even for the smallest things.

"I can't fasten my necklace," she says.

Claire could easily fasten her own necklace. Instead, she calls on me to handle the task. It's all part of the romance.

Claire appears in the doorway, as slender and beautiful as the day we met in grad school, then moves regally across the room. "Here," she says, holding the diamond and sapphire collar, for which I traded a lovely Renoir.

As always, I oblige. I gently grasp the clasp and slide the two ends into place. I smell her Arpège and drift for a moment to the streets of Paris, where I first purchased the scent for her. "There you go," I say, slipping in a kiss on her neck.

The glow of light behind her makes her look like an apparition. She wears a dark blue ball gown, made for this evening's festivities. Her blond hair has been arranged in a chignon, and I notice three jeweled butterflies in her updo.

She glances at herself in my mirror and turns to give me a quick kiss on the cheek. "Porter, let's go. We don't want to be late."

"It can't start without us. Besides we live across the street."

Perfectly framed by my dressing room window is the view of the Metropolitan Museum of Art. The silk drapes are drawn back, allowing light from the full moon to cast a glow on the dressing room carpet. I momentarily dim the crystal sconces for a better view of the museum's columns, which have been swathed in burgundy fabric for the evening's event. They stand tall and majestic like sentries guarding the treasures within. Long banners that sway slowly with the changing wind patterns herald the opening of the Roth Collection.

My great-grandfather, Meyer Rothstein, was an art dealer in Paris during La Belle Époque. His business became the family business, and it was continued by my grandfather Maurice, known as Mori to friends, then by my father, and now by me. Most major art openings garner some attention, but this one is a coup for the museum's director, Jeffrey Bell. The centerpiece of my two-year, forty-painting loan to their Masters Collection is a treasure that has New York's elite talking—a permanent loan of Caravaggio's *The Expulsion of Hagar*, a masterwork with breathless detail and eye appeal.

Unfortunately for them, the painting is a forgery.

1

Thursday, April 9, 1942, Paris

As he did every morning, Mori Rothstein descended the front steps of his well-appointed home just off Avenue Montaigne at 7:30 sharp. Dressed in a well-tailored, pinstripe suit, with the early edition of *Le Petit Parisien* tucked under his arm, he headed to the foot path on the Champs-Élysées. He enjoyed the daily walk to his art gallery in the quiet hours before the city was fully awake. Today, however, that small pleasure was threatened. He didn't have to look over his shoulder more than once to know that the two men in brown raincoats, whom he'd spotted across the street from his home, were now walking a short distance behind him. The hairs on the nape of his neck stood on end, and he listened intently for their footfalls on the pavement. Since the Germans had taken control of the city, Mori trusted no one. He was not alone; fear shadowed the thoughts of most Parisians since the Nazis had overtaken the city.

The previous night's rain had dampened the ground, forcing Mori to dodge puddles on the gravel pathway beneath the blooming horse-chestnut trees. Trim and erect, he moved quickly for a man in his fifties. The wind kicked up, sending pink blossoms swirling, petals alighting in the muddied street beneath the wheels of cars, taxis, and German army transport trucks filled with soldiers.

Mori increased his speed; the men following him did the same. It would be foolish to run, he thought. He had reached the Place de la Concorde with its neoclassical fountains and the grand obelisk that had once stood at the entrance to the Luxor Temple in Egypt. Traffic rumbled up and down the wide boulevard, filling Mori's nostrils with auto exhaust. He strode past the grand Hôtel de Crillon, its splendor unmarred by its current use as the headquarters of the German High Command. Guards stood at the entrance doors as well as atop the roof. The ubiquitous Nazi presence, with its air of superiority and arrogance, littered the city.

When Mori paused to watch the activity surrounding the Jeu de Paume Museum, the two men shadowing him crossed the street. The tan granite building at the north corner of the Tuileries Gardens, which had been commissioned by Napoleon III, had originally housed tennis courts. Now it was one of many city museums. Today Nazi soldiers surrounded the structure. There appeared to be a great deal of activity within that human barricade. Why all the trucks and soldiers? Mori rubbed his thumb and index finger together, a nervous habit.

He veered onto Rue Royale, and—in a small, private act of defiance in the face of Nazi occupation—he allowed the beauty of his city to delight him. This lasted only a moment before he spotted the two men turning the same corner, still following a distance behind him. He picked up his pace, moving past once-fine shops, most now without merchandise. He turned left onto Rue du Faubourg Saint-Honoré, stopping at number 23, just across the street from Hermès.

"MEYER ROTHSTEIN" was painted in gold on the paned windows at the front of the art gallery. Mori touched the letters, a ritual that had sprung up following his father's death. I'm glad you don't have to see what the Nazis are doing to the world, Papa.

Meyer Rothstein had represented an assortment of aspiring

artists when his sale of Monet's *Terrasse à Sainte-Adresse* in 1867 had brought him to the forefront of Paris society. Later that same year he'd represented the sale of *Les Régates à Sainte-Adresse* and *La Plage de Sainte-Adresse*, also by Monet. The three paintings had sealed his prominence in the Paris art world and attracted customers to his gallery. His keen eye and knowledge of art history gave him the credentials for entrée into the inner circles of Paris's bel monde, including that of Moïse de Camondo, and Nathan Rothschild, who regularly visited Meyer's gallery and relied on his guidance for acquisitions to the Rothschild collection. His acquisitions included works by Fragonard, Rembrandt, and Joshua Reynolds.

When Mori had come of age, he followed in his father's footsteps, but his first years were filled with self-doubt. Although educated at the École des Beaux-Arts, he often questioned his decisions. Would they meet his father's approval and keen eye?

He eventually created his own specialty—the authentication and appraisal of rare fifteenth-, sixteenth-, and seventeenth-century canvases. Time honed his expertise and bolstered his confidence. While early masters were his passion, changing trends pushed Mori to develop a sharp eye on the current art scene, as well.

While dining at a wealthy patron's home one evening, Mori was shown their newest acquisition, Picasso's *La Vie, 1903*.

"So, what do you think?" his host asked proudly.

Mori examined the large canvas, painted during the master's Blue Period, moving close to the figures of the nude couple who gazed at an infant child. "It's remarkable," Mori said, though his words were measured. "Where did you get it?"

"Rosenberg."

Mori's eye alighted on the male figure's arm. There was no question; he knew it in his gut. The outline was not bold enough for Picasso.

Mori gently declared the canvas a forgery. To the chagrin

and embarrassment of Paul Rosenberg, one of Mori's contemporaries and a well-known and respected Parisian art dealer who'd represented the painting, the declaration proved correct.

In Rosenberg's defense, it was an assistant who had placed the copy among available works and sold the canvas as an original. This did not fare well for Rosenberg, who refunded the purchase, lost the client, and immediately terminated the assistant.

Now, years later, Mori was sought out by every major museum in France, Great Britain, and America for his keen eye and vast expertise in art history and appraisal. With the Louvre in Paris, the Tate and National galleries in London, and the Metropolitan in New York, Mori held sway over his counterparts. When the Louvre decided to change the painting displays surrounding the Mona Lisa, Mori advised on the proper order of the other canvases to be hung nearby.

He was respected and admired for his ability to understand the art market, and for his mastery at selecting important artists and their work.

Mori pulled a small ring of keys from his vest pocket. The keys captured the morning sun and cast a fleeting flicker on the door. Before he could turn the lock, he heard a man's voice. "Vis maxda?" What's new?

Mori spun around to see his friend Albert, the owner of the café across the street, standing at his elbow. "You startled me." Mori said.

"I didn't mean to scare you," Albert replied.

Mori glanced around the street. The two men who had been following him were nowhere to be seen.

In his mid-forties with thinning brown hair, Albert stood with stooped shoulders, the result of years of lifting crates of sugar and flour. "Hannah and the girls are leaving Paris." Angst resonated in his voice.

"This is sudden."

"The papers arrived this morning. My wife's health is poor. Travel was approved for her, Blanche and Estell, but not me. They have passage to England, but from there, who knows?"

"What about you?" Mori asked.

"I don't know." Albert shrugged. "Maybe soon, but there's no guarantee."

"When do they leave?"

"Tomorrow."

"I'll pray for their safe journey," Mori said. The aroma of café au lait and fresh baguette wafted across the street. "What about the café?"

Albert blew out a breath, "I'd sell it for half its worth. It's not large, but it never lacks customers." A man and woman sat down at one of the sidewalk tables. "I must get back to work." He nodded to Mori then crossed the street.

The very rich had left Paris before Hitler had arrived, when the Fascists had been climbing to power in Eastern Europe. They'd been smart to escape; Mori already had heard of Jews being taken from their homes, disappearing during the night.

How disappointed Mori felt. No papers would be coming through for his family to leave Paris. There was no hope of that happening. He chided himself daily over his poor decision to remain. He felt trapped in a vise each time he considered the future in a city occupied by the Nazis. He had never imagined his beautiful Paris would fall to the Reich. Even with his vast clientele and numerous connections, he was in the same situation as any other Jew who attempted to leave. The exit gates to the city were tightly locked. Forged travel papers were difficult to acquire.

Newspapers being censored, the only source of news about the outside world came from a conversation with a friend—for those who had telephones—or a story passed from one person to another. Everyone whispered about Nazi prisons for Jews.

Once proud Parisians now walked with their heads down for fear of being noticed. Day-to-day life continued, but a shadow of fear blanketed the city. Mori felt a constant chill of threat surrounding him, following him. Most of all, he feared for his wife and sons.

Mori sighed and adjusted his wire-rim glasses, then pushed open the tall wood and glass door with his shoulder. He strode to the rear of the gallery, turned on the lamp, and tossed his copy of *Le Petit Parisien* on his desk. On the front page a face he knew and loathed appeared in black and white. Hermann Goering glared at Mori from the paper. Goering's reputation had arrived in Paris before the Nazis had. In disgust, Mori flipped the paper over.

Mori's trips to the gallery these days represented habit, rather than necessity. He had paintings, but no buyers. He continued to consult with museums and patrons, but the art market was practically comatose. On the gallery walls hung a few seventeenth-century paintings and several by Picasso; everything else was in storage in the back, for fear of theft by the Nazis. The gallery felt unnaturally vacant, displaying— more than anything else—the fraying burgundy velvet walls originally installed by his father.

As he took off his jacket, the phone rang. Mori grabbed the receiver. "Hello?"

"Mori?" The voice was a familiar one.

"Yes."

"It's Nathan Van Dernoot."

"Bonjour, Nathan! How is Vienna?" Mori shouted. The phone connection was scratchy, and Mori strained to hear. The two men exchanged pleasantries. There was a small delay in the sound; when Mori spoke, his words echoed.

"Two Titians and a Rembrandt were taken off of the market yesterday," Van Dernoot said.

Mori couldn't recall ever hearing of anyone making such

a major purchase. Paintings still occasionally sold, but not multiple paintings and not to the same buyer.

"To whom?" Mori replied.

"I said they were taken off of the market, not sold."

Mori didn't understand.

"I think the Germans have them."

Mori expelled a deep breath and held the receiver tightly against his ear.

"Hitler's building a museum in Austria, according to rumor."

"I am aware," Mori said. "Which paintings? I can check the ownership from here."

"These aren't sales, Mori. They're thefts."

Mori sat in stunned stillness for a moment. The closing of local art dealers and the disappearance of Jewish collectors painted a horrifying picture.

There was silence on both sides of the conversation. Then the connection was lost, leaving Mori staring at the wall and wondering if someone might have listened to their call.

Mori paced the gallery. He had memorized the space—eighteen meters long by twelve meters wide. He could reach one corner and turn without looking up from the newspaper. He was reading about a train wreck six kilometers from the Gare du Nord, when the gallery door opened. Startled, Mori looked up.

Two Germans stood framed by the doorway. Both men were tall, fair haired, and solidly built. "Herr Rothstein," one of the men said in a strong yet respectful voice.

Frozen for a moment, Mori struggled to keep his composure. Perspiration dotted his forehead. He'd seen soldiers daily, but never had they set foot in his gallery.

The stench of body odor preceded the men as they approached him. "Please come with us," one of the soldiers said.

With his hand in his pocket, Mori rubbed his thumb and

index finger together. His mind raced. Was this it? Was it his turn to disappear as other Jews had? His legs felt weak, his mouth dry. He knew the rumors. Everyone in Paris whispered about the horrible things the Nazis did to their prisoners.

Mori finally took a step backward. What would happen to Ruth and the boys? How would they know where he was? Who would take care of them? A million questions swirled through his head.

"Where are you taking me?" he asked.

The men did not answer. They moved toward him with great authority.

"I'm coming," Mori said softly.

Gripped by fear, his mind reeling, he kept his eyes on his captors. Both wore brown uniforms with gray medals pinned to their breast pockets and the now-familiar spider-like swastika on their arms. Mori had seen men in uniforms like this in front of the Hotel de Crillon. They looked like officers. What could German officers want with him?

The men positioned themselves on either side of Mori before they escorted him out of the gallery.

"Where are we going?" he asked again.

There was no answer.

2

Émile Rothstein, Mori's younger son, walked through the cloisters of the more than three- hundred-year-old École des Beaux-Arts. Slender and lithe with a fair complexion, he darted in and out of the arched openings, making his way to the school's café. Small patches of moss had formed where ground met building in the large courtyard. The stone walls reminded Émile of the Louvre, where he spent as much time as he did at the school. He loved to paint; it was all he had ever wanted to do.

The campus sat at the heart of the lively Saint-Germain-des-Prés district, across the Seine from the Louvre Museum. Paris's premier art school had come under the auspices of the government of Louis XIV in the 1700s in order to guarantee that artists would be available to decorate the palaces of French royalty.

Acceptance to the school involved rigid requirements. Upon final admission into the academy, a new member was expected to present a *morceau de réception*, an example of their craft. In 1783, Jacques-Louis David had presented *Andromache Mourning Hector* as his reception piece, which was now part of the Louvre Museum's collection. Émile's acceptance to the École proved equally dramatic. His natural aptitude for bringing brush to canvas made a deep impression on those who reviewed his work for the École. One of his instructors said, "I have never seen a painter so young express himself on the canvas with such maturity." Another commented, "Émile's understanding of light, space, and emotion is unmatched by any other student I have known." Émile was more than aware of his talent and was not shy about others knowing it too.

Inside the café, Émile breathed in the fragrant aroma of roasted coffee beans and freshly baked bread.

It was crowded and noisy. A long bar spanned the rear of the restaurant. Small, marble-topped tables and bentwood chairs dotted the floor. Its large black-and-white, octagonal-tiled pattern was worn, and the green walls needed paint. Photographs of generations of students decorated the walls.

He spotted Alena, who sat with their friends François and Michel near a window. Alena worked in the school's office. The only thing he loved more than school was Alena. What had first captivated him was her full red lips and dark eyes, and her rounded curves and full breasts reminded him of a Rubens painting.

Alena's long dark hair flowed around her face and shoulders, a blue ribbon encircling her hair. She wore a dress of brilliant, sky-blue cotton with red flowers. She turned to face Émile. "You're late," she said, wiping a smear of coffee from her lips.

He bent to kiss her cheek. She smelled like lavender, and he paused for a moment to draw her into all of his senses. There were few girls in his school and of those, Alena towered over them in grace and intelligence. Her upbringing had been simple, her father a laborer. Everything about her was real, unlike the girls he had been introduced to through his family.

"Ah, the master is here. You're just in time," Michel said. "Sit. You can settle the argument."

"It's not an argument," Michel's twin brother François chimed in. "It's a disagreement."

Both men loved to argue politics and chase beautiful women. Their darkly handsome features made them popular.

"What's the difference?" Michel asked.

"It's just not an argument, that's all," François snapped.

"*OK*." Michel was fond of using the American slang he had heard in the cinema. Émile smiled.

He ordered a café au lait, then turned back to his friends. "What are you disagreeing about, anyway?"

"It's the soldiers outside the school." François pointed at the men beyond the front gate visible from the window. The tall walls that towered over the soldiers made them resemble children's toys.

"What about them?" Émile asked. "They look like all the rest in Paris, and they're just as annoying." *Hitler's brigade.* They wore the same uniform, same badges, same Nazi symbol.

"No," Michel said. "They've been pacing back and forth for most of the day. It's not just those two, either. There are others. They're watching everyone."

"We must be a threat to Hitler," François said. "Maybe he thinks we can paint him into a corner."

"Do you think they're going to close the school, or invade it?" Michel asked Émile.

The question was not out of turn. Everyone knew the Germans confiscated anything they wanted. *What could they possibly want with an art school?* Émile wondered.

"Why else would they be here?" François snapped. "The Fascists are taking over everything."

"You worry too much," Michel said.

Alena looked at Émile, whispering in order not to disturb the flow of François and Michel's discussion. "There's so much drama with the French." She laughed. "I have to get back to the office."

"I'll walk you. I have a class soon anyway." Émile downed the rest of his coffee, then pushed back his chair and stood. "You'll have to argue this out between yourselves," he said to the brothers. "We're leaving."

"It's not an argument," François said, a sly grin settling into his dark eyes.

Alena and Émile stood outside the café for a few minutes, their arms wrapped around each other. "You should be concerned," she whispered.

He looked into her eyes. "About what?"

"You're a Jew, Émile. There's no safety here for you. They're right, something is happening. Why all the attention to this school?"

He looked at her, a gentle smile on his face, and bent near to kiss her.

She shifted out of reach. "Émile, I'm not kidding."

Rumors of violence by Nazi soldiers ran rampant. Everyone knew someone or had heard of someone who'd disappeared in the middle of the night.

"You're safe," he said, gazing into her eyes.

"Why, because I'm not a Jew? No one is safe." She pulled him closer and put her mouth near his ear. He could feel her breath on his neck, which excited him. It was warm, wet. "You need to be careful," she whispered. "And stop joking about the Germans."

"We should all get together and strike in front of the school," Émile said, jaw clenching. "Let the damn Nazis know we don't want them here. There's nothing in this place they could need."

"Not a great idea," she shot back. Then she grabbed his necktie, pulled him close and brought her lips to his. They pressed against each other, arms entwined and lips meeting for several seconds. When she pulled free, she said, "I need to get to work, and you need to see the reality of what's happening here."

3

The soldiers walked on either side of Mori to a waiting Daimler-Benz staff car parked in front of the gallery.

"Wait." Mori jerked backward, pulling free of one of the men. "The door." He worried for the safety of the paintings inside the gallery. The other man gripped Mori's arm and pushed him to the car.

Mori bent to step into the back seat. Peering out the rear window, he saw Albert wave before closing the gallery's front door. Mori sighed. There were still kind people.

The car backfired then sped up Rue Saint Honoré and turned left into Place Vendôme. Small pools of water between the cobble stones reflected the emerging sunshine, creating abstract designs on the stone buildings surrounding the square. Military transport trucks and assorted cars emblazoned with the swastika lined the perimeter.

The Daimler-Benz circled the plaza's central column which had been forged from melted cannonballs from the Battle of Austerlitz and erected by Napoleon I. The car pulled in front of the Ritz Hotel where a boy barely old enough to be in the military opened the vehicle doors.

"Out," one of the soldiers ordered, pushing Mori's shoulder.

Keeping his panic in check, Mori stepped out of the vehicle and looked up at the domed awnings above the hotel entrance. Its imposing facade no longer held the glamorous allure Mori had enjoyed on his many visits to the grand hotel for parties and dinners with wealthy patrons. The outside of the stoic structure now was draped with large flags emblazoned with the red and black Nazi insignia, and armed soldiers had replaced the formally dressed doormen.

Mori sucked in a breath before he walked through the entrance doors, the soldiers at his back.

"Wait here," one of them ordered, pushing Mori into a small chair.

The interior walls of the hotel also were covered with swastikas. Gone were the beautiful floral arrangements famous for their size and style. Gone, too, were the finely dressed wait staff that had served morning café au lait in the opulent lobby. Soldiers carried large boxes through the front entrance and across the spacious lobby to the salon at the rear of the hotel. Mori knew that the Ritz management never would have allowed a delivery through the front doors. *Not in the past.*

"This way," one of the tall, blond soldiers said, escorting Mori to the far end of the lobby.

The man stopped before a pair of carved wooden doors, and leaned in to open one of them. The stench of his sweat-soaked uniform assaulted Mori's nostrils. The soldier tightened his grip on Mori, and led him into a large room that had previously served as the hotel's restaurant. Mori surveyed the salon in which he'd dined so many times, and the sight broke his heart. There were no white linen topped tables, set with sterling flatware and sparkling crystal goblets. The room had been transformed into a sprawl of desks, typewriters, radio receivers and transmitters. Formally-attired, white-gloved waiters had been replaced by secretaries and Nazi soldiers.

"This way." His abductor pushed Mori through another set of doors, into an almost vacant ballroom, but for one man.

Mori froze. *Impossible.* Across the room behind the grand desk stood the most feared man in Paris, Reichsmarschall Hermann Goering, the head of the Gestapo.

What could he possibly want with me?

The guard led Mori across the room. Mori's heart pounded and he felt as though his shoes were filled with concrete—each step more difficult than the last.

Then came the bellow he had heard on the radio. "You're the Jew Rothstein?" Hermann Goering called out in German, his voice echoing in the empty space.

Shocked not only by the presence of one of Germany's most feared leaders before him, but by the fact of being referred to as "the Jew," Mori stared at the thick-framed man, who looked to be two hundred pounds. His hair was a dull brown, his skin unexpectedly smooth and pale.

Droplets of perspiration trickled down Mori's side. Still, he managed, "I am Maurice Rothstein."

"Sit." Goering pointed to a chair in front of the desk. Mori obeyed. "You're the art expert?" Goering's voice had softened.

Mori took a deep breath.

"I asked you a question," Goering snapped, his voice once again loud and commanding.

"Yes, yes, I'm sorry. My profession is art." Mori felt squeezed by the painted walls with their gold-framed panels and gesso details.

"Your reputation is well-known to me, Rothstein." Goering's tone relaxed again. He sounded almost friendly.

"I'm flattered, sir," Mori said wondering if this officer of the Reich felt distain speaking to a Jew who possessed great knowledge, knowledge he himself might not enjoy.

Two men entered the room, wheeling a statue covered in cloth. Goering motioned to a nearby spot, "Put it there."

As the men moved the statue across the floor, Mori recognized the distinct shape of Aphrodite de Milo, or as most people knew her, Venus de Milo. Her beauty and grace were unmistakable. He was not only surprised to see her, but dismayed that she was being taken by Goering, removed from public view, where she belonged.

Goering eyed Mori. "I have work for you."

"I'm listening."

"The Führer wishes a museum."

"I am aware."

A look of surprise crossed Goering's face and then he laughed. "Of course you are."

Mori's tension eased. He had heard that Albert Speer and other architects had been commissioned to design a grand center, which would be erected on the site of the Linz railroad station in Austria. It would include a museum, an opera house, a theatre, a hotel, and parade grounds.

"And what is it that you wish of me?" Mori asked.

"The Führer desires to acquire only the finest paintings and sculptures."

"Of course." Mori nodded.

"There are fine examples of art," Goering stated, "and lesser, so to speak."

Mori glanced at the Venus de Milo. "And where will these works come from, Commandant?"

Goering ignored the question. "You are the expert and you will determine which paintings are of the finest quality, and which are fine, but not in a premier category."

"Where are these paintings you speak of?" Mori asked.

"You will be taken and shown tomorrow. Separate out those that are of the best quality and explain your conclusions. You will report your findings only to me."

"Determining the value of a painting or its historical importance is not something I can do by a simple inspection," Mori said. "I would need to research comparable pieces to determine why one painting might be superior to another. This certainly isn't something that can be done quickly."

"I didn't give you a time limit, just get the work done."

Mori nodded.

"You have a family." Goering's tone was icy. "They are safe—for the moment. Keep them that way."

Mori felt as though a boulder had landed on his chest. He could barely breathe.

Goering nodded to the soldiers standing nearby. They escorted Mori from the room.

4

Friday, April 10, 1942

The following morning, the massive Daimler-Benz pulled up to the Jeu de Paume on Rue de Rivoli. Mori stepped out of the vehicle, escorted by two soldiers, who led him down a path to a door at the rear. His eyes darting, he scanned his surroundings as he entered the exhibition hall. The air was warm and damp and smelled of mildew, most likely the result of inadequate maintenance of the stone walls.

German soldiers, maybe thirty or forty of them, carried paintings in and out of the large open space, their voices echoing off the walls. A labyrinth of tables occupied the center of the poorly lit room. Hundreds of paintings stacked fifteen to twenty deep lined the walls.

Mori observed a soldier stamping the Nazi swastika on the back of a small painting. When the worker turned the canvas over, Mori was horrified to see it was Vermeer's *Astronomer*. His fear and dread evaporated instantly, replaced by fury. He wanted to yank the painting out of the man's hands, but he knew he was on Hitler's turf now.

Someone behind Mori coughed. He turned to see a tall, wiry man with fair hair, broad shoulders, and bloodless lips.

"I am Colonel Claus Bertolt," he said in German. "I know who you are and why you are here. What I don't know is why someone like you would be chosen for this position."

Mori met Bertolt's gaze, still feeling the anger boiling beneath his skin. "I was instructed to appraise works of art and to report directly to Mr. Goering."

"It's Commandant Goering," Bertolt said firmly. "And we have German professionals who can do the appraising."

Mori clenched his jaw. "Are you referring to the man whom I saw apply a swastika to the back of a Vermeer a few moments ago?"

Bertolt looked at Mori with a sinister expression. "This way," he said after a long, cold minute.

With two soldiers at his back, Mori followed Bertolt to a small office adjacent to the large work space. The faded beige walls were filthy from years of neglect. A large table served as a desk. Bertolt pushed aside a chair, Mori caught a whiff of the pungent stench of the colonel's hair tonic. "This is where you'll work."

A dark-haired soldier with a strawberry birthmark on his cheek appeared in the doorway and clicked his heels together.

"What is it, Weimhoff?" Bertolt said.

"There's a rather large delivery . . ."

"Handle it!" Bertolt shouted and turned to Mori.

"I can't work here," Mori said.

"Do you think the Führer is going to build you your own art gallery?" Bertolt asked with a sneer.

Mori noticed that the two guards had quietly slipped away.

"I wouldn't know where to begin," he said, "and I don't have my reference material available to me, or my contacts for that matter."

Bertolt nodded to a book shelf. "Reference books."

Mori examined a few of the volumes. "These books are outdated and not nearly extensive enough."

"You'll use these," Bertolt insisted.

Mori's blood was boiling, but he was careful to keep his demeanor steady. "May I ask you a question, Colonel Bertolt?"

Bertolt eyed Mori.

"I'm curious about your certificates."

The colonel frowned. "You're questioning my credentials?" His voice grew louder. "I graduated the University of the Arts, Bremen, with honors. I went on to Bauhaus University, Weimar, for advanced studies."

"Then why do you need me?" Mori asked.

"We don't," Bertolt said. "But Commandant Goering has requested your services."

Now he understood Bertolt's contempt. He also understood who was in charge; Goering wanted the Jew.

"Colonel Bertolt, you are aware that the combination of the temperature and the moisture in here is less than ideal for the paintings you are housing."

Bertolt scoffed. "They won't be here long."

"Are the paintings sorted into some order?" Mori asked. "Categories?"

"No."

"I would like to have them separated by artist and year."

"You don't give orders to me, Jew."

Mori's shoulders tightened.

"And, that's impossible. It would take too much time."

The phone rang. Bertolt lifted the receiver and began speaking in German.

Disgusted Mori walked out of the office, in search of a soldier who might assist him; Bertolt clearly wasn't going to help him carry out the duties Goering had assigned. However, the first person Mori spotted in the adjoining room was anything but a soldier.

"Rose?" he said.

Rose Valland looked up expressionless from her desk. She wore a shabby dress and appeared exhausted.

Mori felt a chill from her glance. *Could she be working for the Nazis too?* In the background he heard Bertolt shouting after him in German: "What are you doing?"

"How are you, Rose?" he managed.

"Fine," she said. Her answer was short and curt. She seemed almost angry at Mori's presence. He knew her from her position as an art historian at the Jeu de Paume. Who else might be helping the Nazis?

Mori sensed disdain in her voice and returned to the office. Bertolt stood with his fists balled. "What do you think you're doing?"

"I had a query for one of the soldiers sorting paintings."

"You don't ask questions of anyone other than me," the colonel growled.

"Colonel Bertolt, my priority is to meet Commandant Goering's expectations." Mori did his best to sound respectful, while still standing his ground. He needed to have this endeavor succeed, and he would do whatever it took to keep his family safe. "These are not the proper working conditions for what the commandant has requested. If I am to provide any information, I will need suitable tools. Even if I brought my reference material here, the lighting is inappropriate."

"You'll work with what you have here!" Bertolt ordered.

Mori took a breath, struggling to keep his voice even and his gaze steady. "Colonel, I need the paintings separated into groups. I can separate them myself, but that will take quite some time, and I believe that Commandant Goering wants this work completed sooner rather than later."

Bertolt's jaw dropped. He appeared to be speechless, but his fair skin was flushed red.

"I would like the paintings separated by period," Mori continued, "Renaissance, Late Renaissance, Baroque, Rococo, Neoclassicism, Romanticism, Modern, and Impressionism."

"It's impossible to do what you ask," Bertolt said. Although well versed in art history and in charge of assembling the paintings, Bertolt clearly failed to appreciate the beauty that surrounded him.

Mori frowned and steadied himself with a breath.

Bertolt spoke his next words slowly, deliberately: "It would be in your best interests, Mr. Rothstein, not to question my authority."

Mori stared. "Please tell Commandant Goering that I am more than qualified to accomplish the task he has requested. However, it is impossible to do so under these conditions. The lighting is fine for sports, but not for master art." He turned to leave, then at the door looked back at Bertolt. "I'm going to my gallery. It might be best if I work from there. Once the paintings are separated, I can inspect groups of them at my gallery and make my reports accordingly."

Mori left with his heart pounding and hands trembling. This act had taken every ounce of his courage and self-control.

5

Mori stood for a moment on the street outside his home in the upscale neighborhood on Rue François, dwarfed by its grand limestone façade. He took a deep breath and rubbed his face, then smoothed out his vest and jacket, hoping the day's strain didn't show.

He walked slowly up the eight steps from the street to the large landing flanked by ornately carved columns. Each pillar was trimmed with bronze leaves that hung as garlands at the top. He unlocked one of the tall glass doors and walked in.

"Hello," he called out. From the intricate design of the spiral stairway's gilded banister to the carved gesso roses on the ceiling, every detail of the home's elaborate features had been meticulously overseen by his wife, Ruth.

"Cheri, I'm in the kitchen," she answered.

Mori took another steadying breath before pushing open the door from the dining room to the kitchen. "Here you are," he said, kissing her cheek.

Mori waved to the maid, who was just leaving through the laundry room door. "Thank you," he said.

"Where else would I be at five o'clock?" Ruth stood at the stove, stirring a pot of beans. A large game pie dish rested on the next burner, filled with sizzling sausage, duck, and butter. Behind her, two trays of freshly baked plum pastry sat on the countertop. Ruth's community of friends had quickly learned how to get the unattainable. Black market purchases had become the norm for housewives with means. Still, Ruth was a shrewd shopper.

He pictured her childhood home, which he knew from her stories, a meager two-room cottage in Poland, a small town called Zamosc. She had cared for her parents and tended chickens in the yard. A million years ago, and in another universe.

Mori stepped in again, put his hands on her shoulders and kissed her neck. "I love you."

She turned her head and smiled, that same sparkling smile he had fallen in love with so many years ago. "I love you, too."

Ruth's slender figure and porcelain skin were accentuated by a belted, rose-colored dress trimmed with lace. She wore only the subtlest rouge on her cheeks, and her eyebrows were penciled discreetly.

He looked around the kitchen. "You've been busy." He glanced at the riches she had created.

"I played Mahjong with the girls this afternoon." Ruth played the tiles weekly with her friends Belle, Inas, and Perla. "Belle shared a new chicken recipe so I got to work in here when I got home."

Mori bent over the pastries and took a long, slow sniff. A dusting of sugar glistened over the golden sweets. "De-licious," he said.

Ruth was extremely discerning; her smile told him he was putting up a good façade, hiding how restless and uneasy he felt. How could he share with her all that had been happening? He didn't want to alarm her. Plus, she had spoken for months about getting their family out of Paris, and he had assured her over and over that it would all blow over soon, that the Nazis would leave their beautiful city, that Paris would never succumb to such nonsense. How could he now say, "It's over, I'm Goering's prisoner. There's no leaving Paris. Not now, maybe not ever." And yet, he had never kept secrets from Ruth, in all the years they'd been married. It made him uncomfortable.

"Are there soldiers on the street?" she asked.

"Avenue Montaigne, yes."

She turned to face him. "Mori, we should leave. Maybe try to go to the south?"

And here it was again—the plea that broke his heart almost daily now. Mori sighed. "Oh Ruth, how I wish we could leave. But I don't know how. You know I've tried to get travel papers."

"You must keep trying. It's not safe for us here."

Mori tensed and stepped away from her.

"What is it, Mori?"

"It's nothing," he lied.

6

Wednesday, April 15, 1942

Émile approached the École just in time to watch the sun rise. Streaks of soft pink and orange reached up from the building tops as though left by an Impressionist's brush.

To his surprise, François, Michel, and a group of other students stood at the entrance, holding up signs. One placard read, "Our School Is None of Your Business." Another said, "Leave Our School Alone!"

Across the street a dozen or so German soldiers congregated near a large military truck.

"What are you doing?" Émile demanded. He grabbed Michel's arm and dragged him out of earshot of the others. "Are you in charge of this?"

"It's enough!" Michel said. "We need to take a stand."

"Are you crazy, this isn't a stand," Émile shot back. "These guys are dangerous. You think they give a shit about us?" Alena's warning had sunk in. The Nazi presence was not going to change because a group of paintbrush-wielding students had joined a cause. Europe was at war; this wasn't a game.

"What do they want with us?" Michel said. "We're just students, and we don't need them spying on us every day."

"I agree, but this isn't wise or safe." Émile wondered why he hadn't known in advance about this demonstration, small as it was. Word traveled quickly around the school, and this seemed to have appeared overnight. He glanced across the street at the soldiers. "You're just provoking them."

"Who cares?" Michel said.

"I do!" Émile said. "Call this off. It's crazy. Someone's going to get hurt or killed."

Michel glared at Émile. "Who put you in charge?"

"Do it now, Michel."

Michel bit his lower lip in defiance, but took Émile's advice. He turned to the other students and shouted, "All right, enough. They know we're unhappy. We made our point."

After a moment a few of the students backed off, but others continued to brandish their signs.

Michel hesitated, then yelled, "Come on, it's done."

"Let's get to class," Émile said.

"Where's your passion?" Michel asked, bumping Émile's shoulder with his own and tossing his sign to the ground.

I'm passionate, Émile thought, for *Alena and for my painting.* He looked across the street. The soldiers appeared uninterested in the senseless display, a few of them chuckling.

Émile paused. Someone was clearly in their sights.

7

Thursday, April 23, 1942

Traffic was minimal, the consequence of restricted travel and petroleum rationing. Everything the Nazis could touch was used for the war effort. For the rest of Paris, goods exchanged hands at premium prices.

While the Germans continued to advance throughout Eastern Europe, newspapers gave differing accounts of Hitler's actions, and *Le Petit Parisien* was closely monitored by the Nazis. Accurate news remained almost unattainable.

Mori jingled the keys in his pocket as he walked up Rue du Faubourg Saint-Honoré. The morning air felt light, the sky the softest of blues.

Mori smelled the aroma of coffee and changed his destination to Albert's café across the street. Large windows behind sidewalk tables displayed assorted cakes, pastries, candies, cheeses, and breads of every shape and size. Mori could almost taste the tang of lemon when he entered and passed a round silver tray of citron tarts resting on a table. Of course, like other businessmen, Albert was shopping the black market, as Ruth and her friends did.

Albert stood behind the highly polished bar. "You're alright?" he said, reaching across the wood and brass counter to grasp Mori's arm. "I worry about you."

"I'm surviving, thank you."

"Where did they take you a couple weeks ago? Why? They let you leave?" Albert's questions came at Mori rapid-fire.

"Albert, really, I'm fine. And thank you for locking the gallery. I appreciate that."

Albert nodded. "Café? Maybe a biscuit?"

Mori smiled. "Yes, that would be nice. Did your family leave?"

"Yes, thank God," Albert said. "They're safe, away from Paris."

How had Albert done it? Mori's numerous attempts during the last few weeks to get his family out of Paris had failed, every travel request denied. He would never forgive himself for missing the window.

A waiter placed a steaming espresso and a white plate rimmed in red with two small cookies on the counter in front of Mori.

"Thank you," Mori said, and the waiter left. To Albert, he said, "You'll be lonely without them."

Albert sighed. "I am."

"Where are they?"

"England, Newcastle. It's in the north."

"Will you go?"

"If I can, but so far my request for a travel permit has been rejected."

The two men stood in silence for a moment.

Mori breathed in deeply. "I must get to the gallery, but you'll come for dinner this week?"

"That would be such a nice change from eating here and going home alone."

"I'll speak to Ruth about it."

Albert smiled. "Thank you, my friend."

Mori turned, holding up the cup and saucer. "I'll bring this back later."

Mori headed to the gallery. One of the first things he had to figure out was where to store the fifty or so master paintings in his inventory. Currently he had them tucked in the rear of the storage room, each piece meticulously wrapped to guard against scratches. He didn't want his paintings confused with those being delivered from the Jeu de Paume.

8

Wednesday, May 6, 1942

Mori slammed the desk drawer. The two guards turned toward the sound. They had been stationed daily at the front of his gallery ever since Goering had turned his life on end. "Sorry," Mori said, sucking in the warm, wet air of the cramped gallery. He felt the walls tightening around him.

Mori squeezed between several rows of paintings. "Can you help me, please?" he called.

The two men edged their way to him.

"We need to make some space, at least a walkway from the door to my desk." Mori began restacking several paintings. His thoughts to separate the canvases by artist, date, or period proved impossible thanks to the constant arrival of new work. Mori pointed. "Please, move those paintings there," he said, motioning to the far side of the room. He knew Bertolt was deliberately sending more paintings than Mori could process. He had requested that the colonel slow the pace of the daily arrivals, but the arrogant bastard had simply ignored him. Although Goering was in charge, Mori had to cooperate to some degree with his underling.

The guards moved several paintings, bumping and scratching the frames.

"No! No!" Mori said in frustration. Both men looked blankly at him. "I'll do it myself."

34

The guards returned to the front of the gallery, one slipping a pack of cigarettes from his pocket.

"Outside," Mori insisted.

The soldiers lumbered out the door and stood beside a small green transport truck.

Mori removed his jacket and hung it on the back of his chair. "Idiots. Bertolt's idiots," he muttered.

The deep burgundy walls seemed to vibrate from his anger. One by one he began to move the paintings, creating a narrow path from the front to the rear of the gallery. He carefully placed frame against frame, protecting the precious canvases.

He paused at one particular painting—a medium-sized gilt frame containing Antonello da Messina's *Portrait of a Young Man.* The somber darkness and wandering eyes of the subject fascinated him. He inhaled, as though the beauty of the work had allowed him suddenly to breathe, to forget his current situation. After several moments, he finally slid the painting aside to continue the work at hand, but what was revealed behind da Messina's portrait produced an audible gasp from Mori. Resting against the wall was Caravaggio's *The Expulsion of Hagar,* a painting that was as familiar to him as one of his own children. Mori gazed at the workmanship of the masterpiece, allowing himself to dive inside the image, to take in every nuance of the composition—the softness of Hagar's scarf; Abraham's outstretched finger; the setting sun, a reference to the close of this chapter in Hagar's life.

"Magnifique," he whispered to himself. The detail and softness of color applied to the child's tiny hand caused an unexpected upwelling of emotion. Could he protect his own children as Hagar had protected her son? Mori felt her pain. The clarity of the two lost souls against a dark and foreboding background unsettled him. Caravaggio's choice to place Hagar with her son at the doorstep of the biblical Abraham's house showed the uncertainty of their future.

His heart ached at the sight of it. He closed his eyes, but the ache did not leave. This painting belonged to his client and friend, Paul Betone—a Jew like himself. Mori had sold the masterpiece to him more than twenty years earlier. For a time, Paul had given it to the Louvre on a temporary loan. During that period Mori had visited the painting in the museum periodically, as one would visit a dear friend. He grudgingly opened his eyes, and there the painting was, still in line for deportation to the Führer's collection. He had no idea whether his friend Paul found himself in the same predicament as his beloved Caravaggio.

Mori exhaled, trying to shake his worry about Paul and his growing anger at what was surely a colossal theft. He moved slowly to his desk and collapsed into his chair. And there he sat for a long moment, staring into space, as though not aware of his surroundings, until finally the front door opened and startled him upright.

In the doorway the silhouette of a large man blocked most of the light from the street.

Mori jumped to his feet. "Mssr. Goering?" he said, squinting at the shadow. The surprise visit diverted Mori's upset about the painting. Although this wasn't Goering's first visit to the gallery, it caught Mori off guard each time, for Goering never announced that he was coming.

The big man moved down the narrow aisle. "What is this?" he barked, glancing around the cluttered gallery.

"I'm sorry," Mori said, shrugging into his jacket. "Colonel Bertolt is delivering paintings faster than I can examine them."

Goering frowned. "You'll have to work faster."

"I've devised a system to rank the paintings on a scale of one to ten, ten being the most valuable. I've included composition, provenance, historical importance and value. Speed however won't allow me to do what you want."

"Why not? Inspect the paintings and separate them."

"Every canvas is a masterwork. My job is to research each to provide you with proper information. That research takes a bit of time."

Goering settled onto a small chair in front of Mori's desk. The morning light created a glow around his head, which Mori thought looked ethereal. Goering turned to take in the rows of paintings. "Maybe it is a little tight in here," he conceded, his voice softening.

Was the man beginning to understand his dilemma?

"Rothstein, I do expect more progress."

Mori sighed and pushed the wire frame of his glasses up on his nose. "And I want to do a good job for you."

"I'll speak to Bertolt," Goering said.

"Thank you, sir."

Their meetings and conversations were respectful, although brief. Goering came to the gallery, discussed certain works, usually taking several paintings with him, the ones ranked ten out of ten. Following the first of several visits, Mori suspected Goering was keeping artwork for his personal collection.

"Do you have something to show me?" Goering asked. "Maybe a Da Vinci?"

Mori's eyes opened. Leonardo Da Vinci? Would a stolen Da Vinci be arriving soon?

Goering now expected a surprise each time he visited the gallery. His knowledge of art impressed Mori, as did his taste. They had discussed masterworks during several of Goering's visits.

"It amazes me," Mori said.

"What?"

"Your knowledge."

"Why?"

"I'm not sure. It's just intriguing to me that a soldier would have such a love of art and possess the acumen to understand the nuance and history."

"Are you flattering me or insulting me?"

"I'm flattering you," Mori chuckled. "You clearly understand good composition and quality work. Moreover, you always appear to desire to learn the differences between a good painting and a great painting. I respect your interest, sir.

What surprised Mori most, though, was that Goering wanted to discuss art with him in the first place. The question in his mind: Was Goering trying to befriend him, a Jew? Mori didn't trust the man.

"What have you today?" Goering said.

"Well," Mori began, but Goering suddenly turned and bellowed to the guards standing outside the front window, "Open the door!" His voice was strong and vibrant, but the guards didn't seem to hear. "Open the door!" he shouted again, loud enough this time to startle the men. "I can't breathe in here."

Mori shrugged. "There isn't much room for air."

The soldiers opened the front door, securing it in place with a chair.

Goering turned to Mori. "You were saying?"

Mori cleared his throat. "I have a drawing for you. I'll fetch it." He rose and made his way into the storage room across from his desk. The space was nearly as crowded as the gallery. At one end of the storage room, shelves held a vast array of reference books and other materials Mori relied on for research. He removed an elaborate but small gold frame from atop a stack of leather-bound books. He grabbed a cloth, dusted the glass cover, and returned to his desk.

Mori placed the small jewel before Goering, who seemed unimpressed by the item.

"What is it?" Goering unbuttoned his jacket, allowing it to fall from his shoulders onto the back of the chair.

"One of the rarest pieces I've seen in this gallery." Mori watched Goering's face carefully.

"Really?" Now Goering appeared interested.

"A sketch," Mori continued.

"Of what?"

"Captain Frans Banning Cocq."

Mori expected the vacuous expression on Goering's face. Few people outside of the art world would recognize the small yet distinct drawing of the man.

"It's Rembrandt's sketch for *The Night Watch*. The painting is, by far, the master's most important work."

"I've seen other sketches. Not that impressive." Goering dismissed the piece with the wave of his gloved hand.

"Not like this one," Mori pressed.

"Why is this so important?" Goering squinted at the small work.

"Rembrandt added color," Mori said, tapping the glass barricade that separated the warmth and oils of his skin from the fragile paper on the opposite side. "All the other sketches I've seen are in black. This one has red across the sash. From a collector's view, that makes this a very precious work, a small treasure."

Goering removed his gloves, as though he needed to touch the piece to understand its value. He gazed at the red sash and gently ran a finger over the sides of the frame and glass, a smile flitting over his lips. He touched the piece as if it were a favorite child.

Goering had told Mori that he casually shared information about art he'd gleaned from Mori when he entertained at the Ritz. Goering's friends and acquaintances marveled at his knowledge of art.

They would be shocked to know that he was being coached by a Jew, Mori thought.

"It's beautiful." Goering placed the small master—which only a few minutes earlier had represented nothing more than dusty wood and glass—on his lap.

"I'm pleased you like it."

"I'll take this with me."

"Of course, as you wish."

Goering rose from his chair, grabbed his jacket, tucked his gloves into his pocket, and placed the small prize under his arm.

"Sir," Mori said. "May I . . . ?"

"What is it, Rothstein?"

"I need your advice." Mori had decided to appeal to Goering's sensibilities rather than complain. "Perhaps you can think of a way to slow the flow of paintings a bit. This would liberate me from the constant shuffling of frames . . . allowing me more time with the art."

It might also slow down the rate the Nazis are confiscating art, Mori thought.

Goering arched an eyebrow. "I'll speak to Colonel Bertolt."

"Thank you, sir."

9

Thursday, May 7, 1942

Minutes before six o'clock in the morning, Mori heard a thunderous pounding at his front door. He bolted upright and looked at Ruth, whose eyes were wide with fright.

"Who—?" she whispered.

"Shh, stay here."

Mori grabbed his red silk dressing gown, tied a firm knot in the sash, and ventured into the second-story hallway. He flipped a switch, illuminating several crystal sconces in the entry below. From the upper landing he squinted down at the glass entry doors and saw the hazy figure of a tall man on the porch.

The man knocked again.

Mori cautiously stepped down one riser at a time on the spiral staircase until he stood on the stone entry floor, his heart racing.

"Heir Rothstein?"

Mori straightened his spine, approached the door, and moved the gathered lace to peer through the glass.

"Heir Rothstein?" a German soldier asked.

Mori eased open the door a few inches. "What do you want?"

The man extended his hand, presenting Mori with an envelope.

"Thank you." Trembling, he grasped the manila packet marked with the initials HG.

The soldier turned and descended the front steps.

Mori closed the door and tore open the flap of the brown paper. Inside, he found two large stacks of food coupons.

10

Tuesday, May 12, 1942

Alena lived with her parents on the Left Bank in a modest apartment at 15 Rue Jacob, behind the café Deux Magots. Each evening after work, she walked from the École des Beaux-Arts and stopped at the boulangerie on the corner of her street for fresh bread. Although the price was cheaper in the afternoon, there was less selection available. She was happy to get what she could.

From inside the shop she could see her apartment building, which was cast in the fading glow of the setting sun. Two German soldiers waited in a parked truck at the curb.

The baker handed her a small paper-wrapped package tied with twine, his meaty hands dwarfing the round loaf. "Voila," he said.

"Thank you, sir." Alena forced a smile. Her eyes darted back to the soldiers. She handed the baker a few coins, tucked the bundle in the crook of her arm, and stepped outside, never taking her eyes off the Nazis.

She strode quickly to the entrance of her building.

"Achtung!" The guttural command echoed around her. She turned. A stocky soldier climbed out of the truck. Through the vehicle's window she saw another soldier smoking a cigarette.

"Yes?" She gripped the handle of her purse, her heart beating wildly.

"Carte d'identité" the soldier said, extending his hand.

She hadn't been stopped by the Germans before. She feared their presence and kept her distance.

Alena fumbled through her handbag, producing a faded yellow card. Everyone in Paris carried identification papers. It was the law—German law.

The soldier snatched the paper from Alena's hand and examined it carefully. "Hmmm," he said. "Why are you in a hurry?"

Anxious, Alena waited. She struggled to understand his German. She crossed her arms, pulling her purse closer, crushing the bread.

A few moments later he returned the paper. "You're free to go." He feigned a smile.

"Thank you." She reached for the document. He snapped it back and laughed. "Maybe a kiss for me before you leave?" His comrade laughed too.

Alena stepped back.

"Ah, go ahead," the soldier in the truck said. "Give it back to her." Then he flicked his cigarette to the ground.

Alena grabbed the document, turned and ran. Her hand trembled as she fumbled for the key inside her bag.

She slammed the outer door to her building and dragged in several deep breaths. She leaned against the wall for a moment, her heart pounding, then crossed the cobblestone courtyard surrounded by buildings with dirt-stained windows. She entered the door at the far end, and raced up two flights of stairs to her family's apartment.

"Bonjour, Maman." Alena kicked the door shut, still panting.

"I'm in here," her mother called out.

Alena's mother, Elise, a woman in her forties with long brown hair pulled into a bun, stood over a large pan that rested atop two gas burners. Her soft, pale features were moist from the rising steam.

"You look exhausted," Elise said.

"I'm fine." Alena took a deep breath. "It smells delicious."

"Chicken with potatoes, carrots, and leeks." Here, taste." Her mother blew on a large metal spoon and held it to Alena's lips. "You're trembling." She put the spoon back into the pot.

"I was stopped by German soldiers."

"Oh my God!"

"They frightened me, but I'm alright."

"I saw them, too." Elise scowled. "What did they want?"

"My papers."

"Why?"

"I don't know."

"But there must be a reason they stopped you. Were you doing anything?"

"I don't know," Alena said. "He just stopped me, scaring me half to death. Once he saw my identity card he let me pass. Those bastards are everywhere."

"Well, they're not in here and that's all that counts," Her mother said matter-of-factly. "I go about my daily activities quietly and carefully, keeping my distance from the Germans, especially when I go to buy food.

"They were at school again today, too," Alena said.

"The soldiers, why?"

Alena shrugged. "There were a couple of them in a truck just outside the entrance. They were just watching the students. They've been doing that a lot lately. It's unsettling."

"The French government opened its doors and invited them in. Now we're stuck with them. So, we mind our manners, keep our heads down, and go about our business. Hopefully they will go away like a bad cold."

"I don't think so." Alena dragged a small step stool to the counter and pulled a chipped dish from the top shelf. "Do you want this?"

"Yes, thanks." She took the container from her daughter and

began transferring the contents from the bubbling pot. "Will Émile join us for dinner?"

"He will." Alena stared out the window to the courtyard below.

She smiled to herself, recalling seeing Émile for the first time. It was his second day at the École. He was so cute. She checked his school application and saw the comments for his acceptance. She couldn't recall ever having seen such praise for a first-year student. It took two weeks for her to get up the nerve to introduce herself. He was reading a book in the hall.

"Do you always read here while classes are in session?" she asked.

He had looked up at her; his warm dark eyes sparkled in the morning light. "Yes. Actually, I read in the hall and I sleep in class."

She laughed. Émile spread his jacket on the floor and motioned for her to sit.

"Why aren't you in class?" she asked.

"It's boring." He raked his fingers through his dark hair. "I'll have to go back inside in a few minutes, though."

He extended his hand. "I'm Émile."

"Alena."

"Hmm, very pretty. If you meet me for lunch, I promise I won't bore you with talk about school."

"You're not boring me," she said.

"What's your favorite class?"

"Oh, I don't take classes, I work in the office."

"I've never seen you here."

"Your misfortune."

Émile grinned at her. "Meet me for lunch?"

Alena nodded in agreement.

"Les Deux Magots, noon?"

"Alright." Alena pushed herself up, walked toward the office, and glanced back with a smile. "I'll see you at noon."

Brought back to the present by a knock at the door, Alena startled. "Germans?"

"Open the door," her mother said.

Alena swung the door open and stepped into Émile's embrace.

"I thought you'd never get here," she said. "Did you see the soldiers outside?"

"No. Why? Are you being watched? Are you involved in espionage I should know about?"

Alena gently smacked his shoulder. "It's not funny. They were there when I got home."

They walked to the kitchen. Émile placed a small apple cake on the dinner table at the far end of the room that overlooked the alley. "Bon soir, Madame Belcoeur. This is from my mother," he said.

Elise smiled. "Thank her for me." She held the cake to her nose. "I can smell the apples and cinnamon. Delicious."

Alena's parents liked Émile, but they worried about their daughter's safety. Jews were being sought out by the Nazis. Although both Elise and her husband, Andres, had been raised Catholic, neither observed their religion more than the occasional Christmas mass, and only then if friends were attending. Despite the lack of formal religion in the house, a crucifix adorned each room, and although belief to them simply wasn't important, they still feared the unknown. Unions between Jews and gentiles remained uncommon in Paris.

Alena clutched Émile's hand under the table through most of the meal. When everyone had finished eating, Émile leaned close to Alena. "I have to go, *ma chérie*," he said softly. "Meet me tomorrow?"

"Le Petit Coin?"

"Absolutely. Our special place."

Alena took Émile's arm and walked downstairs with him. They paused for a moment on the bottom landing to share a kiss.

Émile crossed the courtyard to the gate and then disappeared.

As she stood in the shadows, Alena reached beneath her dress to caress the small six-pointed star she wore around her neck, a gift from Émile she never removed, but kept hidden from view.

William Ian Grubman

11

Wednesday, May 13, 1942

Émile strode the short block from the École to Sennelier, one of the oldest art supply stores in Paris—the very same shop that had provided pigments and other supplies to Monet, Renoir, Cézanne and Picasso, among other great artists.

"Bonjour?" the petit elderly woman behind the counter said when Émile walked through the door. "How is my most handsome customer?"

"You're a flirt," Émile said.

"At my age?" she chuckled.

"And what age is that? Thirty-five? Forty?" he said, knowing she was probably in her mid-eighties.

"Mon Dieu, you bad boy," she laughed. "What do you need?"

"Pigment, a few brushes, and some oil."

The shop was small with dark wood-paneled walls, and the metal ceiling showed signs of leakage and age. The place reeked of mold and spirit of turpentine. Tall maple cabinets with glass fronts lined the walls. On top of them sat unopened boxes filled with small containers of paint pigment neatly marked with their color. A rolling ladder made selections from high places easy.

Émile unlatched a cabinet door, its broken hinge causing it to swing out at an odd angle.

"Ooh la la," the woman said, coming to Émile's aid. "It's old. Like me." She smiled. "Eighteen eighty-seven."

"What?" Émile gave her a quizzical look.

"Eighteen eighty-seven. That's when my father opened the shop. Nothing much has changed since then." She shrugged.

"Well, not this door, anyway," Émile said, reaching for a sable tipped brush.

Émile would give anything to follow in the footsteps of the masters who had bought the ingredients to make their paints from this very shop, to make his own mark on the art world, to hang in a major museum. That was his dream.

"What are you painting?" she asked, inspecting him through her thick glasses.

"Anything, and nothing in particular."

"Then what makes your work special?"

"Because I'm good."

"Good isn't enough. If you want to hang in the same halls as the greats who came before you, you'll need to be exceptional. You must be unique."

Émile paused for several moments, turning this statement over in his mind. "The problem is I'm not unique," he confessed. "I still haven't found my special style, something that sets me apart."

"You forget, Émile, I've seen you work in the Louvre, and you've been shopping here for years. You're just being modest. You have immense talent."

"You're flirting with me again."

She shook her head and cleared several items from the countertop. "You must be different, Émile. If you're not, how will you shine brighter than the rest? How will you stand out?"

"I think about that." He placed two brushes and a container of azure blue powdered pigment on the counter. The woman slowly listed his selections in a ledger and showed Émile the total.

"Thank you." He placed several coins on the countertop.

"Thank you, monsieur," she said with a wink.

Émile laughed.

He left the shop and turned on Pont du Carrousel. His lighthearted mood faded when he spotted a German soldier across the street. Not just any soldier, but one who was definitely watching him.

12

Several follies were scattered across the verdant grounds of Parc Monceau, a gem among the renowned parks of Paris. For Émile and Alena it was the perfect getaway from the turmoil of the city, a peaceful rendezvous for two lovers. When they wanted to be alone, they escaped there, to the small stone pyramid beside a copse of camellia bushes. They called it their petit coin, or small corner.

Quiet time was difficult for them to come by. Émile's class agenda and Alena's work schedule didn't often allow them time to be together.

With the art supplies tucked under his arm, Émile arrived while the spring's early evening sun hovered over the rooftops of the limestone mansions surrounding the park. After a short wait, he spotted Alena hurrying toward him. He pulled her close. "Were you followed?"

"Just by a little dog," Alena teased.

He pressed his body to hers, and drew her into a long, ardent kiss. Her arms encircled his narrow waist, her fingers intertwining at the small of his back.

"I missed you," he whispered, pulling her close.

"I saw you last night," she giggled.

"I know, but we barely had any time alone."

"We do now."

He looked into her eyes, then kissed the tip of her nose.

They sat on an old iron bench with a wood-slat seat that

needed painting.

"You're chilled."

"A little," she admitted with a faint shiver.

He removed his jacket and draped it around her shoulders.

"Mmm," She wrapped herself in the garment. "You always take care of me."

Émile slid his arm around her, pulled her close, and gently kissed her. "I love our little corner."

The sun had set and the ancient lamps in the park shed a soft glow.

Émile reached into his sack and removed a bottle of wine, some Camembert and a baguette. Hungry?" He broke off a piece of cheese.

He fed her a morsel, then popped a piece into his own mouth. The strong aroma filled his nose and throat. Émile slid the loose cork from the already open bottle. He offered Alena a sip and then helped himself.

A rustling came from the bushes. Alena stiffened. Émile stood and squinted into the darkness. The sound moved nearer, each step scattering leaves. Then Émile spotted a pair of eyes reflecting the lamp light. The owner of the eyes sauntered out from behind a tree—a stray dog with a scruffy coat. Émile collapsed onto the bench and Alena's laughter echoed deliciously around them. A moment of joy in a somber city.

"Same dog that followed you into the park?" Émile said.

"I thought it was a soldier," she whispered.

"Me too." Émile remembered the soldier who had been watching him as he'd left Sennelier. He didn't mention this to Alena.

"They're everywhere. I always feel like I'm being watched," Émile said. "Like last night at your parents."

"Well . . ." She paused. "They probably just wanted some of your mother's apple cake." She playfully tousled his hair.

Émile felt a raindrop, then two. A drizzle could quickly

become a spring storm.

He tucked the bottle and cheese into his bag and stood. "Come." He extended his hand. He led Alena to a diminutive door on the side of the pyramid. Dropping to his knees, he withdrew a battery operated light from his sack and handed it to her. "Hold this."

He removed a key from his pocket and unlocked the padlock, which he had placed on the rusted latch when the two of them had discovered their secret spot. He opened the metal door separating them from the dry shelter, and they ducked in through the small opening. Once inside the pyramid, they stood in the narrow space no more than ten feet square.

Émile tugged at an iron ring attached to a wooden trap door in the floor. He propped open the hinged, decaying wood, then scooted backward, feet first, through the square hole. He climbed down a ladder that led to an even smaller storage space. There he pulled a wrapped bundle from the corner and took out a large blanket, which he handed up to Alena. She spread the woolen cloth on the floor as Émile climbed back up.

They lay side by side, shining the torch to the pyramid's pointed top. The mottled stone walls loomed above. With the door closed, anyone passing by would assume the barricade was locked. However, no one ever came here at night, and their light wasn't visible from the outside.

Émile turned on his side and gently touched Alena's cheek. "You make me feel like the outside world doesn't exist, and when I'm at school all I do is think about you."

She smiled shyly and cupped his cheek. "I love you, my brilliant artist."

He slid his arm under her shoulder. "Are you warm enough?" She nodded.

After a long silence, she asked, "How long do you think we'll be free to come here?"

Without a word, Émile leaned in and kissed Alena.

13

Friday, May 15, 1942

At eight o'clock the following morning, Émile arrived to a commotion in the courtyard at the École. Instructors and students were fleeing the confines of the school's stone walls.

"What's going on?" he asked a passing student.

"Someone's missing, and there are soldiers everywhere."

"Who?" Émile said.

The young man shrugged his shoulders, clearly unnerved by the chaos.

"Who's missing?" Émile repeated.

"They beat him." The student darted past Émile and joined the flurry of people running in all directions.

Two soldiers moved quickly past Émile. Careful to avoid eye contact, he made his way through the crowd and up to Alena's second-floor office.

She sprang from her chair. There was panic in her eyes. "You're here."

He drew her close. "What happened?"

"Michel! They took him away."

"Why?"

"The soldiers came into the school, grabbed him, and loaded him into their truck. Émile, you know why."

"I don't know. I'm just hearing about it."

"He's a Jew, and he's vocal about the German presence."

"Where did they take him?" Émile asked.

"Who knows? A cold dark prison somewhere," she said, her breathing shallow. "If they can come in here and seize him, who's to say they won't be back for us?"

Émile had never seen such terror in her eyes, and her body was trembling. He gripped her arms, bringing her closer. "This isn't a safe place for us," he whispered, "not right now."

Émile glanced out Alena's office window and noticed a German soldier at the far end of the courtyard below, gazing up at him.

"Don't look," he whispered. "There's a soldier in the courtyard."

Alena reactively turned her head.

"No." He stopped her. "When I left Sennelier the other evening," he said in a hushed voice, "there was a soldier on the street across from the shop. I think that's the same one."

Alena moved away from her desk.

"I wonder if it's one of the men who was outside your apartment?"

"You're scaring me," she said.

More soldiers filled the courtyard now. There was a commotion below, as well as just outside the door. "Let's go," he said. "I want to go to the gallery to talk to my father. Get your things."

Alena grabbed her purse and sweater. Émile took her hand and led her into the corridor. Students were scrambling in every direction.

Émile looked up and down the hallway. "Come on," he said.

Alena instinctively turned to the right, her usual path out of the building.

"No," Émile said. "This way." He pulled her by the hand.

"That won't take us to the gate," she said resisting.

"Trust me. It's how I get in and out of the school without anyone seeing me when I need a smoke, or if I feel like skipping a class."

They made their way up a narrow set of stairs through the crush of bodies charging down. There was noise and shouting in every direction. At the third-floor landing, they turned into a deserted hallway. On the far end they entered a room. Small and poorly lit, the space smelled of stale air. It was a deserted office filled with old furniture and used books. By the far side of the room, a door led to an adjoining private office. Inside, a bank of tall bookshelves with years of dust, grime, stacks of papers, and assorted collectibles hid Émile's escape route.

They heard the door to the outer room open. "Shh." He placed a finger to her lips. He led Alena by the hand. Behind the shelves an open door led to a dark staircase. Once they were through the opening, Émile quietly pulled the door shut.

They descended the wood steps to a landing at the second floor. Their only light appeared from a rooftop window, which was partially obscured by repair materials and years of dirt. The darkness protected them from anyone who might follow, but it also slowed their pace.

They continued down the steps. When they reached the door at the bottom, Émile turned the knob and pushed. They stepped out into the bright sunlight facing the Seine.

"Come on," he said. "We need to get away from here. Don't run, just walk casually with me."

As they headed toward the Tuileries, Émile wondered why that soldier kept following the two of them.

14

Émile and Alena strolled through the Tuileries, trying to appear inconspicuous. The crowded park provided cover for the two lovers who walked hand in hand. However, keeping Alena safe remained his primary concern.

The walk from the École to Émile's father's gallery took less than twenty minutes.

Émile noticed a telephone box at the far end of the park. "Maybe we should have telephoned him," he said as they approached the Place de la Concorde.

They turned up Rue Royale, then took a left on Rue Saint Honoré. Émile stopped abruptly and grabbed Alena's arm. "Wait."

"What is it?"

"The curtains."

"What about them?" she said.

"The curtains in the gallery, they're closed."

"I don't understand."

"Papa never closes the curtains, not unless he has a client inside." The curtains only covered the lower half of the windows, giving privacy to a prospective art investor, while allowing light in at the top. But Émile knew his father had had no clients since the war had come to Paris.

Then he saw it. The green military transport truck parked a few doors up and a soldier seated inside the cab. The traffic on the street seemed normal. Pedestrians behaved as though oblivious to the military presence. Émile's uneasiness grew. Taking a steadying breath, he led Alena up the street. They slowly approached the gallery, stopping in front of the door. Émile glanced across the street, behind and ahead, his gaze coming to rest again on the transport truck. The soldier inside appeared unfazed by their presence. Was this supposed to be normal now—soldiers everywhere? He didn't even know what normal meant anymore.

Émile grasped the doorknob and cautiously pushed the door open. He stepped inside, Alena in tow, but before the door closed behind them, a hand gripped his shoulder and pulled him around. A large soldier threw him to the floor and restrained him. Alena screamed.

Émile lay sprawled face down on the carpet, with the boot of a German soldier on his back.

The front door opened and a second soldier burst into the gallery. Alena gasped.

"What is this?" Émile shouted. "How dare you!" When he saw Alena being restrained, he yelled, "Get your hands off of her!" He thrashed beneath the German soldier, who was kneeling on his back now. Alena tried to jerk free of the man holding her.

Mori rushed from the storage room into the gallery, his face red with rage. "Let him be, he's my son. And her too."

The two men released Émile and Alena and wandered back to their posts.

Mori raced to Émile and offered his hand. "What are you doing here?"

He helped his son to his feet.

Émile glanced around the gallery. There were paintings everywhere—hundreds of them. He had never seen more than a few dozen canvases displayed at any one time.

"What on earth?" Émile said. "What's going on?"

Alena stood motionless.

"Papa?"

"Not now. We can talk later."

Émile had seen some of these paintings before. He knew that many belonged to his father's patrons. "Papa, what are all these doing here?"

"Not now, Émile."

He was worried for his father's safety." Are you alright?" he whispered.

"I'm fine. We'll talk this evening. Come home early for dinner, and please bring Alena." He sounded calm, but Émile knew better.

Mori approached Alena and put a protective arm around her shoulders. "I hope you didn't have too much of a fright."

Alena offered a faint smile. "I'm fine." She paused and smoothed out her skirt. "Thank you."

"Join Émile at our house this evening. We'll talk then."

Mori guided them toward the front door.

"Papa, why don't you—"

Mori stopped Émile mid-sentence with a shake of his head.

Émile and Alena stepped outside onto the sidewalk. Émile turned and watched his father close the door. There was fear in the older man's eyes.

15

Mori looked around the dinner table. Ruth, Émile, Alena, and his eldest son Jacob sat in silence. He tinkered with his fork, unable to eat. The others picked at their food.

"I thought if I kept quiet about Goering, the paintings, everything, I could keep you all safe. Now you know."

The details of his relationship with Goering and Bertolt had stunned them. He had described what he was doing with some of the greatest master paintings in the world, which were in the process of being swallowed up by the Nazis. Mori dropped his fork in the center of the dish. His servitude to the Reich now threatened his family.

"How long will it take?" Ruth said.

"To finish the work for Goering? I don't know, but it will come to an end."

"Then what?" Émile said.

"Then—that's the problem. I need to protect you now, and my only concern is how we're going to survive in Paris until the war ends."

Mori sat at the far end of the dining table, Ruth beside him. He gently touched her forearm. The early evening sun cast shadows across the wall. The days were lengthening with the approach of summer. He was aware of this moment of calm in a world of turbulent hatred and violence that surrounded them.

"What are you going to do?" Émile asked. "There are only so many paintings. What happens once they run out and the

Nazis have no more use for you?"

Ruth paled. "I wonder if our friends and neighbors think we're Nazi collaborators."

Mori's older son, Jacob, leaned his arm on the dining room table and awkwardly forced himself up. He took a cane from the back of his chair and limped to the sideboard. His leg injury was the result of a childhood fall that had broken his femur. Although the leg had healed, growth had been impaired, leaving one limb slightly shorter than the other. At the lace-draped credenza, Jacob picked up a box of matches. He pulled a Gauloise from his jacket, struck the match, and inhaled deeply, expelling a plume of smoke.

"You're walking slower. Are you in pain?" Ruth said.

"Some days it hurts, some not," Jacob said. "Today is one of those days it hurts." Limping back to his chair, Jacob flipped Émile's collar up—a boyhood taunt.

Ruth jumped up to silence a whistling tea kettle in the kitchen then returned and began removing the plates from the table. Alena helped.

"Why did you wait to tell us?" Jacob asked, lighting another cigarette.

Mori was searching for the right answer, of which he knew there was none. He needed to get his family to agree with his plan. But how? Ruth wouldn't like it. He took a deep breath, "I didn't have much choice," he said.

"There's always a choice," Jacob snapped, ever the argumentative one. His son couldn't see the complexity of the problem but Mori was sure in time he would.

"You don't know what you're talking about," Mori barked back in anger.

"Stop it, both of you," Ruth said as she carried a teapot and a milk jug from the kitchen. Alena followed with a platter of sweets. "Émile, sugar." Ruth motioned to the sideboard. "And Mori, the mouse is back again, under the stove."

Mori sighed and nodded to Émile and Jacob. "If you two would stop dropping macaron crumbs I wouldn't have to take care of mice. I hate the rodents!"

Even with a cleaning woman who came daily to maintain the large home, Ruth couldn't keep up with a stray intruder. That mouse had to go.

Émile leaned back on the two rear legs of his chair, grasping the floral-painted Limoges sugar bowl. The spoon inside clanked when he swung it over to the table. Behind Émile, above the sideboard, was a delicate Renoir, a gift from Mori to Ruth on their first anniversary. Mori always said it reminded him of his bride.

"What happens now?" Alena asked.

"I don't know," Mori said. "When it first started it seemed harmless, or at least not dangerous. I went to the gallery, I did what was asked of me, and I went home. Simple." He lifted his arms in frustration. "I thought it was a way to keep all of you safe. I am sick about Émile and Alena's confrontation with the German soldiers at the gallery."

Émile drew circles on his mother's table with the blunt end of a spoon. Émile's table cloth art reminded Mori of the staircase at Chambord, the largest chateau in Val de Loire. He and Ruth had taken the boys there on a summer holiday many years earlier.

"Papa!" Émile said, lifting Mori from his reverie. "You can't keep helping them." Émile stirred sugar into his cup. Concentric circles appeared on the top of the caramel-colored liquid.

"And what do you think I should do? I've got an idea. Why don't I just go to the Ritz tomorrow, walk into Goering's office, and tell him that I've decided to take my family on holiday and won't be available to examine any more paintings." Mori's face was red with anger. He saw fear in his family's eyes.

"What if you just stopped?" Jacob blurted out.

"This isn't an American movie with Douglas Fairbanks as

the hero. If I don't do what I'm told, we'll all be shipped off."

"So, what's next?" Ruth asked.

Mori straightened and heaved a sigh. "Of course I know this is wrong."

At that, Jacob looked satisfied. Émile frowned and stopped tinkering with his silverware.

"At first it was just artwork, paintings I had no emotional interest in. Then I started to receive paintings from every major Jewish collector in Paris."

Silence settled over the table, and Émile leaned in.

"Now I'm seeing more and more paintings that I sold to my own clients. God knows what has happened to *them*, to their families." Mori pressed his palms to his cheeks as he tried to make sense of it all. Many of his Jewish patrons had left France before the Nazis had arrived, some even abandoning their belongings. Others remained, foolishly thinking they could weather the storm. Mori was one of the foolish. Now Jews just disappeared. Everyone in Paris spoke in whispers about it.

"I have an idea," Mori said. "It's dangerous but possible."

All eyes were on him.

"If I change my daily behavior, I put all of you in jeopardy, so I have to keep working with them, but . . ." Mori paused and refilled his teacup. He was uncertain how the others would react to his next statement. "I want to steal some of the paintings I've received at the gallery."

Émile's jaw tightened. "How, Papa?" he said.

"It doesn't sound practical," Jacob said. "Under the watch of the Nazis you're going to steal paintings?"

"Do you always have to think practically?" Émile said.

"Do I have to remind you I'm a graduate student of economics and accounting at La Sorbonne?" Jacob said.

"You remind me of it often enough. You're the family scholar," Émile said.

"Stop it you two," Mori said.

"Speaking of school, is it even safe for the boys and Alena to return to school?" Ruth asked.

Mori took a deep breath. "Where did they take your friend, the one that got arrested?"

"Michel?" Émile said. "I don't know, maybe where they take other Jews?"

"And how safe are we?" Ruth asked, mouth pinched with worry.

"For the moment, we're safe," Mori said.

"Safe enough to start stealing from the Nazis?" Jacob said.

Ruth frowned. "If they're roughing up Émile at the gallery and watching the school, who says we're not next on the list. Not to mention the soldiers watching Alena's house."

"I've tried to get travel papers—again and again denied. If I don't continue to do what I'm doing, Goering will come after all of us," Mori said.

"My parents don't have much money, not enough for travel papers," Alena said, her face tightening. "We're not even Jewish."

"Exactly! We are," Mori said, "which I think might be putting your family in danger." His heart contracted. Émile would be disappointed by his next words. "Maybe the two of you should stop seeing each other."

"No!" Émile said. He put his arm around Alena's shoulder.

Her eyes filled with tears and she grasped Émile's hand.

Ruth reached out, taking Alena's hand. "Steady," she said.

Alena blinked back a tear.

"There must be another way. You don't just stop seeing the one you love." Émile said. "The one you want to marry, the one you want to have children with."

Alena sat up taller and stared at Émile, then began to cry.

Ruth put her hand over her heart.

Mori hadn't expected such an extreme reaction. He hadn't realized the depth of feelings the two young people had for each other.

Émile bent and kissed Alena's cheek. "This is not happening," he whispered.

Mori was unsettled by the thought that his association with Goering affected not only his family, but possibly Alena's, as well.

"What do they do with all of the paintings?" Alena asked.

Jacob cut the air with his hand, smoke trailing. "What do you think they're doing? The greedy bastards. They're stealing them."

Mori nodded. "I've seen the paintings picked up, but I'm not sure where they go from the gallery. It all happens rather quickly. They're shoved into a truck and from there who knows?"

"Shoved?" Émile said.

"These soldiers are pigs," Mori said. "They have no idea of the value of the works they're moving. The more I tell them to be gentle, the more they ignore me."

"And you don't know where they go from you?" Alena asked.

"All I know is that Hitler is building a museum in Austria," Mori said. He didn't share with them that Goering was plucking up some of the most valuable paintings for himself. And perhaps Bertolt was doing the same. Vultures over carrion.

"How do you know?" Ruth asked.

"Nathan Van Dernoot told me about the museum, and Goering confirmed it," Mori said. "Most of the paintings gathered at the Jeu de Paume are inspected by Bertolt; then perhaps they're sent to Hitler's museum. No way to know for certain."

A hush descended over the table, until Mori broke the silence: "He hates the Jews."

"Who?" Ruth asked, putting her teacup in its saucer.

"Bertolt. He hates Jews. He hates me. I can see it in his eyes. I saw it the first day I met him. He's a pompous, arrogant son of a bitch. I wonder if he's sending his soldiers to Alena's house to show me his power."

There was another long silence, and Émile resumed doodling on the tablecloth with his spoon.

"I'd like to figure out a way to keep some of the paintings from returning to the Jeu de Paume," Mori said, "or wherever it is they go."

The clock chimed eleven. During the tense conversation, no one had noticed the sun had set. "Alena," Ruth said, "it's getting late, *ma chérie*. I don't think it's safe for you to go home at this hour. Call your parents and tell them you're going to stay here."

Émile looked up with excitement.

"Émile, you'll sleep on the sofa; Alena will use your room."

"That's not necessary," Alena said.

"It's very necessary," Ruth said firmly. "It's after curfew. German soldiers are out."

Émile turned to his father. "Do they ship them to you in boxes?" he said.

"The paintings?" Mori said. "They handle them the same way you and I handle a baguette. They just stack them on end in the back of a military transport truck, wrapped in some blankets, and drive them to me. It's the same when they pick them up. A couple of soldiers arrive, they collect the paintings, stack them in the back of a truck and leave. It's outrageous. Great works driven like cattle to the stockyard."

"I'd like to see some of them, Papa," Émile said.

"I've put some of my clients' paintings near the rear of the storage room. The pickup and delivery paperwork is so mishandled, no one has asked about them yet. Problem is I don't know what to do with them, not to mention my own paintings. I'm surprised the Nazis haven't confiscated them already."

Mori had heard gossip in art circles that Nazi soldiers were destroying what they referred to as "degenerate" art. Canvases by Picasso, Van Gogh, and Matisse had fallen to the flames of Hitler's fires.

"What are you going to do?" Émile asked.

"This evening, nothing, but I have an idea I'm still working on," Mori said. "The most important thing is keeping all of you safe." Mori's life was wrapped around his family. From Ruth's kiss each morning before leaving for work, to hugging his boys each evening, family came first. "Boys, Ruth, Alena," Mori continued, "go about your normal day. Don't bring any attention to yourselves. Most of all, don't discuss any of what you've heard tonight with anyone." Mori shifted his gaze to Alena. "I'm sorry, but I think it would be best that you not mention this to your family. They might panic."

"No," Alena said, shaking her head.

"If you tell your family, they'll surely be concerned. They might speak of it to close friends for advice. Word travels quickly. No one must know of my involvement in this mess."

Alena nodded her understanding, but fear lurked in her eyes. Mori knew she didn't like the idea of keeping something so important from her parents, but Alena was a smart girl. She wouldn't want to put them in harm's way.

"Are the guards always in the gallery?" Jacob asked.

"During the day, yes. At night, just one soldier in a truck out front."

"What about the rear?" Émile asked. At the back end of the storage room was a large door used for shipping and receiving. It opened to the courtyard and alley behind.

"I never see anyone out back," Mori said.

"I wonder why they don't deliver to the rear," Jacob said.

"The storage room is too small. It's easier to have the paintings come through the front door."

"So," Émile said, "if you put something outside of the rear door, no one would stop you?"

"I put trash out there every week," Mori said.

His eyes met Émile's, and they stared at each other for a moment in silence.

16

Monday, May 18, 1942

A steady drizzle had been falling over the city for more than two days. Mori took his usual route along the Champs-Élysées, which had turned into an obstacle course of puddles. Making his way along the garden path, he hopped around the small water-filled potholes.

When he got to the gallery, he walked past it, crossed the street, and ducked into Albert's café.

Albert stood behind the bar. "How are you, my friend?" he asked.

Mori shed his wet raincoat and hat, hanging them on a hook near the entrance. "Fine, busy. Best to be these days. You, and your family?" Mori removed his glasses, wiping the tiny droplets of rain from the lenses.

"They're in London now," Albert said, frowning. "I'm still here."

Mori sighed.

A customer approached and placed a few coins on the bar.

"Adolfo," Albert said, "thank you for coming. It's always nice to see you." Albert turned. "Mori, this is Adolfo Kaminsky."

"Nice to meet you," Mori said, shaking the man's hand.

"It's a pleasure, sir," the man said before leaving.

"He's been coming for years. He lives to the west in Vire but visits family here. Let me get you a coffee." Albert motioned

Mori to a nearby table. He returned quickly with a small cup and saucer and a plate of sweets.

Mori drew in a deep breath. The fragrance of Albert's wonderful baked goods filled his senses. The café was a daily treat. "Thank you," he said.

Albert motioned to the gallery. "The curtains are always drawn now, and I see a German truck parked in front," he said.

Mori had become so involved with the world inside the gallery, he'd forgotten what it looked like to those outside.

"I'm just trying to keep my family safe." Mori knew he looked exhausted and that Albert could easily see the comings and goings of artwork across the street. "It's complicated."

The café started to fill up. Albert's name was called from somewhere behind the bar.

"I've got to get back to work," he said.

Mori needed Albert's help. He just wasn't sure how to go about asking, and he dreaded bringing another person into the complicated web of his life. If Albert became part of Mori's plan, he, too, would surely be in jeopardy.

"Come for dinner," Mori said quickly before Albert disappeared.

Albert turned. "When?"

"Friday, come to the house for Shabbat dinner. Eight?" The Jewish Sabbath began at sundown each Friday and lasted until sundown Saturday. Mori and his family celebrated Shabbat every week at dinner together, although that was the extent of their religious observance, other than Passover in the spring and the High Holy Days each fall.

"Friday at eight. I'll be there."

"Perfect," Mori said. He finished his coffee and popped the remaining sugar cookie into his mouth, the one with the piece of apricot on top that he'd saved for last, and then brushed the crumbs from his jacket.

The rain had grown heavier outside. He put on his raincoat

and hat, bent his head down, and hurried across the street to his gallery.

For the next few hours, Mori tried to create some order in the chaos of paintings that cluttered the space. He found himself distracted by both the disarray and the beauty that surrounded him.

Mori studied Fragonard's *Girl at the Window*. The delicate pale blue of her gown shimmered in the light of a summer afternoon. Layer upon layer of lace fell gracefully over her rounded shoulders. She peered from her window to the garden below, while a small dog lay sleeping beside her. He considered every inch of the canvas. He knew this painting. He knew its rightful owner, but the Nazis had it now. The guilt was destroying him, and his loyalty to his clients tugged at his very soul.

The door to the gallery opened. Both German guards rose immediately, dropping the cards from the game they were playing.

"It's me, it's me." Émile raised his palm, warning them off.

The guards stood in place, watching him.

Mori walked to the front of the gallery. "What are you doing here?"

"I came to see you, Papa." Émile kissed his father on both cheeks.

Mori took Émile's arm and led him to the storage room, out of view of the guards. "You shouldn't come here," he whispered. "We spoke about this, it's not wise."

"You spoke about it," Émile said.

"Émile, please. I don't want you in any more danger."

"Papa, there are Germans everywhere—school, our house, Alena's. How much more danger can there be?" For a long moment Émile stared at the rear door, which led to the courtyard and alley. He then glanced around the gallery. "There are more paintings than last time."

"Another delivery this morning."

Mori moved to the rear of the storage room and tipped a stack of paintings forward, creating enough space to slide the last canvas, the one nearest the wall, from the stack.

Émile's eyes widened. Caravaggio's *The Expulsion of Hagar.* His gaze darted from the painting to Mori and back to the painting. He stood frozen in place.

Émile was as familiar with this work as his father was, if not more so. He had grown up knowing this painting; Mori had often taken his son with him on visits to the Louvre when the piece had been on loan to the museum. Émile had later come to know every detail of the painting with the intimacy that one knows a lover's body, for he had chosen it as the subject for his morceau de réception—his entrance presentation—for the École des Beaux-Arts. He had spent days in the Louvre sketching, refining, then painting his copy of the work.

"Where . . ." Émile said. "How did you . . ."

"It arrived a few days ago."

"But you sold it to . . ."

"Paul Betone." Mori said the name slowly, deliberately, as though speaking the name might conjure the man.

Émile stooped down and carefully inspected the canvas. It was virtually impossible to tell the original from Émile's copy, but for a small addition Émile had made to the straps of the satchel Hagar's young son carried. They had discussed the change at a family dinner one night. Émile had expressed concerns about copying the work and felt the minor adjustment separated the two pieces.

Mori slid the painting back into place and tilted the others against the frame.

"How long did it take you to copy it?" Mori asked softly.

"Not long. The problem was figuring out a way to make the surface crack, to give it age. Albert's oven took care of that."

"Can you do it again, if I ask you to?" Mori whispered. "And very quickly?"

17

Wednesday, May 20, 1942

Mori placed the package of bread and cheese on the back seat of the 1930 Citroen 7 Coupe, then drove from the garage of his home toward the city limits. From there he would head to the estate of his friend and patron Paul Betone.

On the outskirts of the city he approached a barricade at a traffic crossing. Not finding his identification papers in his suit pocket, Mori panicked for a moment and fumbled through his raincoat, which lay on the passenger seat. He checked each pocket, and wasn't able to breathe again until his hand had grasped the tucked-away document. Without these papers, you were as good as imprisoned.

A scowling German soldier looked into the car's window. "Carte d'identité," he growled.

"Bonjour," Mori said, trying his best to sound calm. He both feared and loathed the uniform, the Party, Bertolt, Goering. He hated them all.

"Where do you go?" the slender soldier said in a sour voice.

"Versailles."

"Purpose?"

"A friend of mine lives there. He's ill. I'm taking him lunch." Mori motioned to the package on the rear seat.

Glaring, the soldier perused the car's interior. Would he take the cheese and bread from him? Everything had value, and

German soldiers seemed eager to line their own pockets. The man examined Mori's papers. "Jew," the soldier said, his mouth twisting ever so slightly.

Mori said nothing.

The soldier tossed Mori's papers into the window of the car. "Move on," the man barked.

From Mori's home to the countryside surrounding Versailles, the twenty kilometer drive took about an hour. He rarely made such trips anymore. Petrol was rationed, and these checkpoints were best avoided all together by staying within the city limits. But he no longer could sit idly by and wonder whether Paul was all right. Mori had placed several calls to Betone's home the previous day. No one had answered.

The countryside seemed calm and peaceful. There was virtually no sign of the war and struggle so prevalent in the city; he saw few soldiers and only one parade of German trucks. A relief.

As he passed Versailles Palace, Mori spotted German flags adorning the estate. The sight angered him and caused his stomach to tighten. He turned off the main road, choosing to take a longer, yet more private route to Betone's home.

Three kilometers from the palace, Mori turned into a large, gated property.

His heart rate sped when he saw the condition of the grounds. He recalled stately gardens, never a leaf out of place. Now overgrown plants and hedges sagged from lack of proper care, appearing like ominous shadows of a magnificent past. Where once romantic statuary reigned, barren pedestals and stone body parts lay broken.

Mori inched his car slowly into the courtyard and stopped. He sat motionless for a minute, surveying the front of the house. A light drizzle prompted him to don his rubber shoe covers for the walk across the pebbled granite paths. Umbrella in hand, he approached the classic French chateau and ascended the massive steps to the entrance.

On the stone landing, in front of the tall glass and iron doors, Mori's heart sank. Behind shattered windows he saw the tattered remnants of Paul Betone's once-glorious home.

He passed his hand through the broken pane, turned the handle inside the front door, and walked into the massive stone entry with double curved staircases. Dead leaves drifted over the floor in the breeze and dust blanketed everything. The chamber was damp, with darkened corners.

Gone were the enormous antique rugs and Gobelin tapestries. Paul's art collection, one of Europe's finest, missing; so was the furniture, crystal chandeliers, silver Judaica dating back to the Romans in Jerusalem. Nothing. Just an empty shell of a once-vibrant home.

He wondered what he'd expected to find. Was he foolish enough to think his friend was safe? Betone would never be overlooked by the Nazis. After all, he was Jewish and wealthy. Mori feared he was with the other Jews who'd disappeared without a word. The Germans didn't need Paul; they'd just wanted his belongings, and certainly his money. But Mori was a different story. He had something they needed—a set of skills they would suck dry before they discarded him.

The house creaked and whispered its ghostly sounds. Mori moved down the hall to Paul's study. It was a grand, carved-wood paneled room with a fireplace at the far end large enough to roast a steer. The tall exterior doors stood open to the elements, and the wind rattled their glass, blowing brown leaves from the corpses of Asian Sycamore trees into the space. The bare floors—once highly polished inlaid wood, covered with beautiful Aubusson rugs—were dull and scratched.

Mori leaned against the wall, sighed and rubbed at the tightness in his neck. He felt a sadness greater than anything he'd known. He pushed the glass doors closed and secured their locks, a feeble attempt to aid his missing friend and protect his home. He could only pray that Paul had somehow escaped before the house had been ransacked. Mori turned to leave, then saw the empty space on the wall where Paul's most treasured painting, *The Expulsion of Hagar* had once hung.

He recalled his first conversation with Paul about securing the piece for the Betone collection. It had belonged to Baron Philippe de Rothschild. The young baron had purchased the treasure at Sotheby's for his London townhouse. Since Rothschild was also his client, Mori had arranged the sale at a hefty profit to Rothschild. Brokering the purchase and sale to Betone gave Mori commissions on both ends. Paul loved the painting and shared its beauty with guests invited to his home, and later with visitors to the Louvre during the loan of the work.

Mori gently touched the dry wood wall where the masterpiece had hung. He wiped a tear from his cheek, turned and walked out.

Had all of his Jewish clients met with the same fate?

18

Friday, May 22, 1942

More and more paintings arrived daily at the gallery, among them a growing number of works which had once passed through Mori's hands to his clients. With the appearance of each of these familiar canvases, his sense of duty to his clients—whether they were still alive or not—grew, as did his anger.

The true anguish had begun with the arrival of *The Expulsion of Hagar* in his gallery, and had grown heavier upon witnessing the state of Paul Betone's home. Now the ache had swelled into rage. This was wrong. These paintings belonged to his clients, and he was determined to do everything in his power to make it right.

Mori had a plan that would endanger his family. Yet he now agreed with Émile. How much more danger could they be in? What was done was done. He had finally absorbed the fact of his gross error; he had put his family in horrible danger by not getting them out of Paris when it was still possible. Now it was too late. Together, he, Ruth, and the boys would have to ride out this storm. He prayed they could survive and make it through until the war was over.

For now, his aim was to rescue as many paintings as possible. Although the handling of inventory and paperwork was lax, surely the disappearance of major works would be noticed, and he would find himself and his family, Alena included, on a truck headed to wherever the Germans sent the Jews.

Mori knew he was walking on thin ice. His plan needed to be foolproof, and he needed help to make it so—the help of both Albert and Émile.

Throughout the day, Mori considered how to approach Albert. Would he come right out and say it? How could he expect a person to put himself in harm's way for the sake of art, valuable though the paintings were? He knew not everyone felt as he did about the masters, and he couldn't expect others to have loyalty to his clients. Perhaps he could get Albert's help without letting him in on the details, and thus not put him in danger. The less he knew, the better.

That evening Ruth made a wonderful Shabbat dinner, with a home-baked challah, and the whole family gathered around the table, with the addition of Mori's friend. Albert seemed to have a good appetite, which made Mori happy. Mori had noticed that his friend had lost weight since his wife and children had left. It was good to see him eat well.

At the conclusion of the meal, Ruth walked into the dining room with a pot of tea and a plate of sweets. Émile and Jacob excused themselves from the table.

"That was delicious, Madame Rothstein."

"You're too kind." Ruth smiled. More than anything, she enjoyed feeding and caring for people, especially those without family nearby. It was one of the things Mori loved about her.

Albert settled his hand on his belly and sat back in his chair. "I'm usually the one doing the cooking and serving," Albert said, "in the restaurant, that is. At home I barely prepare anything." Albert's voice became somber. "Since the family's gone, I take my meals at the café."

Mori leaned forward and put a hand on Albert's shoulder. "You must come more often. Your family is far, and I know how difficult that must be for you."

"I'll let you two talk," Ruth said. "I've got dishes to wash," and she walked back into the kitchen.

The room felt still, and the air seemed thick. Mori was nervous and tapped his finger tips on the table. "I have something I need to speak to you about," Mori said, not sure how to broach the subject.

He rose from his chair, picked up his cup and saucer, along with the teapot. "Let's go into the library. I have an exquisite bottle of port. Can you bring the sweets, please?"

Albert collected his tea and the plate of macarons. He followed Mori across the entry hall and through the large double doors into Mori's library.

The elegant room, just off of the entry hall with its paneled walls and windows overlooking the street, was dimly lit. At one end, above a large fireplace, hung Picasso's oil sketch for his masterpiece Saltimbanques. Albert studied the brightly colored painting while Mori turned on the lamps.

"It was a gift," Mori said.

"A gift?"

"The painting. It was a gift from the master."

Mori could tell by the expression on Albert's face, he didn't understand.

"The artist gave it to me. He painted it about thirty years ago. I saw it in his studio shortly after I began representing him. About a month later it arrived. He's one of my finest artists, although these days no one's buying."

"I don't know much about art," Albert said.

"No bother." Mori didn't want to burden Albert with an explanation of Picasso's Rose Period. "Sit, please." Mori gestured to an olive green velvet sofa. Albert placed the sweets and his cup on a low table, then sank into the overstuffed down cushions.

Mori took a small crystal bottle of port from an elaborately decorated tantalus on the table and filled two glasses. He extended one to Albert.

"Thank you."

Mori moved to the windows and pulled the tasseled cord on the brocade drapes, closing them for privacy. "I'm not sure how to start this conversation."

Albert gazed at him, kindness in his eyes.

"I have a problem," Mori said.

"Who doesn't these days?" Albert sipped the port.

Mori was momentarily silent, and tense.

"What is it?" Albert finally asked.

Mori sucked in a deep breath. "I don't even know where to begin."

Mori spent the next several minutes explaining his involvement with Goering, the paintings from the Jeu de Paume, and his clients' paintings. Sorrow swept over him. He hadn't intended to tell Albert even this much; he risked putting him in danger . . . and yet, they were already in danger— all of them, even Albert—just by the fact of being Jewish. "What would you be willing to do to stop the Germans?" Mori said.

Albert's dark eyes widened. "You have something in mind?"

There it was, the pivotal question. Resolute, Mori said, "I need to use your oven."

"What?" Albert looked shocked. Mori started to laugh.

Albert laughed too.

"It's funny," Mori said. "I need your oven. It sounds funny." He couldn't help himself. The situation was stressful, yet the solution seemed comical.

"Why?" Albert asked, still chuckling.

"That's the tricky part," Mori said. "The more information I give you, the more danger I put you in. I can't even imagine what the Germans would do to you."

"Mori, you know I'll help you. Of course you can use my oven.

"We'll be gone by the time you need to begin baking in the early morning hours," Mori said.

"What is it you want to bake?"

19

Saturday, May 23, 1942

Mori spent the morning at the gallery.

Thunder, wind, and rain created a cacophony of sounds as the storm pummeled the city. Neighboring streets overflowed from the downpour, sending water up over the curbs and into shops and restaurants. Few ventured out, yet the gallery delivery and pickup that had been scheduled in advance arrived on time.

Two soldiers unloaded four paintings in elaborate gilt frames and carried them through the downpour into the gallery. Manet's *Bar at the Folies-Bergère*; Rembrandt's *Homer*; Raphael's *Madonna*; and Delacroix's *Lion Retreat*, a medium-sized romantic work from the mid-eighteen hundreds. Mori quickly slammed the front door brushing water from his sleeves.

"Be careful," he said to the delivery men. He raised his voice so the guards at the front of the gallery would hear his concerns. He grabbed a clean cotton cloth to dry the paintings. "Please bring them back here," Mori said, guiding the men to the rear of the gallery.

New paintings were always set down near the front door for inspection. Mori placed paintings for pickup in the same area, keeping the delivery men out of the tight spaces created by stacks of canvases. It appeared to be the best format for safety. Today was different. Care was not necessary. Calculated timing was.

The two men hoisted the precious treasures and made their way through the narrow aisle toward Mori's desk.

"Careful," he repeated with raised volume.

Grumbling, the guards on duty stepped outside of the crowded gallery to smoke under a neighboring awning, apparently not wishing to hear Mori shout at the delivery men. Ill-prepared paperwork was exchanged, and the delivering soldiers went on their way.

Mori returned to the rear of the gallery, his stomach in knots. He had thought about it for days. It was a carefully considered plan that had now fully formed. In his head, everything made sense, but now he questioned his every move. It was now or never. The timing was in his favor; he was alone, both guards still outside under the neighboring canopy.

Mori took a deep breath. *Could he do it?* He glanced around then quickly moved to the desk and withdrew a pair of scissors from the top drawer. He hurried to the new arrivals, and paused. He was flooded with doubt. How could he possibly defile a masterwork? His life was the world of art, and now he was at a crossroads. Although his next move would jeopardize one, it was the only thing that might help save others.

He longingly studied Rafael's masterpiece as he gently dabbed the rainwater from the *Madonna*, her brow, cheek, neck. The softness of her skin, the tenderness of the Christ child in her arms—these carefully wrought details spoke volumes to him. The dark background made this the perfect choice.

He set aside the cloth and gripped the scissors. One more glance around the room and then, with speed and precision, he brought the scissors down onto the wood panel, scraping the upper corner of the *Madonna*, yet taking care to preserve her flawless face.

There it was. A clean scratch about four inches long.

He hurried to his desk and threw the scissors back into the drawer as though the metal were hot. Then he quickly switched the positions of the paintings, sliding the damaged one behind the Manet. His heart raced and he began to sweat.

Mori ran for the rear door, unlocked the massive bolt, threw it open, and vomited on the step. He was shaking with fear and rage, filled with disappointment at his "now-too-late" decision. He wept for the precious *Madonna* and the predicament he found himself and his family in.

After several minutes outside the back door, taking one deep breath after another and wiping his face on a handkerchief, Mori managed to pull himself together enough to step back into the storage room. It was done. Now it was time to set his plan in motion.

A few minutes later, the guards returned to their post just inside the gallery. Mori asked one of them to move the newly arrived Manet to the storeroom, which would expose Raphael's *Madonna*. His request seemed normal; he often asked the men to move paintings.

When the large canvas of Manet's beautiful bar maid was moved to reveal Raphael's *Madonna*, Mori gasped in horror. "Oh my God!" he cried.

The guards appeared confused.

"Those idiots, look what they've done!" Mori knelt before the damaged painting. He needed to convince them that the delivery men had ruined the master work. "God, no. They've destroyed it!" He put his hand over his mouth, eyes wide.

The two guards stood frozen in silence.

Mori pushed up from his knee. "Get out of my way." He shoved his way past one of the guards and shouted profanities. The guards were taken aback.

So far, so good, he thought.

Continuing his rant, Mori pulled rubber covers over his shoes, put on his raincoat and hat, and stormed into the downpour, umbrella in hand. He turned right onto Rue du Faubourg Saint-Honoré and began the trek to the Ritz Hotel.

His walk gave him time to think about the next part of his plan. He went over in his mind the role he would have to play for Goering, detail by detail. Once his mission was set, there would be absolutely no turning back.

Soaking wet and stomach still in knots, Mori arrived at the Ritz just before mid-morning. The rain had slowed, and the temperature had risen. He was drenched in sweat.

"Halt," shouted one of the soldiers when Mori approached the entrance. The tall yellow-haired boy couldn't have been more than eighteen. "Papers," he demanded.

Breathing hard from the quick journey, Mori fumbled through his pocket, then produced a document.

The young soldier inspected the papers and hesitated. "Hmm," he murmured.

"Young man, I must see Mssr. Goering immediately. I mean Commandant Goering," Mori corrected himself.

"Sit there." The soldier motioned him inside to a chair against the wall. Mori slumped into it.

Mori recalled his last visit to the hotel and his meeting with Goering. He was just as frightened this time but for a different reason. He kept his eyes focused on the once-luxurious floral carpet, now dirty and damp from the comings and goings of soldiers and guard dogs.

He fidgeted with his pocket watch. Had he made a mistake coming to the hotel? Would Goering take the time to see him? It had to be now; he needed to move his plan forward. He took a deep breath, stood, and began to pace.

Hung with the elegance of Gobelin's tapestries, the lobby was fouled by red German flags bearing the familiar swastika. The memory of the opulently dressed women and tail-coated gentlemen who used to fill the lobby was seared in his brain.

"Sir."

Mori turned.

A tall, broad-shouldered German in full military uniform

adorned with medals motioned to him. "This way."

Mori grabbed his raincoat and followed the man. They walked through the large outer room and entered Goering's office. When Mori had first met with Goering, the walls had been bare but for a few small paintings. Now, he was surrounded by some of the most valuable artwork in France.

Goering sat at a large Empire desk with a gold-tooled, leather top. He handed a large stack of papers to a waiting soldier. "That's everything," he said. The soldier took the papers and left.

Goering looked up.

"Thank you for seeing me," Mori said. "I know you're busy, and I'm sorry to disturb you."

Goering stared at Mori, hands on his desk. "Why are you here?" he demanded.

The relationship between the two was usually cordial, respectful, and at times Mori even liked the man. Now he was cold and distant. Mori nervously squeezed his raincoat.

"There's been an accident, sir."

Goering looked annoyed. "What kind of accident?"

Remain calm, Mori told himself. *Stick to the facts of the story.* "It's the delivery men," he said. "The soldiers who bring paintings to me at the gallery."

"What about them?"

"Rafael's *Madonna* was delivered today with a rather large scratch on the panel. There was no mention of damage on the accompanying paperwork."

Goering glared. "Gott verdammt."

"It's a new scratch," Mori said.

Goering bolted from his chair.

"I'm certain it can be repaired," Mori said quickly.

"Why didn't you go to Bertolt?"

Mori hated Bertolt, and he knew the colonel would accuse him of being careless. He would never believe one of his men had damaged the painting while moving it, and that's what Mori needed Goering to believe. "I stopped by the Jeu de Paume earlier," Mori lied, "but he wasn't available. I felt this was something that needed to be reported immediately, sir. I hope I haven't upset you, but with Bertolt absent, I thought you would want to be informed."

The veins in Goering's neck expanded, his face flushing.

Mori pushed on, hoping his next utterance didn't send Goering over the edge. "There are other paintings I've noticed with marks and nicks," he continued to lie. "I think the men delivering them don't realize their value, or how delicate they are." He did his best to keep his voice innocent, controlled, and calculated.

Abruptly, Goering marched out of his office. Mori heard him shouting in the next room. "Get me Bertolt!" Mori couldn't make out what was said next, until Goering ordered: "Replace the delivery men!"

Goering returned to his office. Not taking his eyes off Mori, he sat behind his desk.

Mori took a deep breath to keep his fear in check. "I can have *The Madonna* repaired," he said.

"How?" Goering said.

"My son, Émile—he can repair the damage."

Goering scoffed.

"He's the right man for the job. Émile's a master student at L'École des Beaux-Arts. His painting techniques are brilliant." Mori spoke quickly. He didn't want Goering to appoint someone else for the task.

"I want to see the damage!" Goering roared.

"Of course, sir." Mori turned to leave.

"Today!" Goering shouted.

He looked back at Goering and nodded. "Of course."

When Mori departed the Ritz, he was trembling, filled with a horrified excitement. His plan was in motion. He needed to return to the gallery to create damage to additional paintings before Goering showed up.

20

When Goering entered the gallery in the early afternoon, Mori looked up. The two guards rose to attention and clicked their heels together. They took up new positions outside the front door.

Goering's eyes darted around the room. "Where is it?" he barked. His mood was unchanged.

Mori motioned Goering to the storage room. The *Madonna* rested on an easel.

Mori turned on a small spot light and adjusted it to shine directly on the scratch in the panel.

Lips pursed, Goering inspected the damage. His breathing sounded labored. "Where's the man?"

Mori furrowed his brow. "The man?"

"The painter," Goering said.

"Ah, my son, Émile. He's in school."

Goering touched the graze as gently as he would stroke the cheek of a delicate child. He looked closely at the damage, then stood back. "She's magnificent," he said.

Mori nodded, looking carefully at the man. He saw Goering wipe his eyes. Mori was unexpectedly moved by the man who sent innocents to die, yet could weep for the beauty of a painting. "Would you like to sit?" Mori said.

Goering moved from the storage room to a chair in front of Mori's desk. "How long will it take to repair?" Goering's voice had become calm and respectful.

"Most likely several weeks," Mori said, sitting down behind the desk. He went on to explain the process, embellishing each step to justify the length of time for the task.

Goering listened. Mori could see by his pursed lips that Goering wasn't convinced.

"The process takes time because each step requires a period for drying." He needed to buy time for Émile. "Not to mention the other damaged paintings," Mori said.

"Hmm." Goering bit his lip.

"I do have something special to show you."

Mori gently slid a painting aside to expose a lovely work by Charles Meissonier. The small picture of a countryside inn— with brightly clothed men and women enjoying freshly made wine— seemed the perfect choice.

He hoped Goering would find the piece to his liking, that it would create nostalgia for the man's homeland.

Although the painting was of a French gathering, the view could easily have been Germany.

Goering's eyes opened wide. "It's charming," he said. "It reminds me of home.

The man was hooked.

"This piece is unique because of the number of people in the scene," Mori said, handing the work to the commandant.

Goering inspected the piece more closely.

"Meissonier rarely painted more than four or five people in such a small work. There are eighteen in this piece, making it truly unique." Mori embellished his story for the man's sake. Goering preferred all things rare.

Goering laid the small painting flat on the desk. "And what about the other damaged paintings?" he said. "How many?"

"Eight, possibly ten, and I'll keep my eyes open for any others."

"Get them fixed, all of them. Get your son to work immediately."

"I'll have him start in the morning. He can begin with the one on the easel, the *Madonna*."

"Not here," Goering said. "The work can be done at the Jeu de Paume. Bertolt will oversee the restoration."

Goering's words threw him, into a panic. If Émile was sent to the Jeu de Paume, his plan would fail and he would have ruined a masterwork for nothing. He had to think quickly. He needed Émile in the gallery, not under Bertolt's nose.

"Excuse me, sir, but that's not the best choice."

"Why?" Goering snapped.

"Well," Mori said, searching for his answer, "most importantly, the lighting at the Jeu de Paume is insufficient for painting. Matching color would certainly be difficult and problematic."

Goering rubbed his cheek. His skin was fine, showing little trace of facial hair.

Mori knew he needed to convince the German beyond a shadow of a doubt. He stood and lifted the small painting of the colorful country scene and propped it at a slight angle on top of the desk, facing Goering. "The lighting in this gallery was created to display artwork in the very best way," Mori said, pointing to several features of the tiny canvas. "Its softness allows the viewer to see every color and detail in the way the artist intended."

Goering frowned, and paused to consider the statement.

Mori's heart raced.

Goering said nothing, but he seemed unable to tear his eyes from Meissonier's work. After several long moments of gazing at the small jewel, he heaved a sigh. "Alright," he said. "Get him in here."

"I'll get him to work right away. I'll take him from school."

Goering's face had lost some of its red. He snapped a salute to Mori. "Heil Hitler!" He picked up the tiny painting from Mori's desk, slid it under his arm, turned, and left the gallery.

It took several minutes for Mori to recover after Goering had left, though he was pleased with how his plan was shaping up. Even the weather had improved. Light poured through the front windows above the half drapes; the grayness had given way to soft billowy clouds floating against a parish blue sky.

But the game was far from over, and Mori felt unsettled. He closed the large reference book with the tattered, brown leather cover. Although there was a great deal of research to do, what he needed most now was Émile!

Mori decided to walk to the École rather than take a taxi. It had been a difficult morning. His mind and spirit needed a rest; he wanted time to think. He crossed the Tuileries, deserted because of the storm, and headed toward the river.

Classes ended early on Saturdays; Mori knew Émile would just be finishing up. He walked across the cobblestones at the main entrance. "Excuse me," Mori said to a young woman he encountered. "I'm looking for my son, Émile Rothstein?"

"I saw him earlier in the café." She pointed to the far end of an open air corridor. "It's over there."

Mori thanked the girl and moved briskly in the direction she'd indicated. He crossed the wet courtyard, zigzagging around puddles.

The café was jammed with students, but there was no sign of Émile. Mori felt a pang of panic. His plan depended on his son. Where was he?

Mori backtracked, running up a flight of stairs to the school's office. Water-soaked stacks of papers lay everywhere. The damp stench permeated his nostrils. "Is there someone in charge?" Mori said.

A worker on top of a tall ladder, pulling large pieces of plaster from a leaking gash in the ceiling, looked down at Mori. "The secretary was just here, but she left."

Mori's stomach tightened. He raced down the hallways, peering into each classroom. He was sweating and short of breath. Where was Émile? He stopped to rest at a window on the third floor, sucking air into his exhausted lungs.

Through the closed window, he spotted them—Alena and Émile walking across the courtyard. "Émile!" Mori shouted. "Émile!" He pulled at the latch, trying to open the pane of glass.

Neither of them heard his cry. They continued past the large stone classical statuary lining the quad and headed out the front gate. Mori sprinted to the stairway, running down the spiral steps two at a time. At this pace he could easily catch up with them.

Halfway between the first and second floor, Mori was stopped by storm debris—fallen plaster and water. The route was blocked. He had no choice but to backtrack and find another way out. Down a long hall, he spotted a staircase. He followed several students, moving around those who walked slowly.

A few minutes later Mori reached the empty courtyard. He ran to the street and looked in every direction, but Émile and Alena had disappeared.

He was exhausted, and without his son. Mori leaned against a vine covered stone wall to catch his breath. "Merde."

21

Émile and Alena strolled the Tuileries to Place de la Concorde. From there, the streets narrowed behind Rue du Faubourg Saint-Honoré. The walk from the school to Parc Monceau took no more than forty minutes.

Émile spotted the large gate columns that marked the entrance to the park. "I'm so glad it stopped raining." Holding Alena's hand, he walked faster, eager to get to their spot. She smiled at him and clutched his arm.

"Halt."

Émile and Alena stopped abruptly and turned toward the sound.

Four German soldiers on foot approached. Their brown uniforms repulsed Émile.

"Where do you go in such a hurry?" one of the men demanded. His hand rested on a semiautomatic Luger PO8 holstered at his hip. The other three soldiers stood to the side.

Émile opened his mouth, but no words emerged. His heart was racing, his ears ringing.

"We're going to the park," Alena said, her face flushed.

"Why the hurry?"

Émile could feel Alena trembling beside him.

The soldier glared at them.

"It's getting late." Émile finally found some words, despite his fear. "The sun will set soon, and we want to enjoy the park before dark."

"There are nice paths for walking and there's a lovely sitting area near the pond," Alena said.

The soldier held out his hand. "Carte," he demanded.

Émile pulled his identification papers from his jacket and handed them to the soldier.

Alena searched her purse. She pulled at its contents, dropping a small tube of lipstick and a handkerchief. "I can't find—"

"Carte!" He shouted.

"Alena, give him . . ." Émile began.

Alena knelt and emptied the contents of her bag on the damp ground. "It's not here." She tore through the bag, her eyes filling with tears.

With lightning speed the soldier slapped Alena across the face, throwing her to the ground. Her purse flew from her hands, and the carte fell out.

Émile reached for her but lost his balance, falling to his knees. He was steaming but held his tongue.

Alena spotted it. Sniffling, she crawled to the folded paper, then handed it to the man.

The soldier mumbled something disparaging about Jews to his buddies, which neither Émile nor Alena understood, then tossed the documents to the street.

After the four soldiers walked away, Alena burst into tears.

Émile helped her to her feet. She trembled violently. "Fucking bastards." He hugged her to him. "Are you alright?"

She touched her cheek. "It stings," she said, rubbing at the swelling flesh.

Émile kissed her forehead, then recouped her identification papers from the wet street. He put his arm around her shoulder. "Come," he said and guided her to a bench just outside the park. They sat for a moment when he noticed the gold chain at her neck. "It's not safe for you to wear the star anymore. Give it to me and I'll guard it for you."

22

Atop the desk in Mori's home library sat a small gilt bronze statue of an elephant; its outstretched trunk held his father's gold pocket watch, which had once been owned by Otto von Bismarck. Its highly polished case was engraved with the likeness of the Prussian statesman.

Mori unhooked the small timepiece and wound the stem. It was shortly after nine in the evening. He felt restless and moved aimlessly about the room. Where was the boy? Now that his plan was in motion, he felt driven by an urgency to take the next step, but that couldn't happen without Émile. At the same time, he felt torn about getting his son involved. He turned on the lamps in the fading light.

Ruth joined Mori in the library, and another half hour passed before they heard the front door open. Mori rushed to the hall.

"Bon soir, Papa," Émile said.

"Where have you been?" Mori snapped. "I've been looking for you all afternoon. Why weren't you at school? I saw you and Alena leave." These words had rushed out in a harsher tone than he'd intended.

Émile flushed. "I went to the park with Alena. There was damage from the storm. She couldn't work, my classroom was flooded. What were you doing at school?"

Mori took a deep breath. "Come," he said, taking Émile by the arm and guiding him into the library.

"Good evening, Maman," Émile said before sinking into a

large upholstered sofa near his mother. He plumped a down-filled cushion behind his back. "What's going on? You're making me nervous."

"I went to the Ritz earlier," Mori said, and he began pacing the room as he explained his visit to Goering and what he had done to the *Madonna*.

Émile's face reddened, his eyes wide.

"From there I went to the school to find you," Mori continued. "I have a plan. It's going to shock you, but I think it's going to work, and I need your help."

Émile stared hard at his father. "You damaged a Rafael? What were you thinking? How could you?"

Mori stopped pacing and returned Émile's glare. "Don't lecture me. It was the only way."

"The only way for what?"

"It was the only thing I could think of to get Goering to agree to allow you into the gallery. You need to repair the painting."

"Can you slow down, please?" Émile said. "Why would you damage such an important work of art only to have me repair it?"

"There's more to do than the *Madonna*. There are other paintings."

"Other paintings?" Émile said, incredulous.

Mori had never seen Émile look so angry. "Several," Mori said and he began pacing again.

Émile's jaw dropped. "You damaged others? They'll throw you in jail, or worse. What were you thinking?"

Jacob entered the library while Émile was mid-sentence. "Am I interrupting something?" Jacob said.

"No, you're just in time to hear Papa explain why he stabbed Raphael's—"

"You killed Raphael?" Jacob said.

"Émile, stop. Sit down, Jacob," Mori ordered. "Nobody

killed anybody."

"Might as well have," Émile snipped.

Jacob sat on the sofa between Ruth and Émile. Mori repeated the day's events for Jacob's benefit.

"How can I help?" Jacob asked.

"You can't, I need a painter," Mori said. "Émile needs to do this. I've already spoken to Goering. He knows Émile's name. You don't paint, and we can't afford to anger the man. He's mad enough about the damage." Mori sat down in a chair facing Jacob. "You might help later, but for now, sit tight. And we don't discuss this with anyone."

Mori turned to Émile. "Can you find old or used canvas that shows its age?"

"Probably."

"Good," Mori said, and he was up on his feet pacing again. "You'll need stretchers too, and something to cut them with."

"Papa, you're way ahead of me. I'm very confused."

"I'm sorry." Mori took a deep breath, picked up a cup of tea from his desk, took a sip, and placed the cup and saucer on the cocktail table. He dropped into a burgundy velvet wingback chair. "I want you to repair the *Madonna*," he said to Émile, "and a few other paintings with minor damage. I repeat, minor damage that I caused."

Émile stared at his father.

"At the same time, I want you to create forgeries of several other paintings," Mori said.

"Forgeries?" Émile said quietly, as though confused by the word itself.

"I know you can do this. I've seen the copy you made of *The Expulsion of Hagar*. The difficulty will be hiding quickly what you're working on should Goering or anyone else come into the gallery."

"There's a war all around us, Émile. The rules are different now."

Émile took a breath and nodded. "How many paintings do you want . . . forged?"

"I don't know yet. There are several I've found that I sold to clients."

"Why do you need forgeries?" Jacob said.

Mori heaved a sigh and leaned back in his chair. "I know I can't be the caretaker for all the art in France, but I can try to protect the paintings I sold to families who have been faithful to me." He looked around the room, taking in the beauty that surrounded them. "It's those families who've made life easy for us." His eyes alighted on a large Sevres figurine of Cupid, which he'd given to Ruth when he'd courted her. What a different world they now inhabited.

Mori turned to his boys. "You go to fine schools, we have food on the table, and plenty of money. I make a very good living, at least I did before the war. All because of the paintings. And now it's my job to protect those works and the people who trusted me." The more Mori thought about his clients and their collections, the heavier his heart grew—so heavy he feared it might burst. "When the canvases began showing up, I tried contacting some of the families—" Mori's voice cracked, his eyes filling with tears, and he lowered his head.

Ruth squeezed his hand and smiled weakly.

Jacob rose. "Papa, what is it?"

"It's his life," Émile said softly. "It's breaking his heart."

Mori couldn't recall his boys ever seeing him cry. It was a time of many firsts, and this was not the worst among them. Ruth handed her handkerchief to her husband. He wiped at his cheeks, then told his family about his visit to Paul Betone's home and how sickened he'd felt when he'd seen the devastation.

All four were silent for a moment.

"Do you know where he is?" Ruth asked.

"He's gone. I haven't a clue, but if he's not dead, he's in a camp for Jews and probably will be soon." Mori took a deep breath and fixed his gaze on Émile. "That's why I need the copies. I'll safeguard as many of the originals as I can, which I'll return to their rightful owners when this mess with the Nazis ends. I plan on giving the Germans your forgeries instead of the real works. If your copies are similar in quality to *The Expulsion*, there shouldn't be problems."

"The paint will smell," Émile said. "If someone comes into the gallery, they'll smell it."

"That's why you repair the *Madonna* slowly. Should someone arrive, you simply slip the forgery behind other paintings, and put the *Madonna*, or another piece you're repairing, on the easel."

Émile rose and walked to the fireplace. He paced, appearing deep in thought. "Depending on the paintings," he said, "I would need to heat the canvases for aging."

"You can use Albert's oven. I've already spoken with him," Mori said.

"How am I going to get a forged painting out of your gallery without anyone noticing?"

Mori hadn't thought that far ahead. The gallery was guarded night and day.

Jacob leaned forward on the sofa. "Can the painting be removed from the stretchers and moved to Albert's? Can it be rolled?"

Émile pursed his lips. "I guess. But how are we going to take a canvas out of the gallery, even rolled, without creating suspicion?"

"I'll walk it," Jacob said.

All three looked at him, Ruth's face tight with worry.

"But how?" Mori asked.

"Because I've got a limp. We can roll the painting, tie it, and slide it alongside my leg. No one should notice since I use a cane."

There was silence. Mori rubbed his chin. "Your idea is good." Mori felt as tortured inside as Ruth now looked. He feared for the safety of his sons. Was this wise? Was he putting them at further risk?

"It's an excellent idea," Émile said.

Jacob seemed grateful for his support.

"If I roll and tie a painting and put it into the trash behind the gallery," Émile said, "Jacob could come along in the evening, pick up the canvas, and move it to Albert's, where I can meet him. That would mean the painting would have to already be dry."

Mori nodded, listening intently.

"From Albert's, we simply reverse course and Jacob walks it back to the trash at the rear of the gallery. I'll retrieve it there in the morning, re-stretch it, and place it into the original's frame. I'll roll the original and Jacob can carry it off the same way for safekeeping."

Mori held his gaze steady on Émile. "There's only one ending to this journey."

Émile nodded. "Of course."

Mori slid forward in his chair, "Émile," he said and paused, as pained by what he was about to say as he knew Émile would be. "You know this means the end of the École."

Émile's face dropped. "For how long?"

"I don't know, son." They stared at each other for a long moment.

Ruth put her hand on Mori's shoulder and nodded her head in support. "Where will you store the originals?" She asked.

"I hadn't gotten that far," Mori said. "We can't store them here. If Bertolt or Goering ever showed up . . ." He let his voice trail off, not wanting to complete the thought and further worry Ruth.

Émile spoke up. "I have a place."

23

Monday, May 25, 1942

The German guards, playing cards just inside the door, rose immediately when Émile arrived at the gallery carrying his easel.

"It's alright," Mori shouted from his desk at the rear of the room. "It's my son. He's going to repair the paintings the delivery men damaged."

"No one told us of any repairs or another person in the gallery," one of the soldiers said blocking Émile's way.

"Commandant Goering has approved the work. I'm sure Colonel Bertolt has been informed. You can check if you like." Mori flipped the switch on the Veritys Zephyr fan. The day had hardly begun, and it was already sweltering in the gallery.

The guards stepped aside.

"I'll have to bring brushes and paint later," Émile said, winding the serpentine path to the rear of the gallery. "I tied the easel onto my bike, but I couldn't carry more. Where's the painting?"

Mori led Émile to the storage area. On the far wall, in an ornately carved gold frame, the *Madonna* held sway over the other masters in the room.

Émile inspected the painted wood panel with great care. "You're lucky Jews don't go to hell," he said, keeping his voice down.

"Trust me," Mori said. "I feel worse than you about harming the it."

Émile surveyed the space, focusing on a corner near the rear door. "I think this is where I should work."

"There's not much room," Mori said.

"That's alright. I'll move some paintings to create an area large enough to move around in." Émile sighed. "I'll get the rest of my supplies here this afternoon and start working on it in the morning. Do you have a table for my things?"

"There." Mori pointed to a folding table propped against the wall.

"I'll need something a little larger. I'll take care of it." Émile moved a few paintings, then came upon several Picassos belonging to Mori. "They didn't take these?" Émile said softly.

"Not yet."

"I wonder why."

"They've confiscated 'degenerate' paintings from every gallery in the city, but from mine, nothing." Mori shrugged his shoulders. "They need me. Maybe it's incentive to keep me working?"

Émile continued to move things around, creating a workspace inside the storage room appropriate for their plan.

"I'll set the easel facing away from the door," Émile said. "We don't want anyone to see what's on it."

Mori put his finger to his lips, and Émile stopped speaking. Mori stepped outside the storage room for a moment and saw that the guards were deeply involved with their card game. He returned and nodded to Émile.

"We should slightly block the access to the storage room," Émile whispered. "This will give me time to switch from the painting I'm working on to one I'm repairing, should someone come back here." He looked up. The few hanging lamps in the storage room would not be sufficient to work by. "I'll bring a couple of lights, too."

Émile continued to adjust paintings, moving some out into the gallery, creating a tidy corner for work in the storage room. "I'll borrow another easel from school," he said, then more quietly, "I'll need to have them side by side."

Émile checked the *Madonna* once more, this time using his father's magnifying glass. "The scuff is clean," he said quietly. "It should be easy to fix."

Mori sighed. Although he was pleased with his handiwork, he was disgusted by his crime.

"I'll be back later with more supplies," Émile said.

Mori walked his son outside.

"Choose the first painting you want copied," Émile said. "I'll get canvas and stretchers."

"I'm sorry. I dread dragging you into this," Mori said. Would this plan cause more harm than good; would it further threaten his family?

"It's too late for doubt or regret."

Mori accompanied Émile to Rue Royale. The blue sky helped soothe the gloom inside him a bit. "Be safe," he said, kissing his son's cheeks. Émile turned to go, but Mori stopped him. The two men stared at each other for a moment, then Mori said, "I know you're sure of yourself, Émile, and that's a good thing. I also know you can get a little cocky, that's normal for a young man. But this is different. Unusual times mean you've got to grow up fast." He held Émile's shoulders for a moment and peered into his son's eyes. "There is no margin for error."

Émile returned his father's steady gaze. He nodded, and Mori knew he understood.

24

Tuesday, May 26, 1942

Mssr. Jacques Brenier
École des Beaux-Arts

Dear Mssr. Brenier,

It is with a heavy heart that I commit pen to paper this day. I have been deeply honored to be a student of the esteemed École des Beaux-Arts. Alas, for family reasons, I find it necessary to take leave of my studies at this time.

It is my fondest hope to return to the École at the earliest possible date.

Sincerely,

Émile Rothstein

After Émile dropped off his written notification to the office of the École des Beaux-Arts, he hurried back to his bicycle, his breath shallow, eyes burning. He sat on the curb, buried his face in his hands, and wept. His dream of becoming an important artist had been snatched away by the loathsome Nazi occupation and he was going to do all he could to seek revenge. His father's plan seemed the perfect answer.

Émile gave himself only a few moments. He pulled a handkerchief from his pocket, sniffed back the tears and wiped his face. He threw his leg over his bike. There was no more time for grieving. He had an important job to do.

Out in front of the gallery, the two guards were leaning against their dirty transport vehicle and smoking. Émile wondered if they ever moved that truck. He shielded the sun from his eyes and smiled at the guards, neither of whom responded to his cordial gesture.

Émile entered the gallery and untied the bundle of supplies he had strapped onto his bicycle—including two flexible Leviton metal spot lamps. Jacob had arranged for two saw horses and several six foot planks to be delivered outside the gallery the night before. A couple of pieces at a time, he carried his supplies into the cramped storage room, his work space. Émile moved a few more paintings, then set up the sawhorses and laid several pieces of wood across the top of them, creating a worktable. He attached the lamps he had brought to the storage room's wooden shelving and positioned them so they lit up the Madonna, which sat majestically on the easel. Émile held the magnifying glass above the graze and assessed the damage once again. He cautiously touched the surface of the paint, inspecting every millimeter of the scratch. "Simple," he mumbled to himself.

When Émile smelled his father's shaving soap, he greeted him without turning away from the painting. "Bonjour, Papa."

"Good morning," Mori said from the doorway that separated

the gallery from the storage room. "Do you have enough space to work?"

"I think so." Émile had traded the spacious studios at the École for this tight space. Although he would miss the school terribly, he felt honored that his father had entrusted him with a mission more important than anything he'd ever done. He was determined not to fail.

"How long will it take you to repair it?" Mori asked.

"Not long," Émile whispered. "It's clean, and there's very little paint loss. An hour maybe. But I can drag that out for a couple of weeks, at least."

Mori leaned close to Émile's ear. "Take longer if you can," he said. "Be meticulous and precise and, most of all, very slow."

Émile understood his father's tone. There were several paintings belonging to Mori's clients that he wanted Émile to copy. If Émile worked too fast on the repairs, there would be little reason for him to remain at the gallery. Working slowly would not seem unusual to the uneducated art collector. Goering would not suspect the truth.

With Mori looking over his shoulder, Émile took his magnifying glass and again inspected the fragments of paint that outlined the scrape. He removed a small bottle of cleaning solvent and dipped a clean brush into it. With a smooth and precise move he applied the liquid to the damage. "The scratch just needs to be smoothed and painted," Émile said quietly. "Here, see? That's just dirt and wax from years of never being cleaned."

Mori nodded his understanding.

Émile set down the magnifying glass and turned to his father. "Which painting do you want copied first?" he whispered.

25

Thursday, May 28, 1942

While Ruth and Alena tidied the kitchen, Mori and the boys moved into the salon. Tastefully decorated in tones of greens and gold, comfortable chairs and sofas mixed easily with antique tables, lamps, and assorted sculptures. Fragonard's *Le Parasol de Mademoiselle Céleste* dominated the room from above the mantle. Through gilt-framed windows, Mori could see the evening sun, which cast long shadows across the room.

Mori settled into an armchair and looked at Émile. "How long will it take?"

"Speed isn't really the issue, Papa."

"Speed is an issue, Émile. I don't know how long you can remain in the gallery."

"I can paint very fast. After all, it's a copy; there's nothing to figure out. The problem is drying time."

Mori closed his eyes leaning his head against the back of the chair.

"I can probably knock out a canvas in several days to a week," Émile said. "And I can work on multiple canvases while I wait for paint to dry."

"Okay," Mori said, readjusting the plan in his head. "I think it might be best to place the copies at the rear of the storage room until they dry. I'll keep the originals in the same area. We can set other paintings carefully in front of them to keep the copies hidden."

Émile nodded. "Makes sense."

"The paperwork from Bertolt is so erratic," Mori said. "If a few paintings aren't returned to the Jeu de Paume quickly, it might not be noticed. I'll think of an excuse if I need to."

Jacob sat silently taking it all in.

"As of today," Mori said, "there are six paintings that need to be copied. Now that you're set up, you can start tomorrow. It sounds like this can be done rapidly."

"Papa," Émile said, sitting forward in his chair, "let me just clarify. Although I can work on multiple paintings simultaneously, the process is not exactly fast. And it's not just about the drying time."

"I'm listening," Mori said.

"First, I must prepare a canvas the same size as the original painting. Then I have to copy the painting." Émile spoke slowly and deliberately, glancing up into his mind, as though envisioning the process. "Once dry, the canvas will need to be removed from the stretcher bars and rolled, and those needing to be aged will be taken to Albert's, re-stretched, and heated. Again, the canvas will have to be removed from the stretchers, rolled, and returned to the gallery, re-stretched again, touched up, and inserted into the original frame. At that point, the original canvas can be rolled and removed."

"It is a complex process," Mori agreed.

"Sounds exhausting," Jacob said.

Ruth and Alena entered the salon, carrying tea and cakes on two large silver trays.

Ruth took a chair next to Mori.

Alena sat beside Émile on the sofa. He gently kissed her bruised cheek.

Mori couldn't help but notice the gesture. "I'm furious the soldiers hit Alena," he said. The incident reinforced the dire need to keep his family safe. Every time he looked at her bruise, anger boiled inside him. "Fucking Germans."

Alena handed Émile a cup of tea and offered him a sweet.

"This is going to be a huge task," he said, taking a small bite of cake.

Alena smiled and settled back against Émile's shoulder.

"We should have gotten out of Paris last year," Ruth said, her jaw set, her frustration palpable. "Now, it's constant fear; we're never safe."

Mori settled a hand on his wife's knee, hoping his touch might calm her. His failure to get his family out pierced him through the heart over and over again.

Ruth placed her cup on the coffee table. "I can't count how many of our friends have either left Paris or disappeared, and now Émile and Jacob will be in the line of fire," she said.

Mori tried offering some reassurance. "As odd as this sounds," he said, "we're probably safer now than any of our friends. If I didn't have something the Nazis needed, we all would have been shipped out of here."

Ruth put her hand over his and held his gaze for a moment, eyes moist. "And what happens when they're done with you? What then? We disappear with the rest?"

Émile had raised this question before, but Mori had chosen to disregard that reality, praying instead that the war would end before his job with the Germans was done. "These repairs will prolong their need for me."

"Even so," Ruth said, "There's no ignoring this, Mori. When your work is finished, so are we."

A heavy silence descended on the room, no one making eye contact.

Finally Émile looked at Mori. "Papa, perhaps we can save the original masterpieces, but Maman's right. We must find a way to leave Paris."

26

Sunday, June 7, 1942

Mori picked up the morning copy of *Le Petit Parisien* from the front stoop and sprinted back up the steps and into the house.

Ruth was in the dining room.

"Good morning," he said, sitting at his place.

Ruth poured coffee and slid a plate of croissants in his direction.

Mori opened the newspaper revealing the front page. The enormous print of the headline hit him like a slap across the face.

All Jews in France Now Required to Wear Yellow Star

Mori was stunned. In horror, he read the accompanying article that explained every detail of how the Germans now demanded that French Jews be immediately identifiable, just as they had in Germany, Poland, and other countries before this. He had not expected France to ever agree to such a decree. His heart pounded and he said aloud, "Oh God no!"

Ruth grabbed hold of his hand. Her face was ashen. "What is it?"

Mori swiveled the paper toward his wife.

27

Wednesday, July 8, 1942

The heat from Albert's bread oven, combined with the sweltering summer weather, created a taxing working environment for Émile and Jacob. They were exhausted and wanted to get home for some rest.

This was the fourth night in a row Émile had worked into the wee hours, preparing and painting canvases. Before he rested, however, he had to finish aging the canvas. He had not carried out this process since his copy of *The Expulsion of Hagar* upon entrance to the École. He'd used Albert's oven for that painting as well.

Although the aging process had been successful that time, there was no guarantee it would work so well again. Earlier that day he had finished treating the back of the canvas of Édouard Manet's *Opera Ball*, which featured several men in dress coats as they admired a beautiful dancer descending a sweeping staircase. Now it was literally trial by fire to find out whether Albert's oven could work the same magic on *Opera Ball* as it had on *The Expulsion*.

Émile glanced at Jacob, who was assisting him in the overheated kitchen. "Here goes," he said.

Jacob smiled and gave his brother a nod.

Émile carefully lifted the medium-sized canvas, which he had just finished re-stretching and securing onto its wood supports. Jacob opened the oven, the heat blasting them both in the face, and Émile slid the painting onto the oven rack. He left it in there for a few seconds, then pulled it out and slid it onto the marble-top counter to cool. He eyed every inch of the canvas and, after a few minutes, slid it back into the oven.

Émile repeated this process multiple times throughout the evening, pulling the painting out frequently and keeping a close eye on the progress, watching the paint slowly crack and tighten on the surface of the masterpiece.

After a couple of hours, both Émile and Jacob were drenched in sweat. Jacob handed a glass of wine to Émile, who turned for just a moment from the oven and took a gulp, grateful for the liquid.

"Émile!" Jacob pointed to the oven.

The corner of the Manet was smoking. "Merde," Émile said dropping the glass, which shattered on the floor. He frantically pulled the canvas from the heat, tossing it to the marble-top table. Jacob dabbed the edge with a towel extinguishing the smoke.

Émile held his burned fingers to his mouth but did not tear his eyes away from the painting. Despite the mishap . . . there it was; the awaited changes had begun. The paint was now thoroughly dry, the lighter colors developing a yellow tinge from the heat, and the rabbit-skin glue Émile had used to treat the canvas before he'd begun to paint was developing a fine craquelure across the expanse of the canvas. The result was a painting that reflected age and damage from airborne elements.

The two stared at the artifact, Émile almost as amazed as his brother. "It worked," Émile said, exhaling in relief.

"I'll bet you're glad you don't have to do this part for all the paintings," Jacob said.

"I am," Émile said. "Keep in mind, not all the paintings I'm copying are hundreds of years old. The process is different for each one."

Émile had spent days at the gallery copying the Manet. Now the cracked surface made it truly mimic the real thing. The original treasure belonged to Mori's dear friend, Edmond Rothschild, who had had the piece hanging in his large hunting lodge near the Loire Valley, a family estate held for generations by his father, grandfather, and great-grandfather.

After completing a couple more rounds of the heating-and-cooling cycle, Émile stood back from the canvas and said, "One more step." He pulled some raw umber from his bag and mixed it with a light oil to the consistency of water. He dipped a small cotton cloth into the liquid and, with quick even movements, he wiped the face of the painting. The dark mixture filled in the cracks and instantly finalized the aged appearance of the canvas.

"That's amazing," Jacob said.

Émile immediately placed the canvas into the oven again for one last time. He moved the work around equalizing the heat to all corners of the painting. A few minutes later, a masterwork lay on Albert's marble-top bakery table—the same table on which Albert would make brioche in a few hours.

Jacob stared at the work for several moments before speaking. "I am in awe of you." He couldn't stop studying the canvas. "I know you paint well, yet every time you finish something, I just can't imagine that I'm related to you."

"Hopefully what we're doing will work," Émile said.

"I just admire your skill. I love the way you paint," Jacob said. "I wish I had your talent."

Émile looked his brother in the eye. "Thank you. That means a lot to me."

Jacob grinned.

When the painting had cooled enough Émile said, "Okay, help me here."

He slid the painting to the end of the table, kneeling on one knee. "Hold this in place. I need to remove the tacks."

He pointed to the small brads that affixed the canvas to the stretcher bars.

Émile placed the sharp edge of a tack puller under each brad, prying the tiny copper supports from their resting places. "It will need varnishing to really bring out the color, but I'll do that at the gallery tomorrow. The smell won't bother anyone. I've been using varnish all week on repair work."

After finishing one side, Émile turned the painting 180 degrees and repeated the process. After that he alternated as he removed the remaining tacks. First one tack from one side and then one from the other side, thus stabilizing the pressure on the canvas.

Jacob watched his brother's every move.

"Almost . . ." Émile pulled the last tack. "There."

The canvas sagged slightly, resting on the stretchers and the cool top of the marble table.

Émile turned off the oven. "I hope this works." "What do you mean, the greatest forger in the world fail? *Incroyable*."

The two men stood over the table, admiring Émile's masterwork. Émile ran his fingers across the dry paint. He felt the texture of his work, the small cracks, the tiny variations of the paint's thickness. He looked up at his brother's face, flushed from the heat, bluish circles under his eyes. "You look as tired as I feel," he said. The restaurant was dark, the small light in the kitchen not visible from the street. It was getting quite late. Soon Albert would arrive to begin making baguettes.

Émile removed the stretcher from the table, disassembling it into four parts, two each of varying lengths. He tied them together with two cotton ties, then leaned them against the wall behind the table. He took a deep breath. "That's it. Time to move this out of here."

Émile slowly began rolling the canvas, half expecting the paint to peel off. Each time he did it, he felt just as nervous, even though it had worked every time. When the painting was fully rolled, he enclosed his hands around it. "Here, hold this," he said to Jacob.

Jacob placed his hands around the center of the cylinder, copying Émile's position. "Okay, I have it."

Émile gently lifted the end of the roll and slid a narrow strip of cotton cloth beneath the painting. He brought both ends together, tying them with a loose-fitting knot. He repeated the same action at the other end while Jacob held the roll still.

"Alright, I'm going to tie one more piece of cotton where your hands are. Just raise the painting a bit, so I can get the cotton underneath."

Jacob lifted the roll slightly above the table, and Émile slid the cotton strip into place at the center of the roll and tied it. "That's it." Émile took the finished roll, covered it with a thin layer of cotton material for protection, and placed one final cotton tie to keep the fabric in place.

The brothers sat down on small café chairs at the marble table, their bodies limp with fatigue. Émile poured himself another glass of wine and held it in the air. "To you, Jacob."

"Me?" Jacob said. "Why?"

"Because I couldn't do this without you."

Jacob smiled, clicked his glass to his brother's and took a long final gulp.

Émile stood, put the two glasses into a nearby sink, recorked the wine bottle, and swept up the broken glass. "Okay, you ready?"

Jacob nodded and slowly stood, stretching his leg. He loosened the button at the top of his pants.

Émile took the rolled painting and helped his brother guide it down the leg of his pants. "If we tuck the lower part into your sock, that should keep it from falling out."

"That's a good idea. I didn't do that before, when I brought it over here."

Émile bent down, raised the hem of Jacob's pant leg and

guided the lower end of the painting into his stretched sock. "How does that feel?"

Jacob buckled his pants. "Okay, I think."

Although Jacob was the elder, Émile felt responsible for his brother's safety. Life had dealt Jacob a more difficult hand. "Please be careful," he said.

"I will."

"I don't mean for the painting, I mean for you." It was well past curfew. He hated seeing his brother walk out of here so late with a forgery on him, and with that horrible yellow badge on his chest.

Jacob smiled, took a deep breath, and reached for his cane. "You did it, Émile. Another one finished. I'm off to the gallery. Don't forget to look in the dust bin tomorrow morning."

117

28

Thursday, July 16, 1942

Émile tucked the four stretcher supports behind a table in Albert's kitchen and rolled and tied the canvas with his brother's help. After doing this for so many nights, the two of them were getting the process down and worked well together.

"How many is this?" Jacob said as Émile adjusted the position of the canvas under his brother's pant leg.

"This makes eight, and there are still more," Émile said. Some were easy; others, not as much. "Thank God most of them haven't had to come over here for this type of aging." All the rolling and heating, stretching and re-stretching was wearing Émile down.

This canvas had taken longer than the previous ones, and the two men hadn't finished until almost four in the morning. Émile felt uncomfortable with the hour as they stepped out of the restaurant onto Rue Saint Honoré. He desperately needed to get home for a few hours of sleep. "I'll walk you to the corner."

"You walk me every evening. It's not necessary," Jacob assured him. "Besides, your bike is parked behind the café."

"No, I want to," Émile insisted, concerned about leaving Jacob while the painting was still on him.

"Stop worrying," Jacob said, rolling his eyes. "I'll be fine." He patted the rolled canvas inside his trousers.

"Jacob, I'm only taking you to the corner. It's a half block. I just want to make sure you're alright."

The brothers turned left outside the café and began a slow walk down Rue Saint Honoré.

From the opposite side of the street, they passed their father's gallery. A lone German guard slept soundly in a transport truck parked directly in front of the door. It served as a permanent guard station with a scratchy sounding radio.

In the glow of golden lamp light, Jacob limped slowly to Rue Royale, Émile at his side. "Alright," Jacob said, "Get home. I'll drop this off behind the gallery and be right behind you."

Émile agreed that Jacob should approach the rear courtyard alone, so as to avoid drawing attention to two men entering the area at such a late hour. "Be safe," Émile said.

Jacob rounded the corner and began his slow walk to the mid-block gates that opened into the rear courtyard.

Émile ducked into a darkened doorway to watch his brother make his way down the street. From the shadows he watched him open a small door within one of the gates that led into the dark open courtyard at the rear of the gallery. He imagined Jacob's slow progress across the courtyard, which was surrounded by buildings fronting on Rue du Faubourg Saint-Honoré and Rue Royale. Now he would be at the rear door of the gallery, removing the scroll from his pants, placing it in a dust bin beside the rear door.

Hurry up, Émile thought. Exhausted, all he wanted was to get home for a few hours sleep. He leaned back against the wall of the dark alcove, waiting for Jacob to reappear. A sound startled him to attention. It was the growl of a truck. Émile's heart lodged in his throat. A vehicle—now two, now three—accelerated through the intersection and would pass the gate in a second. He stepped back into the darkest corner of his sanctuary, hoping now that his brother did not appear.

All three trucks parked to the curb. French police officers exited the vehicles and moved rapidly in both directions on the street. What were the police doing at this hour? This couldn't be about the painting, could it?

Jacob was still somewhere in the courtyard, behind the gate. *Stay back*, Émile thought, sweat dripping from his temples. *Stay behind the gate*, Jacob. His heart was pounding. Although the air was not cold, he felt a strange chill. *Don't let this happen, don't let this happen*, he prayed silently, *don't open the gate*. Émile thought Jacob would surely hear the noise of the trucks and the gendarmes and stay hidden.

A few minutes later, although the police remained, the urgency seemed to have eased.

From the shadows Émile prayed, *Don't come out yet*. But a moment later, the gate slowly swung open, and Émile cringed. Jacob stepped onto the sidewalk. He looked both ways. Then he froze.

No! Émile looked on in horror.

After a moment, Jacob turned right toward his bicycle, which he'd parked on the street earlier in the evening for his ride home.

Act normal, Émile thought.

Jacob moved carefully with his head down, no more than a few steps, before a sharp shout came from behind him: "Jew!"

Jacob reeled around. His head turned from side to side, attempting to make sense of the crowd. The yellow star on his dark jacket shone brightly in the glow of the street lamps.

"You! Stop!" the officer ordered. "Our first--"

"Me?" Jacob said, trying to get his bearings.

Émile watched his now motionless brother. *What do they mean, first Jew?* he thought. He watched three police officers approach Jacob. He clearly heard the word "Jew" repeated several times. These were not German soldiers; why would French gendarmes be singling out a Jew?

"When I want to hear from you, I'll speak to you," the officer shouted, kicking the cane from Jacob's hand and causing him to lose his balance and fall. Another officer kicked Jacob's leg.

Émile looked on in terror. He had to hold himself back from running to his brother.

A second gendarme picked up the cane, striking Jacob several times in the leg before breaking it in half over his knee. "Now you'll know when to talk and when not to."

The other policemen watched their comrade and laughed. Then they grabbed Jacob by the arms and pushed him into the rear of a nearby truck.

In a panic and unable to do anything to help his brother, tears streamed down Émile's cheeks. He could barely catch his breath. He wanted desperately to run to Jacob's side but if he did, he would surely meet with the same fate. Then their parents would never know what had happened to them.

With a rumble, the trucks pulled away from the curb. Émile felt light-headed and couldn't keep his thoughts straight. He stepped out from the shadows, grabbed his belly, and vomited. Everything seemed to be spinning, and he wept uncontrollably for not going to his brother's aid. Where would they take Jacob? What would happen to him?

Émile wiped his face, took a steadying breath, and tore the yellow star from his pocket. Then he ran up Rue Royale toward Jacob's bike. When he passed the door to the courtyard, where moments before Jacob had stood, Émile found the broken pieces of cane.

With an ache in his heart, Émile mounted the bicycle, and with as much energy and speed as he could muster, he raced toward home. He needed to get to his father.

29

Every time the vehicle rounded a corner, Jacob slid from one side of the truck bed to the other. "Where are you taking me?" he yelled.

"Shut up, Jew," a voice in the front shouted.

"I haven't broken any laws." He thought about that statement. He had just dropped a forged painting behind the gallery.

The Peugeot flatbed engine ground and rumbled. The truck sped through the streets of Paris, the two officers talking and laughing in the cab.

Crouched and trembling, Jacob massaged his injured leg. It had all happened so fast. He still didn't quite understand what had occurred. Where were they taking him and why? He glanced around at the canvas covering. Could he cut through it and jump from the vehicle? He searched his pockets for his folding knife. Nothing.

Why would the police want me? he thought. *Could it be the painting? How could they know?* He had dropped it off just as he and Émile had planned. *There was no one there.*

The truck turned sharply and braked to a stop. Jacob heard the officers jump to the street. He crawled painfully a few feet and lifted a small corner of the canvas where it met the wooden siding. He tried pulling, but the fabric was attached to the outside of the truck. It was dark but for the glow of a street lamp that crept through a small opening in the trucks canvas cover. He wondered if he should call for help. Would his cries meet helpful ears, or would it further endanger him? "Help me!" he tried, then waited a moment. "Help Me!" he shouted louder. "I'm here in the truck."

Then he heard the officers again. "Hurry up," they shouted.

Jacob beat his fist against the wood siding of the truck in frustration.

Voices outside became louder, closer. An officer was yelling to someone to get in line. There were other voices too, voices of men and women filled with fear and panic. He heard the cries of young children.

With a sharp crack, the rear of the truck opened, not to release Jacob, but to force others in. The light from the street lamps illuminated the yellow stars sewn to everyone's clothing. Yellow stars everywhere.

Chaos ensued. Mothers cradled their babies in their arms, consoling them as much as possible.

"Where are you taking us?" a woman asked.

"They're taking us away," a man called out, "Like the rest of the Jews."

"What's happening here?" Jacob asked a woman pressed tightly against him on the floor.

"We're going to the prison for Jews," she said.

Fear coursed through Jacob's body. His leg still throbbing, he pulled himself up to a standing position, using a wooden bar on the side of the truck for leverage. People were tightly packed against one another, and the early morning air stank of body odor inside the closed and airless tomb.

After a while, he could no longer stand and let himself slide slowly to the floor, pinned against the side of truck. It felt like hours before the vehicle began to move again.

30

Émile turned Jacob's bike into an alley that ran parallel to the Champs-Élysées. Peddling like a madman, he flew past dust bins overflowing with garbage.

He had never ridden so fast. His heart pounded, and sweat soaked his clothing, nausea lingering in his belly. He turned onto Avenue Gabriel and rode past stately stone homes with mansard roofs. Their windows reflected the glow of scattered street lamps; each one mirrored Émile's image as he sped by.

As he pedaled, he played the scene on Rue Royale over and over in his head, yearning for a different ending, but nothing changed. Jacob was still gone.

Avenue Gabriel was sheltered by large elm trees that blocked the light of the moon. Émile could see the Champs-Élysées across the park to his left. Headlights moved in both directions on the large boulevard, which struck him as odd. It was half past four in the morning. Why so many cars? He stopped to get a better look. From the darkness beneath the trees he observed French police and German soldiers in the distance. He saw both Army and police trucks parked together on the Champs-Élysées.

A quick left turn put Émile on Avenue Montaigne. From there he was just one block from his home on Avenue François.

Almost there. The only obstacle appeared to be the entirety of the Paris police department and an assortment of German soldiers.

And no clear path.

31

Jacob hugged his legs to his chest as the crowded truck hurtled through the streets. He peered through a small gap where the canvas cover met the wooden side of the truck's bed. Even if he could tear open the fabric and somehow jump, that made no sense; his legs were his enemy now. He rubbed his throbbing shin, where the gendarme had kicked him; it was swollen and warm. His body would surely fail him if he attempted to flee. He closed his eyes, dropped his hands into his lap, and prayed while the truck swayed from side to side. His heart beat in time with the knock of the wheels as they bumped over cobblestone streets. Bump, knock, bump, knock. Noxious fumes from the engine filtered in through a narrow flap at the rear of the truck, causing everyone to cough.

The wail of a frightened child rose up from the huddle of bodies. Jacob looked into the faces surrounding him and cringed. Fathers and mothers sat in dim stillness on wooden planks that stretched from the front to the rear of the rolling, canvas-enclosed box. Like fish suspended in a bowl of water, minimal movement; just shock and fear.

The truck took a sharp turn, and people braced themselves, one man tumbling over a child, others over luggage. They were Jews—no longer people—not men, women, small boys and girls. Just Jews. Were people now categorized simply by the badge on their chest? A yellow star. It meant nothing, and yet it meant everything. *Are we humans first, or are we just faceless bodies distinguishable by a bit of yellow fabric?*

He glanced at his wristwatch. He'd received it from his parents on his eighteenth birthday. The inscription on the back read, "For your 18th, for life. Love, Maman and Papa." At the top, the engraved Hebrew symbol, "chai," its meaning, *life*.

How much time did he have? Was he going to prison? Was he going to be killed? Tears streaked his face.

When the truck finally came to a stop, it was half past six in the morning. Loud voices added to the tension and chaos. The women seated near him sobbed. He ached at the thought of his mother someday enduring this humiliation and fear. Fathers, husbands, stoic men brandished the only weapon they had, their solemn faces, attempting to stand strong for their families. His father would do the same.

The rear canvas flap swung open, flooding the interior of the truck with an explosion of light and noise. Shouts from the police. Confusion.

"Sortez, sortez!" commanded the officer standing on the street holding a large rifle. A deep scar ran down his cheek. He kept his face slightly averted.

"Out, out!" another man shouted.

Jacob limped toward the light, momentarily blinded by the sun's glare. In the distance he spotted the Eiffel Tower. "My house, it's just over there." He moved to the edge of the truck. Jacob pointed, hope surging in him. To the scarred officer, he said, "There, I need to go there."

"Get in line," the man snarled.

"There's a mistake. I shouldn't be here."

"Sortez, sortez!" He jammed the rifle into Jacob's side.

Hope died. Dread gripped his gut. Jacob's chest felt like it was being compressed in a vise.

Without his cane, the step down was too tall. Placing both hands on the truck's floor, he turned, knelt down, and climbed backward from the truck's platform. Without warning, someone gripped his arm. His body jerked backward, and he fell to the street. The smell of oil and tar wafted up from the road, along with the tantalizing aroma of freshly baked bread on the breeze. A woman sipped espresso in a café just across the road.

"Vite!" a rough looking policeman said.

Jacob felt a hand smack his shoulder. He lost his balance once more, falling to the curb.

"Why are you doing this?" he shouted up at the man who towered over him.

"Inside. Move inside."

"Pardon," said a tall dark-haired young man. He edged between Jacob and the officer. With a sympathetic smile and a strong arm, he eased Jacob to his feet.

"Thank you," Jacob said, looking at the crowd of people surrounding them. "What's happening here?"

"They're arresting Jews," the man said.

Jacob had heard this statement several times now, and still it didn't make sense. His mind refused it. He dusted off his pants and jacket and extended a hand. "I'm Jacob."

"Ben. I heard you say you live near here."

"I live there." Jacob pointed. "A short distance from the Tower on the other side of the river."

Along with the rest of the yellow-starred unfortunates, the two men were herded toward a large building, the *Vélodrome d'Hiver*. Jacob knew it well. He and Émile had attended events in the Vel' d'Hiv as it was known. The structure was the first permanent indoor cycling track in France, and was used for other athletic events as well.

"What are we doing here?" Jacob asked.

"They came to our house a couple of hours ago," Ben said. "They told us to pack some things and get into the bus."

"Bus?"

"It just left. It was a big one, like they use around the city."

"I was picked up while I was walking down the street,"

Jacob said.

"Where's your family?"

"I don't know. Home, I think. This is a mistake. I shouldn't be here." His dread deepened.

"Better go inside," Ben said, brushing back his dark wavy hair. "My family is up ahead." He offered his arm to Jacob who gratefully accepted the help.

Hundreds of people crowded them. Small valises, cloth-wrapped personal items, children's fallen toys, all became obstacles for a man who desperately needed his cane. Jacob's jaw tightened. It was the same tightness he'd felt when he'd been bullied as a child for dragging his leg. It was the tightness of anger and of helplessness to do anything about it. "Damn the yellow star," Jacob said.

"Keep your voice down. You don't want to mess with these guys. They're nothing more than Nazi thugs in Parisian gendarme uniforms."

Jacob inched along with the crowd, one small, painful step at a time, while they funneled through the tall entrance into the now crowded arena.

"Where do you live?" Jacob asked Ben.

"Behind l'Opéra."

Jacob's shirt was drenched with perspiration. He tied the jacket he'd been wearing around his waist. His leg ached. He was thirsty, exhausted, and terrified.

He hobbled into the building, where men had once raced bicycles for glory. The glass ceiling, which had previously offered a clear view of the evening stars, was now painted dark blue like a starless midnight sky. Small flecks of paint were missing, which allowed tiny streams of light to filter through an otherwise gloomy stadium.

Thick, pale green iron columns with ornate leaf patterns molded at the joints reached to vaulted arches that supported hanging lights. Rust stains dripped from structural beams, and dirt from years of neglectful maintenance blanketed every surface. The smell of human sweat and waste permeated the cavernous prison.

Jacob felt a hand at the small of his back, then a shove. "Move on," an officer yelled. Jacob stumbled forward, catching his balance on a handrail separating the last row of seats from the mid-level walkway where he'd entered. Below him lay rows of seats filled with strangers; behind and above him, more seats.

"Come on," Ben said.

Several hundred people moved about the arena, whispering with fellow prisoners, searching for loved ones, weeping.

Ben helped Jacob limp up two steps, turn, and sit on the first seat in the first row high above the arena's floor. He motioned to his family, gesturing that he would sit with Jacob.

Jacob massaged his leg. Anxiety and fear wouldn't save him. He needed a plan.

"I wonder how long they'll keep us here," Ben said.

Jacob's eyes darted from one end of the arena to the other. He sucked in the stench of fear and resignation and vowed to find a way out.

32

It was dark outside but for a hanging gas lantern still shining on the front porch. Mori paced the upper hall landing, which overlooked the entry below. Each time he passed Ruth, she said, "Why aren't they back yet?" or "They should have been home hours ago." She stood glued to her spot at the bannister, hanging onto a fistful of her dressing gown, her hair in pin curls. She did not tear her eyes from the glass front doors and the street beyond them.

Mori worried too; how would he even begin to find their sons if they'd been taken? But he kept this to himself, instead saying, "I'm sure they're OK, Ruth. They'll be home soon."

"Maybe you should go look for them," she said.

Mori paused and put his arm around his wife. He stared out the front entry with her for a moment, then a movement caught his eye. A shadow several feet in front of the glass doors. "Shh," he said, drawing her away from the bannister. He lowered his voice to a whisper. "There's a soldier out there."

Ruth's mouth opened, but no sound emerged.

Through the sheer lace curtains on the front doors Mori could see a German facing the street, a few steps down from the stone stoop, a Luger resting at his hip.

A rumbling sounded outside as French police cars and German transport trucks headed up and down the street. Mori pulled Ruth further into the shadows.

Her eyes were wide, "What's he doing?" she whispered.

"I don't know. I think he might be guarding our house."

33

É mile's route home remained blocked. He had to get word to his parents about Jacob. Where had they taken his brother?

He remained in the narrow park and waited there, protected from view behind a row of bushes. For the moment he was safe, but once day broke, he would be exposed. A block of apartments faced the park. His presence would alarm anyone looking out of their windows.

On the opposite side of the park, the French police herded civilians—men, women, and children—along the sidewalk. Sickened, Émile watched them being led, one family at a time, to buses lining the Champs-Élysees. Mothers and fathers carried toddlers; others toted suitcases, Jews, all of them. The yellow stars sewn to their coats glowed under the street lamps.

He was so close but he didn't dare leave the shadows of the park, even with his yellow badge removed.

At just past six the sun peaked over the roof tops, but the coast still wasn't clear. He would be spotted and picked up in an instant. Across the park Émile recognized the faint silhouette of a garbage collector's abandoned trolley—a small metal trash can with a handle, resting on two wheels. Against it, a straw broom leaned beside a long wooden rake.

He didn't have much time before the gendarmes noticed him. Crouching in the bushes, he took two large handfuls of earth and rubbed the grit on his pants and shirt. He dirtied his face and messed up his hair. Then he hid his brother's bicycle in the bushes.

In a slow, deliberate move, Émile walked to the garbage can and threw his jacket inside. He pushed the can to the uppermost border of the park, along Avenue Matignon. Long shadows formed from early morning sun cast eerie shapes across Émile's path. His head down and shoulders rounded, Émile removed the broom from the can, tucking it under his arm; he had seen a street sweeper carry his broom this way.

With what appeared to be most of the Paris police department across the street, Émile walked slowly to the corner of Avenue Matignon and Avenue des Champs-Élysées, his heart pounding. From under his arm he allowed the broom to drag on the street behind him as he walked into the storm of arresting officers. No one noticed him.

Arriving at the corner of the Champs and Avenue Montaigne, Émile stopped. In full view of the French police, he pulled the broom from under his arm and swept an invisible handful of debris from the gutter into his hand, going through the motion of dumping the trash into the already half-full can. He tucked the broom back under his arm, muttered an assortment of inaudible words, then walked slowly down Avenue Montaigne, and turned left onto Avenue François.

He could hardly believe what he was doing seemed to be working. *Almost there*, he thought, his breath short and shallow.

Halfway down the street, Émile spotted a German soldier on the entry stairs to his home. A flash of panic struck through him. *Maman? Papa?* Had they rounded up his parents too? He kept his pace slow and steady, even as he gasped for air. He hoped the soldier was paying as little attention to him as the police had on the Champs.

Once past the house, he inserted his key into a brass lock on a wooden door. He wheeled the trash can into the service courtyard that belonged to his house. Émile closed and locked the door behind him, leaned heavily into the gate for a moment, then he ran across the courtyard to the rear entrance of his family's home.

"Papa! Maman!" he shouted out as he ran inside. "Where are you? He needed to see their faces and know they were alright. He had to tell them about Jacob. Papa knew Goering, he would help. He hurried through the kitchen to the entry hall beyond, then climbed the spiral staircase two steps at a time. "Papa," he called softly, remembering the soldier on the front steps.

"Shhh, up here." Mori stood in a darkened corner of the upper hall.

Upon seeing his father's face, Émile burst into tears. "Papa, they got Jacob!"

Mori was dressed in pajamas and robe; he stepped out of the shadows.

Ruth grabbed Mori's arm. "No!" she cried.

"The police took Jacob on Rue Royale." Émile could barely get the words out. "They took him." His voice broke as he dissolved into tears again.

"Stop, slow down," Mori said.

"Papa, we left Albert's—" Émile began."The gendarmes, the Nazis—they're everywhere."

Mori looked puzzled. "What do the police want with Jacob?"

"I don't know. A bunch of police in trucks pulled onto Rue Royale when Jacob came out of the courtyard behind the gallery. One of the gendarmes shoved him to the ground."

"Shoved him?" Ruth's face looked horror-stricken.

Émile grasped her hand in his. "And they took him away in a transport truck. I couldn›t believe it."

Ruth moaned, "God help us."

"In here," Mori said, his voice hushed, drawing Émile and Ruth into a bedroom. "Keep your voices low." Mori nodded toward the front of the house. "We don't want anyone to hear us."

"What is that soldier doing here?" Émile asked.

"I don't know," his father said. "We've been waiting up here for you and Jacob."

"When I walked past, it looked like he was guarding the house," Émile said.

Ruth stared at Émile in the faint light. "You're filthy, and you stink," she said. "What happened ?"

Émile told his parents about his flight from the scene and through the park. His mind was racing. "We must find Jacob," he said, "but police are all around the neighborhood. Nazis, too."

"Nazis, I understand," Mori said. "But why the police?"

"It looks like the police are taking people," Émile said.

From the darkness of the bedroom, Émile, Mori, and Ruth peered out the window at the street below, careful to hang back in the shadows. Many of their neighbors carried valises as they walked to buses parked on Avenue François. A small yellow star dotted every person's clothing.

"Where are they taking them?" Mori asked.

"I don't care where they're taking them," Ruth said, wiping at tears on her cheeks. I want my son home." She turned to Mori. "You must bring him home." She placed her hands on her husband's shoulders. "You have to get him back. Please." Her voice was forceful. "Speak to Goering."

Mori stared at her. "Goering?"

"Yes," she said. "He is the one with the power."

Mori seemed frozen in place but his eyes were intense as though he was hatching a plan. His gaze darted around the room, finally settling on his son. "Émile," he said. "I need you to do something for me. Get washed up, have some coffee, and then meet me down in the library."

34

While he waited for Émile, Mori threw open the library drapes, leaving the lace curtains behind them closed for privacy. He unfastened a pair of glass-paned French doors allowing fresh air to flood the room while the lace billowed with the breeze.

His collection of rare, leather-bound books with tooled-gold spines stood side by side in long rows. Titles were imprinted in gold on covers of green, brown, burgundy, and black. Mori's gaze combed the books. "Where is it?" He muttered to himself and tilted his head to see the books that lay on their sides. Scattered among history's greatest literary treasures were various antique manuscripts and tomes.

He glanced at the Picasso above the fireplace. It was a masterpiece. He needed a masterpiece, and it would take one to get Jacob back.

Mori moved to the bookcase on the other side of the fireplace and looked at the lowest shelf. *"There you are, Monsieur Da Vinci,"* he thought. *"You're about as masterful as they come."* He lifted a large book, then set it on the leather-topped, antique desk. He turned on two Sevres lamps positioned on either side of the desk and opened the book to the blank page preceding the text. He gently touched the paper, rubbing it between his fingers. He turned the page and ran his index finger to the year printed at the bottom of the second page. "Not the right age," he whispered. This paper was not old enough. "But the book's right."

He closed his eyes as he sorted through his thoughts. *I can make this work. I just need an older book.* He flipped through the pages of the Da Vinci tome, stopping at a low-quality photograph of the Mona Lisa. "Perfect!" He sighed with relief.

Mori stood behind his desk and scanned every shelf in his cavernous library. His gaze landed on a small cupboard below the bookshelf on the opposite side of the room. With a sigh of remembrance and relief he strode to the carved-wood doors and pulled open the bronze knobs. He found the object of his search on the bottom shelf—a massive manuscript bound not in leather, but in cloth. The binding needed restoration, so he used great care as he lifted the delicate treasure from its resting place.

"There you go." He ran his hand over the manuscript, treating the volume like a lost child. He cautiously opened the cover to the blank page preceding the text. Again, he felt the paper between his fingers and checked for the date.

"Wrong date, but you're close enough," Mori thought to himself, *"Goering will never know the difference."*

35

Jacob awoke with a start to the sweltering heat and the din of hundreds of murmuring voices. He massaged his face, then looked at his watch with blurry eyes. Six o'clock. At first he was confused. Was it morning? No. He'd only gotten a few hours of restless sleep. Night was not far off. He had tried lying on the narrow wooden bench, but had found it easier to sit on the floor with his head resting on his arms on top of the bench.

The stale air was thick and close, heated by the masses of people, and Jacob was drenched in sweat. More families poured into the arena, all confused and terrified. Jacob wanted water and a way out of this hell hole. He needed to escape. Carefully observing his surroundings, he appraised the arena once more. Cracks in the ceiling glass assured dripping water during a storm, and the damage to the floor in several areas spoke of years of neglect.

Jacob stood and saw misery in every direction. Mothers could not feed their children. Babies cried. Jacob limped to the toilets near the stadium floor. He said a silent prayer for running water in a sink. Each step was painful. There were guards everywhere.

A day before, he'd joked and shared wine with Émile. Now, he was alone, separated from his family. Did his brother even know he'd been captured? Had he seen the police take him?

He walked around the privacy barrier in the restroom. The stench of puke and feces turned his stomach. He thought he might vomit. *Why don't they open a window?* He stood before a backed-up toilet, unbuttoned his trousers, and urinated into the already filled bowl. He buttoned quickly and turned to the sinks. They were dry.

Back on the floor of the arena, Jacob came upon a line of people waiting to take a turn at a tall metal cylinder filled with drinking water. He hoped to claim a meager ledel for himself.

"Get back! One at a time," he heard a policeman yell. "Don't push. You'll all get some."

The crowd surrounded the water like a swarm of bees. Men, women, and children tucked in tightly for the priceless liquid. Mouth parched, Jacob waited, moving closer one small step at a time. Eventually he obtained a tiny cup and savored each drop while also wishing for more.

"Move on," the gendarme said, shoving Jacob aside once he'd finished his allotment.

Jacob teetered but regained his balance; he felt unsteady without his cane, and his injured leg throbbed. Searching for a place to sit, he continued to limp slowly around the arena, keeping his eyes peeled for a possible escape route. He scanned every dark corner, every crack in the wall. He looked for windows; there were none, except for the glass ceiling.

Did you really think you'd find a way out? He thought. *There is no way out.*

Then his eyes widened as he recalled the small windows in the toilet. Were they large enough for a person to fit through? He quickly pivoted, pushed through the crowd, and returned to the vile corner he'd run from twenty minutes earlier. He held his breath as he reentered the filthy enclosure. The metal-framed windows, just large enough for Jacob to pinch through, sat high above the sinks. They had been painted blue to block any view.

He managed to climb up onto one of the sinks and gripped the metal handle on the window. It didn't move; it had been painted shut. He struggled with the closure, trying to force it open, without success.

Several men entered the toilet, complaining about the stench. Jacob slid off the sink, his legs buckling beneath his weight. He lost his balance and fell to the filthy floor.

"Are you alright?" a man asked, helping Jacob to his feet. He swayed for a moment then settled. "Yes, thank you. I lost my balance."

"What were you doing?' the man asked.

Jacob didn't answer. He brushed himself off and went through the motions of urinating again, taking his time so that the men left before he did.

Now was his chance. The toilet was never unoccupied for more than a moment. With the room empty, he took the jacket from his waist, wrapped it around his hand, climbed onto the sink, and dealt a swift blow to the blue pane. Shards of glass exploded around his wrapped hand. He swiped at the frame furiously to remove the small pointed remnants stuck to the puttied edges, and greedily gulped in the fresh air.

He threw his jacket over the window ledge to buffer against any remaining broken glass, then pulled his chin up to the lip of the window and sucked in the fragrance of freedom. From his portal he surveyed the outside world, taking in the beautiful sky and trees as though he hadn't seen them in days. The distance from the window to the ground appeared to be about ten feet. He no longer cared if his legs didn't work properly; he would find a way.

Using every ounce of his strength, Jacob crouched, then threw his weight upward, hoisting himself to the window. On his first jump he managed to get his chest onto the ledge and gripped the sides of the window to keep from sliding back down onto the sinks. Heaving and pulling his body weight, he maneuvered his body halfway through the small opening, hoping no one entered the restroom before he could get himself all the way out. Freedom was only a few feet away.

36

From his desk, Mori motioned Émile into the library. He was sickened to have to bring his son into another subterfuge, but there was no other way.

Ruth, still in bed clothes, entered carrying a large tray with three cups, a pot of coffee, a baguette, jam and butter. The aroma of warm yeast filled the air. She set the tray on the coffee table in front of the sofa. Everyone helped themselves.

"What are we going to do about Jacob?" Émile said.

"That's what I've been working on." Mori handed Émile a large book with a slip of paper marking a page at its center. He hoped his son could rise above his fatigue to carry out the plan he'd been brewing.

"What is it?" Émile opened the volume to the photograph of the *Mona Lisa*.

"Hopefully your brother's freedom," Mori said. "I need you to create the 'original' sketch for the *Mona Lisa*." Mori gestured to the world's most famous face. "Your mother is right. Goering is our only chance to find Jacob, but I can't approach the man without something to trade."

Ruth set her coffee down and leaned into the conversation.

"While I'm with him, I can speak of Jacob," Mori said.

Émile gazed at the photograph.

"The sketch needs to be incomplete and rough," Mori said, "but unmistakably by Da Vinci's hand." Mori turned to Émile and saw exhaustion in his son's eyes. "I know you're tired," he said, "but do you think you could pull this off?"

"Yes, of course—"

Mori held up his hand. "This has to be perfect."

"I know what you want."

"Do you remember when I told you there was no margin for error in the copies you are doing of the paintings, that there was no space for you to be too sure of yourself?"

"Yes," Émile said, "but haven't you been pleased with my work?"

Mori nodded. "It's amazing."

"So," Émile said, shrugging his shoulders, "I don't understand what the problem is."

"Now there's even less margin for error. This will not be a copy of an actual piece. "This will be fabricated out of thin air. Plus . . ." Mori stood and leaned closer to Émile across his desk, as if to tell him a secret, "unlike the other forgeries, which at some point we'll slip unnoticed into the stream of stolen works, I'm going to be putting this piece right under Goering's nose. It's an implicit invitation to examine every detail of it—and he's knowledgeable."

Émile looked suddenly very awake, sobered by his father's words.

"On top of all of that," Mori said, "Goering has shared with me a particular fondness for Da Vinci."

Mori thought he saw a tinge of fear cross his son's face. He took a breath and exhaled loudly. "Now you understand what I want."

Émile nodded and leaned back into his chair as though under the weight of the task.

Mori picked up the other large book he'd selected and opened it to the blank cover page. He walked to the other side of the desk and set it before his son. "You'll use this page. The age of the paper is appropriate for the drawing."

Émile touched the blank paper. He closed his eyes and

rubbed the sheet between his thumb and forefinger. After a moment he said, "I can do this, Papa."

Mori nodded.

"Give me a minute," Émile said, standing. "I'll be right back."

When Émile had left the room, Ruth said, "He looks scared half to death. I'm scared too. This is dangerous." She was looking directly at Mori.

For the first time since he'd known her, Mori found it difficult to return his wife's gaze. He felt the same pain as she did over the capture of their son, but he also felt a remorse that deepened each time Ruth expressed her worry. He had hesitated about using Jacob as a courier for the forgeries. His firstborn had always been a bit delicate, and now he'd been taken from them. How could he have put his clients and their paintings before his family's safety? And yet the only way out of this mess now was through further involvement of his younger son.

"What choice do we have?" Mori lifted his gaze to Ruth's. "Do you know another way?"

Ruth blew out a breath and leaned back into the sofa.

"We have Nazis at our door, and the police are escorting our neighbors out of their homes," Mori said. "What's next?"

Ruth's eyes filled with tears. She retrieved an embroidered handkerchief from her sleeve and wiped her cheeks. "Who would have thought the world would come to this?"

Mori sat down next to her on the sofa. "We have so much, but without you and the boys safe, none of this matters."

Ruth nodded. "We have to get Jacob home," she said. "Then we need to get out of Paris. Maybe the south, maybe England."

Mori sighed and closed his eyes. He had tried so many times to get travel papers. "First, let's find Jacob," he said. Ruth leaned into him, and Mori wrapped his arm around her, trying to provide some sense of comfort. "Once Jacob's home, I promise I'll find a way to safety." Behind his words, however, he felt no certainty whatsoever that he'd be able to pull that off.

When Émile came back into the library, Ruth stood and gave her son a kiss. From the doorway she shot a worried glance back at Mori, and then left.

Émile carried a few sheets of writing paper and a wooden cigar box with a metal closure that rattled as he set it on Mori's desk. He moved two porcelain figurines, Mori's father's pocket watch and stand, and several books from the desk to the floor making room to work. He opened the box and removed two pencils and several pieces of chalk. He laid out a couple of the sheets of paper before him on the desk. "May I see the photo?" he said.

Mori handed him the book.

Using his left hand, Émile began to sketch with a pencil on a sheet of writing paper.

Mori's stomach lurched. Émile's movements looked awkward and slow. He'd thought his son had understood the gravity of the task. "Émile, we don't have a lot of time."

"Papa, doing this sketch right-handed won't work," Émile said, even though that was Émile's usual hand for drawing. He explained that the circular marks had to mimic Da Vinci's own left-handed strokes. The pressure of the stroke would easily be noticed if Émile attempted to forge the drawing using his right hand.

Mori had momentarily forgotten the master's dominant side. He felt a surge of pride in his son— his knowledge and sensitivity to nuance. But they were a distance from pulling off this subterfuge.

"What will you use for the final sketch?" Mori asked.

"Da Vinci used everything from silver pencils to brush and ink, as well as pen-and-ink for life studies."

"So, which?"

There was silence. "I think sanguine," Émile answered.

Sanguine, a red chalk favored by Da Vinci, was used on a

great portion of his work.

Mori nodded. "Yes, I think so, too."

"It's age appropriate and familiar," Émile said.

While Émile studied the photograph of the *Mona Lisa*, Mori lifted the large book he had chosen for its paper. He opened the old tome to the cover page and carefully tore the ancient sheet from the manuscript's binding producing a sheet of paper approximately eighteen by twelve inches in size. The page was at least two hundred years old. He didn't think Goering would be able to distinguish its age from older material. In fact, Mori was counting on this.

The edge that had been attached to the binding was square and clean, and it didn't quite match the other three sides. Mori carefully tore the upper left corner on an angle, as if the original paper had been damaged. He created a tiny flaw at the lower left of the paper, as well, in order to draw the mind away from any thought that the paper might have come from the inside of a book. He then flipped the paper to the opposite side, turned it a quarter turn, and placed it in front of Émile to examine. "Here," he said. "Sketch it on the horizontal, not the vertical."

"Why?"

"I prefer it to look like a truly rough sketch," Mori said.

"Yes, but the painting is vertical."

"I know, but let's treat this as if it was just an idea, an impression, without Da Vinci actually thinking he would create a painting. Maybe just a quick facial sketch here," Mori said, tapping the right side of the paper. "Possibly, her eyes and mouth here." He pointed to the left side of the paper. "Maybe turn it on a very slight angle. The face needs to be incomplete but suggestive."

Before handling the aged paper, Émile created a few fast sketches on the writing paper, using a pencil, smearing his work for shadows with his finger. Each one varied slightly.

"Turn her head," Mori said. "Maybe a forty-five degree

angle? Don't make her appear in the same view as the painting."

Émile used four sheets of paper to produce four sketches for his father's approval.

"That's it," Mori said. "That view." He tapped his finger on the fourth sheet of paper. "It needs to look enough like her for me to convince Goering she's real."

Émile nodded, and took a sip of coffee, then removed a piece of red chalk from the tiny pasteboard box. He withdrew a penknife from his pocket and sharpened the chalk with it. He set the aged paper on the desk and angled it just so, then moved the chalk into position.

"Stop! What are you doing?" Mori demanded when he saw that Émile was holding the red chalk in his right hand.

"It's ok. I'm just putting a few guide marks down. It'll be faster and more precise this way. Stop worrying."

Mori worried anyway. Without monumental delicacy, he wouldn't be able to convince Goering to help find Jacob. The sketch was his only hope.

Once the guide marks were in place, Émile took the chalk in his left hand, propped up the book with the picture of the *Mona Lisa* against the lamp, and fashioned the first strokes.

Mori peered over Émile's shoulder. His fists were clenched, and he was breathing heavily.

"Papa," Émile said, "you're making me nervous. Even my teachers didn't scrutinize me this closely."

Mori exhaled sharply and stepped away from the desk, but not so far that he couldn't see what Émile was doing.

Within a few minutes, Émile crafted a rough likeness of the young woman. Although crude and simplistic, her face remained recognizable.

"Wait," Mori said, approaching the desk.

Émile looked at his father. "What?"

Mori studied the paper, then the photograph, the paper, and the photograph. For several seconds he moved from one to the other searching for scale and balance. "Here—" Mori moved his finger over the left side of her face. "This is where to start with detail." Then he gestured to her right side. "Keep that area open. It should look unfinished."

Émile nodded, noting Mori's observation. Although Mori was not in the same league as Émile at creating art, his son respected his trove of knowledge about art and its history.

"Bring her left eye into focus," Mori said. "Look . . ." He pointed to the fold of his own eye lid. "Accentuate this area, give it a bit of detail, show the shadow from the eyebrow."

Émile moved the chalk slowly and carefully across the paper.

"I'll need to fill this in last," Émile said, referring to the details of the left side of her face. "I just want to make sure I have the proportions correct."

"It's good. Just keep the pressure consistent," Mori said. "I know Da Vinci didn't have to work with the same pressure you do."

Within a few minutes the young woman's face came to life. The smile and the glance that had captivated the art world for centuries now appeared right there on Mori's desk. When Émile had finished filling in the detail, he stood and stepped back. He looked at his father, a faint smile surfacing.

Mori scrutinized every stroke of the chalk. "Here," he said, pointing to a small area above her nose. "Darken here a little. See? Look at the picture." Mori touched the bridge of the Mona Lisa's nose in the photograph. Émile sat down again to fill in this small detail.

It had to be perfect—or rather, perfectly Da Vinci. Goering would know. He wasn't a master, but he was smart and would be hard to fool. Every nuance had to be on track.

There could be no signature. In the fifteenth century, artists rarely signed their work. Besides, this was just a sketch.

Mori found a large volume of poetry on the floor near several books he had glanced through earlier—a book larger than the sketch. "This will do well." Mori took the book, positioned several pieces of smooth writing paper on the open page, placed the master drawing facedown, and closed it. The sketch was safe there for the time being.

Ruth came to the doorway, as though she had sensed the task was complete. "What now?"

"Now I need to get dressed," Mori said, "and go call on Goering. And you," he said as he looked at Émile. "Are you too tired to work?"

"I'm fine."

Mori could see how exhausted Émile was, but he appreciated his willingness to override it. "Then I need you at the gallery to continue painting. No disruptions in the normal schedule. Once you're there, be sure to get last night's canvas from the dust bin. Just hide it somewhere. Don't attempt to re-stretch it until I get there."

"When should I expect you?"

"After I've found your brother."

37

It was late morning when Émile left home on foot for the gallery. He made a right turn and headed toward Avenue Montaigne. Lying awake in the park bushes the previous evening had left him sore and exhausted. The early hours at Mori's desk with the sketch of the *Mona Lisa* had compounded his fatigue, and the thick, warm air didn't help. But rest was not an option. He needed to retrieve the painting Jacob had delivered to the dust bin the previous night, lest someone discover it. In the wrong hands, that painting could easily destroy his family.

Jacob's abduction weighed heavily on him. He wanted his brother home, and felt guilty for not having run to his defense. Jacob had been a target, his limp making him easy prey. Émile's eyes began to tear. How could this have happened? *Please, please let Papa find him*, he prayed.

Once at the corner, he made another right and proceeded to the Champs-Élysées. The streets that had bristled with French police and German soldiers a few hours earlier appeared calm now. Still, he wondered if he was being followed and threw a glance over his shoulder.

Émile crossed the broad boulevard to the park beyond, where he retrieved the bicycle he'd hidden away the night before. *Avoid the Champs-Élysées*, he thought. Émile took the same route in reverse that he'd followed when fleeing the scene of Jacob's abduction. There was something missing, he realized as he rode his brother's bicycle to the gallery. People. Men, women, and children. Where was everyone? There were a few cars on the Champs-Élysées, but no pedestrians. And no children at play in the park.

Émile turned left from Avenue Gabriel onto Rue Boissy, rode a short block, and then took a quick right onto Rue Saint Honoré. The usual shoppers on their daily excursions for bread, vegetables, and preparations for the evening meal were nowhere to be seen.

Gliding past Albert's café, he glanced through the large glass windows. Two waiters were moving tables. Albert busied himself behind the bar, but no customers. Across the street, the German transport truck was stationed in front of the gallery as usual. Both guards sat in the vehicle, smoking. Steadying his nerves, Émile coasted to a stop and, forcing a smile, nodded to the two soldiers. He put a key into the lock, stepped inside, and closed the door behind him. He leaned against the door a moment and exhaled a sigh of relief.

The gallery showroom was dim from the closed half-drapes. A glow of daylight spilled over the top of the heavy velvet fabric. In the blurred light, Émile breathed in the perfume of his work—brush cleaner and linseed oil, a bouquet familiar to his senses. He walked to the rear and turned on the light from a switch beside his father's desk. Paintings stacked on the floor in tidy rows lined the gallery walls, reaching into the center of the room. An irregular pathway extended from the front door of the gallery to his father's work space. The path took a right turn near the rear, leading to the storage room.

Émile heard the gallery door. He forced himself not to look up too quickly. Act calm, he told himself. *Act natural.* Both soldiers took seats near the front window.

"Good morning," Émile said coolly, nodding to the two men.

Neither acknowledged his greeting.

Émile inspected a few of the paintings near Mori's desk in an effort to not seem overly anxious to get to work. His stomach, however, was tied in knots. He needed to get the rolled canvas from the dust bin out back. Opening the store room door too quickly might alarm the guards. From where they sat, they couldn't see the door that opened onto the courtyard, but they would hear it.

Émile busied himself moving paintings from one location to another. His mind never left the rolled painting in the dust bin. Mon dieu, those guards were always going out for a smoke. He wished they'd go out now. But there they sat, not budging. He dragged his worktable a few feet, making an unwanted screeching sound.

In an instant, both soldiers stood in the doorway to the storage room.

"I'm sorry," Émile said, "I have to move some things around to make space."

The two men glared at him, turned, and resumed their places near the entrance of the gallery.

This might be the moment, Émile thought. Now they were expecting shuffling sounds. Still he would try not to draw attention. With the least amount of noise possible, he unbolted the wooden door to the courtyard beyond. With great care, making as little noise as possible, he pried open the door, allowing only enough space for his arm to slide through. He didn't want the sunlight from an open door to flood into the gallery and alert the guards. Jacob always positioned the rolled painting in the bin at an angle so Émile could reach it in this way from a cracked door opening.

Emile felt around, his hand slicing air. He inched the door open just enough to slide his body through. The dust bin wasn't there. His eyes darted around the courtyard. It was at the far corner. Apparently the can had fallen and rolled sometime during the night.

He scurried to the bin and righted it. Where was the canvas?

He panicked. Then he spotted the rolled painting about five meters away. He grabbed the bin and ran to the artwork, tossing it into the can. He carried the can back to the gallery, setting it down noiselessly in its proper spot. He glanced around the courtyard, then removed the painting. As quickly as possible, rolled canvas in hand, he slid back in through the barely open door and closed it as quietly as he could. When Émile looked up, however, he saw that he wasn't alone in the storage room. A guard stood at the doorway.

"Fucking canvas, it's still wet," Émile said. "Now I have to start again."

The guard gave him a quizzical look.

"The primer I use on canvas . . ." Émile had to think fast. "It has to be dry before I can cut it into pieces for repairs." He threw the rolled Manet copy to the floor in disgust, praying that his thirty hours of work were not damaged by the impact.

The guard gave him a look of loathing and returned to the front of the gallery.

Émile closed his eyes, took a steadying breath, and tucked the bound copy behind a stack of paintings at the rear of the storage room, hoping the guard had bought his act.

38

Lack of sleep, Jacob missing, German soldiers at his home; Mori was exhausted. He hoped he was prepared to deliver the greatest sales speech of his life.

Where might Goering be this morning? he wondered as he stepped onto his front porch and closed the door behind him.

Ducking into a taxi at the corner of Avenue Montaigne and Avenue Champs-Élysées, Mori noticed the sun streaming across a cerulean sky awash with pastel pink clouds. How could a city of such beauty, on a day so glorious, be filled with so much pain? He placed his thin package on the seat beside him.

"Hotel Ritz, Place Vendôme, s'il vous plait," he told the driver. Mori's agenda indicated that Bertolt had scheduled a morning meeting at the Jeu de Paume. What did Bertolt want? He wondered. Why the meeting. The colonel would have to wait though. Mori had something more pressing to take care of.

After a few minutes the taxi turned into Place Vendôme, circled, and stopped. The Ritz Hotel sat in the far corner of the square.

"Merci." Mori handed the driver several coins before he opened the door. Package in hand, he walked to the entrance of the hotel.

"Halt!" He heard the familiar order, the same word he heard several times a day at the gallery. The guards, his guards, used the same word for almost anyone passing the front window. He loathed the word. A soldier with yellow teeth, stained from

excessive cigarette smoking and coffee consumption, barked again, *"Halt."*

Mori complied. "I am Mori Rothstein, here to see Commandant Goering."

The soldier pushed open the entrance door, walking in front of Mori. He pointed to a chair inside, then vanished through a door at the rear of the hotel's lobby.

Mori knew the routine. He had visited Goering several times, although he preferred when Goering came to the gallery. Mori felt more in control in his own surroundings. Also, he could consult his library of reference materials when the colonel questioned something.

Would Goering be receptive to Mori arriving unannounced? Would he be happy with the sketch? Or, would he see through Mori and his ruse, and have him arrested? Mori tapped his fingers on the package resting in his lap. He watched as the Reich flags hanging from the ceiling fluttered.

The soldier returned. "He's not here."

In dismay, Mori nodded. What if Goering had left Paris? He departed the Ritz disturbed by this thought.

The walk to the Jeu de Paume would give him time to clear his head. Surely Goering was still in the city. He removed his suit jacket, slinging it over his shoulder. The temperature continued to rise. Droplets of perspiration beaded at his hairline, and his dampened shirt clung to his body. He took Rue de Rivoli, which bordered the Tuileries. Large, white wooden boxes with small citrus trees and blooming roses dotted the park's border. Stone pathways, overlapping with Imperial Jade green carpets of grass, snaked through topiary hedges in the shape of large balls.

He arrived at the Jeu de Paume drenched in sweat. He hated Bertolt, and the thought of meeting with him was more than unpleasant. However, Bertolt possibly represented the key to finding Goering. Mori would have to be gracious.

There was military activity around the building. German soldiers moved between the stone structure and transport trucks, carrying crates of various sizes. Mori was repulsed. He knew that the treasures of France, especially Jewish-owned treasures, were concealed in those boxes.

Two soldiers stood guard at the entrance doors of the museum. One of the men blocked Mori's approach. The other snatched the package from Mori's hand.

Mori felt his heartbeat throughout his body. His temples pounded. His pulse speed, but his focus remained on the package in the soldier's beefy hands. That was Jacob's ticket to freedom. "I'm Mori Rothstein. I have an appointment with Colonel Bertolt." He hoped he sounded calm.

"Papers," demanded one of the men.

He fumbled and dropped his jacket.

"They're in my coat." He kneeled, retrieving a folded paper from the inside breast pocket. "Here."

The soldier examined the papers with care. "Juden," the man snorted.

Mori stood and faced the soldier, the package never leaving his awareness. He prayed the brute didn't bend it.

"Tell Colonel Bertolt I'm here." Mori kept his rising anger in check. He held out his hand. "My parcel, please."

The soldier ignored him.

"I'm here on official business," Mori insisted.

"What's going on here?" Bertolt demanded, appearing suddenly at the entrance to the museum. The two soldiers snapped to attention. Bertolt glared at them. "Rothstein, inside. You two, out."

"Excuse me, that's mine," Mori said, grabbing his parcel from the soldier, his hand trembling. He slid it as inconspicuously as possible under his arm and stepped into the museum. He expected Bertolt was furious he had kept him waiting.

The heat of the day intensified inside the stone walls. Instead of feeling cool from the thick enclosure, the building turned into an oven. Oscillating fans, scattered everywhere, sent streams of hot air in every direction.

Hundreds of paintings in standing rows, stacked one in front of the other along the museum's walls, looked like bargain items at a flea market, rather than priceless works of art. Soldiers had sorted the canvases by size rather than artist. Mori knew this procedure was a safety measure. Paintings of the same size were stacked against each other, frame against frame, thus preventing one painting from damaging another. It was an identical scene to Mori's gallery, but on a larger scale and with larger-sized paintings.

The familiar German flag hung inside at both ends of the hall, each one flapping every time a nearby fan rotated in its direction. The large open area bustled with soldiers moving paintings from one position to the next. Large tables held canvases to be inspected for quality, period, composition, and artist—each work to be cataloged, detailing the work's creator, date, and provenance. It was the same process he was carrying out at the gallery.

The combination of the heat and the men inside created a stench that in flashes, overwhelmed Mori's senses. A soldier approached Bertolt and handed him a stack of papers.

"What is this?" Bertolt demanded.

"A list of names from the Vél d'Hiv."

Bertolt snapped at the pages, tucked them into his pocket and dismissed the young man. He turned to Mori. "I'm finishing something," he said with a smug expression, brushing lint from his sleeve. "Wait there."

Mori's jaw stiffened.

Just then a voice boomed from the other side of a large partition. "The Durer engravings, I want all twelve!"

Mori's face relaxed. He knew this voice.

"The Rembrandt," the familiar voice continued, "both

Rubens, and the Valazquez. Send them over this afternoon."

Buoyed by the proximity of the man he needed to see, the man who might save his son, Mori spoke firmly: "I'd like to speak to Commandant Goering."

"That's impossible, he's busy."

Mori raised his voice. "I only need a minute."

"Bertolt," Goering demanded. "Who's there with you?" The commandant appeared from behind the panel.

"Good day, sir," Mori said apologetically.

"Rothstein, what is it?" Goering said.

Bertolt grimaced. "We'll have to meet later Rothstein, I'm running behind schedule."

Mori looked at Goering. "I had an appointment with Colonel Bertolt," he said, "but I misunderstood the time. I apologize for disturbing the two of you."

Goering turned as if to leave.

"Excuse me, sir," Mori said." As long as I'm here, I have something at the gallery that I believe needs your attention," Mori lied. What he had was tucked under his arm, nestled in the moisture of his armpit.

Goering nodded. "I'll stop by when I finish here."

Mori glanced at Bertolt, who was scowling.

"Yes, sir. Again I'm sorry for disturbing you." He turned, and departed the museum feeling hopeful.

39

Émile moved some paintings from the storage room out into the main room of the gallery, blocking the snaking path through the stacked works of art. That way he would be alerted by the shuffle of canvases should either guard venture in his direction again.

The day before, Mori had placed beside his worktable Renoir's *Afternoon by the Water*, which depicted a small, charming visit to the sea. It would be his next painting.

He removed his jacket, loosened his tie, and sat on a stool in front of a blank canvas, trying to ignore his exhaustion and his concern for his brother. The endeavor needed to become a masterpiece of grace, just like the others. To compound his fatigue, the outside heat brought the temperature in the gallery to an almost unworkable level. *You know how to do this, he told himself. You could do it with your eyes closed. Trust your hand.*

Émile's two easels were in place. One for the original which he was supposedly repairing, the other for the forgery. Should anyone approach his work area, he would simply remove the forgery and slip it behind a nearby painting leaning against the wall. He always had one set up with enough room to allow for the wet paint not to be smeared. If anyone questioned the second easel, he would indicate that he could use his time productively by working simultaneously on two repairs.

With rapid brushstrokes, he applied a thin base of pale pink paint to the upper third of the canvas. The color would serve as a primer for the blue and yellow sky. The white, billowy clouds would come later.

The soft tone, the almost nonexistent wash of color, resembling the famously silky hues used by Renoir, caused his mind to wander. A memory of his own seaside visit floated to the surface—he and Alena lying together on the sand, the warmth of the sun caressing their bodies . . . Alena! He hadn't spoken to her. She didn't know about Jacob.

Émile slid the nearly bare canvas into its hiding place behind a framed painting against the wall, then headed to his father's desk. Alena would be at work. He dialed the École.

No answer.

40

Mori arrived at the gallery in the early afternoon, knowing Goering would arrive soon. He pushed through the front door and walked past the guards, acknowledging neither. "It's sweltering in here," he barked. "Open the door, please," he said, pointing to the guard. He needed Goering to be comfortable if he was going to get Jacob back.

Mori set the thin package he'd been carrying on a shelf behind his desk and hung his jacket on the back of his chair. He ran his fingers through his hair, damp with perspiration, then moved a fan up from the floor and onto the desk. He set a large glass paperweight on several paper notes to keep them from taking flight.

"They keep closing the door," Émile said. "I can barely breathe in here." He motioned his father into the storage room. When they were out of earshot of the guards he whispered, "Did you see Goering?"

"Yes and no . . . He's coming here. I didn't have the opportunity to speak with him. He was preoccupied, and Bertolt was being an ass." Mori looked at the canvas Émile was working on. Crude brushstrokes outlined two women beside a tree. In the background, water and sky had been primed with pale blue. He stood behind Émile and settled his hands on his son's shoulders. He wished his son could work faster.

"I've got a half dozen in progress now," Émile said. "It's just the wait for the paint to dry."

"Nothing is without obstacles, I guess."

"I don't think I can work on more than this," Émile said. "I keep sliding them behind other paintings, but there will be too much confusion if I add more."

Mori returned to his desk and pulled the wrapped package off the shelf behind it. He unwrapped the paper with care then opened the cardboard supports embracing the Mona Lisa sketch. He gazed at it a moment, wondering if he himself would know it was a forgery if it were presented to him. Unable to answer the question, he closed the cardboard cover and placed it back on the bookcase.

From where Mori sat, he could see into the storage room, though the guards couldn't. He watched his son slide the Renoir copy he was working on behind a stack of paintings. Émile then applied a fixative to a small piece of canvas. With the original Renoir face down on his worktable, he gently positioned the unnecessary patch on the rear of the painting at the lower right corner. "I've just finished repairing this one," Émile called to his father, lifting the Renoir and turning it around to show him the patch on the back side. Émile winked at Mori. Then he propped the framed work upright on the larger of the two easels. A moment later, he set a handwritten note against the seaside scene that read, "Wet paint, do not move."

Mori knew the routine. The paint was neither wet, nor drying.

Émile came to the doorway of the storage room. "There's some cake and peaches on the worktable. Did you have anything to eat?"

"I'm not hungry, and it's too hot to eat." Mori looked at his watch. How long would it take for Goering to arrive? He worried the commandant might not show up.

Émile dried a clean brush and placed it into a jar, bristles upright. "I'm leaving."

"Where are you going?" Each and every departure Ruth

or Émile made now ignited apprehension in Mori's gut. One family member was missing, and he felt helpless to protect the others.

"I can't reach Alena at school," Émile said. "I'm going to her house." He tossed his rag onto the work table. "I'll be back later his afternoon."

Mori pushed his anxiety aside and nodded to Émile. They must all continue to go about their lives and appear as normal as possible.

Émile made his way along the path through the stacked paintings to the front door of the gallery and was gone.

Mid-afternoon, as Mori tried to focus on a small portrait by Holbein, a large-framed shadow appeared at the gallery door. There was no mistaking that silhouette.

"Commandant Goering, thank you for stopping by," Mori said, rising quickly and donning his jacket.

Goering pointed at the two guards. "Out."

Both men jumped up from their chairs, and hurried to the transport truck parked in front.

Goering's face was expressionless, hard to read. He wiped his forehead with a clean, white handkerchief. "What is it?"

"Yes, of course. Please." Mori motioned Goering to the rear of the gallery and to a chair.

Mori took the parcel from the shelf and placed it on the desk. He opened the package with great care and removed the sketch of the Mona Lisa. He set the drawing in front of Goering and turned it to face him.

Goering's eyes widened. He fixed his attention on the drawing for what seemed an eternity. Mori's heart raced. He had to remind himself to breathe.

Finally Goering shifted his gaze to Mori. "Where did you get this?" There was no need for an explanation or a grand sales pitch. Goering was hooked.

"It was left by a client for safekeeping a few years ago."

"Who?"

"Paul Betone."

Goering's eyebrows arched slightly. He gently lifted the paper from the desk, bringing it closer for inspection. He held it inches from his face, inspecting every line, scrutinizing each shadow, just as Mori knew he would.

"Betone received it from his father, who got it from his father," Mori said. "I can't find any other provenance on the piece."

Mori's neck and shoulders had tied themselves in knots. Would Goering buy the ruse? The man was tilting the paper in every direction. He turned it over to inspect the reverse. "No signature?" Goering asked.

"The master never signed his drawings."

"Interesting," Goering said as he held the paper to the light.

Mori felt his throat constrict. *He's taking too long*, he thought. *He should be smiling by now*. He swallowed hard, wishing he had a glass of water. "I traveled with it to London several years ago," he said, attempting to keep the conversation in motion.

"Why?"

"Paul wanted an appraisal, and I suggested showing it to a few of my colleagues there. I rarely see pieces like this. They're too few."

"What's it worth?"

"We never got that far. 'Priceless' was the only value I received. The auction houses wanted it, but that wasn't the purpose of the exercise. Da Vinci drawings rarely come on the market. Frankly," Mori chose his words with extreme care. "I hadn't been aware of its existence."

Goering smiled. "It's more than lovely."

Mori exhaled, relief flooding his chest. He had never heard the man describe a piece of art in such a delicate way. Paintings were brilliant, beautiful, masterful, bold, or stunning; never lovely. The dainty way in which the hulk of a man handled the small work touched Mori. He cradled it with delicacy between his two frying-pan-sized hands. "I'll take it with me."

"No," Mori said too quickly. The word had jumped out before he could stop it.

"What?"

"No, please. Allow me to place it in a frame. It's too delicate and too valuable to be moved around. There are several frames here that would be suitable. I'll have Émile secure it for you. It will be safe behind glass." Mori didn't want anyone inspecting the sketch too closely. Set behind protection that created a glare, the piece could fool even Bertolt.

"Alright, when?"

"I'll have him get right on it as soon as he returns. He went to visit his young lady. May I deliver it to you later, this evening or early tomorrow?"

"Fine," Goering said.

"The Ritz?" Mori said.

"Yes."

"May I . . ." Mori stammered as he fumbled for the right words.

"What is it?" Goering said impatiently.

"It's my son." His eyes filled with tears, and he removed his glasses.

"What about him? He can frame it, can't he?"

"Yes, of course." Mori composed himself. "It's my other son, Jacob." "What about him?"

"He was taken by the police last night. My son, Émile, saw them put his brother into a truck. I don't know where he is. Émile said he and Jacob had just said good night and walked in different directions. Émile heard noise, then saw a police truck stop. He saw the police beat Jacob and throw him into a truck." Mori took a deep breath. "Can you help me find him?"

He hoped Goering didn't ask him if he'd gone to the police.

Mori knew the abduction wasn't really a police matter. He recalled his conversation with Émile. There were police and soldiers. There was a soldier at Mori's house. No, this wasn't a police arrest. This was a German maneuver. This was the arrest of a Jew. Of many Jews. Mori's fingers alighted on the yellow badge on his jacket. It was because of these damn stars.

Goering frowned. Mori had seen this look before. It didn't necessarily mean anything in particular, but Mori wasn't going to take any chances. "Jacob does a great deal of research on the paintings I receive at the gallery," Mori lied.

"Why haven't I seen him before? Your other son is repairing damage. I've seen him here. I've never seen anyone else."

"Jacob does research from my home. What he prepares allows me to work so much faster. I know time is important to you, and he's extremely knowledgeable and efficient. The library is much larger, as well. The gallery doesn't have enough space to house the material I need." Mori was saying too much, but he couldn't stop. "Jacob works in tandem with me. I would be happy to show you or Colonel Bertolt the work he does if you like. Either of you are more than welcome to visit my home." Struggling to retain a calm exterior, Mori clung to the tiny shred of hope he had of ever seeing his firstborn son again. *Oh Jacob.*

Goering appeared perturbed. Had Mori gone too far?

"What's his name?"

Mori's heart beat faster. "Jacob. I'll write it down for you." Mori took a sheet of paper, printed his son's full name, then noted, *walks with a limp.* He handed the sheet to Goering.

"I'll check into this," Goering said, waving the paper. "In the meantime, I'll expect the drawing later today or tomorrow."

"Yes, of course."

Goering glanced at the star on Mori's chest. "And take that badge off—your family too. I'll have letters written for you."

Mori fingered the humiliating yellow patch, and felt a bit of tension drain from his shoulders.

Goering lifted the delicate drawing for a last glimpse before leaving. "Bertolt will truly be impressed when he sees this."

41

Émile sat in a petite, bergère chair next to Alena's bed, tracing the intricate floral pattern on the wallpaper with his fingertips. A small fan propped on a stack of books oscillated, stirring up the warm air. With each pass of the rotor, the faded lace curtains billowed like sails on a ship, and Émile was enveloped in a waft of Alena's perfume.

The afternoon sun didn't shine directly through the window, but the humidity and heat permeated every inch of the small space. Émile's shirt clung to his damp body. Although he was relieved when he arrived to find Alena safe, he couldn't push the gallery from his mind—his father was there bargaining with the fruits of Émile's labor for Jacob's life.

Alena stretched and rolled onto her side. Her tousled hair tumbled around her shoulders. She wore a dress of pastel yellow cotton trimmed with powder blue piping at the collar and sleeves. The front buttons, which ran from the neck to the waist, were partially open, revealing the curve of her breasts.

"Hi," Émile said softly. He smiled, bent near, and pressed a gentle kiss to her forehead.

"What time is it?" She stretched her arms and then pushed her tangled hair away from her face.

"Almost four. How are you feeling?"

"Better. A little tired though."

"Fever?"

"I don't think so. Whatever it was must have passed." Alena

sat up and swung her legs to the side of the bed, inhaling deeply. "Have you been here long?"

"No. I called the school, but no one answered. When I went there, they said you hadn't come in today. So, here I am. I was worried about you," Émile said.

"Why?"

"The police took Jacob last night."

Alena's face froze. "Oh, mon Dieu! Why?

"I don't know. It was late." Émile had replayed the scene over and over in his mind. Now, he shared the details with Alena.

"You were there? You saw everything?"

Émile's eyes filled with tears. "Yes." He moved to the bed, sitting by her side.

"That's horrible," she said. "I'm so sorry." She wrapped her arms around his neck and hugged him tightly. "It's frightening," she whispered.

He pressed his face to her neck and gently kissed her. He swallowed hard, then recounted the events in his father's library earlier that morning.

"Your parents, where are they? They must be in a panic."

"Maman's at home; she's pretty shaken up.

Papa went to see Goering. Maybe he can help."

"I want to go to your parents."

"You're not feeling well."

"Never mind that," she said. Alena slipped her feet into worn, tan leather shoes with low heels. She took a brush from the top of her bureau, faced the mirror, and quickly ran it through her long, dark hair. She looked at Émile, reflected in the mirror. "First Jacob, then who? No one is safe." Tears pooled in her eyes. "This can't be what you want for us." She turned to him. "Your family needs to get out of Paris; we need to get out of Paris."

Alena took a deep breath and continued, her voice steady,

any trace of fear gone. "Émile, I'm not a Jew. My parents and I are not Hitler's enemy; but you are. Your family is. Your father is keeping you alive by working for his enemy. How long do you think that's going to last? What's Goering going to do once your father finishes his work? And how long will that be? A month, maybe two?"

Émile had never seen Alena so strong, so focused. Was she doing this for him? Could she feel his fear and dread? Did she see through his outer mask of calm? "I'll speak to my father."

"Good. In the meantime, I'm going to your house. Your mother is alone and probably terrified," she said.

"Thank you. I have to get back to the gallery. I'll walk you through the park."

Alena finished dressing, and the two of them made their way across the Pont du Carrousel and through the Tuileries.

"Émile, finish your work. Talk to your father," she said softly. "I love my home, I love my family, I love Paris, but I love you more." She gently kissed him on the mouth, and before they parted at Place de la Concorde, she said, "We need a plan to leave."

42

When Émile arrived back at the gallery, the guards were out front, chatting and laughing. Eager to finish his work, he nodded to the men and ducked inside. Although they still didn't acknowledge him, they no longer scowled when he appeared.

A small fan sat on the floor facing the open door, moving warm air.

"You're back," Mori said, sitting at his desk. "Is Alena alright?"

"Yes, she's fine. It was just a stomach ache."

"Goering came in."

"And?"

"He wants the Da Vinci," Mori said, his face drawn.

"What did he say about Jacob?"

"He just asked me for Jacob's name, then left. Jacob's fate is in Goering's hands now."

With his father at his desk and the guards outside, Émile took the opportunity to swap his forged Courbet into the original frame. He could have chosen to stretch and swap the Manet he'd aged in Albert's oven the night before, but he wasn't ready to see that painting again. It symbolized Jacob's abduction. He would do that one once his brother was home and safe.

Émile knew the work he was doing would matter one day when the paintings he was helping save were returned to their owners. For now his hope was that the drawing he created for

Goering would save his brother.

Émile cleared his worktable and spread a clean cloth across the top. With gentleness and respect, a trait he had learned from his father, he removed a petite painting by Courbet from the stacks on the floor. Its oversized frame emphasized the importance of the piece, in spite of its modest size. He placed the gilt framed pastoral scene face down on the table. From a small metal box he selected a set of pinchers and a screw driver. Slowly, and with great care, he removed the fasteners securing the painting to the frame and placed them in a porcelain dish. He then lifted the painting from its housing.

Émile flipped over the small master, holding it by its corners to inspect the placement of the tacks that held the canvas in place on the stretchers. He carefully scrutinized every millimeter of the original canvas, front and back. Would his copy pass the expert eyes of Bertolt? The canvas Émile used was almost identical in quality to the original, but Bertolt was skilled in master art.

He set the empty frame and the painting on the floor, then placed another cloth atop the one already on the table. The first was not soft enough to cradle the painting facedown without its frame to buffer it. Once the painting was in place, he picked up the screwdriver, and prepared to remove the canvas from its stretchers, a process that required focus and the right amount of pressure.

He placed the sharp, flat end of the screwdriver under the first copper tack, and gently pried the aged metal from its resting place. One down, twenty-three to go. He turned the painting and repeated the process on the opposite edge, allowing the pressure on the canvas to remain stabilized. Once again, he removed a tack and rotated the canvas to work on the other side. When there were just a few tacks left, Émile found his focus drifting to Jacob's plight. Could his brother possibly be found? Was he even alive? Émile delivered too much force to the tack he was loosening and his hand slipped, snapping the metal in two. *"Merde,"* he said. He pried out the broken piece. *Come on. Focus,* he told himself. Surely no one would notice if there were only twenty-three tacks on the forgery. He continued until he'd placed all but the broken tack in the dish.

All tacks had been removed and with great caution Émile held his breath, then coaxed the painting from its grip on the stretcher bars. The edge of the canvas had been wrapped over the wood for nearly a hundred years. Once the canvas fell loose, he removed the stretchers. These original wooden supports would be used to stretch the forged painting, adding a crucial element of authenticity to Émile's copy.

With expertise, Émile rolled the master painting in a soft cotton cloth, tying it with cotton ties. He slid the roll behind a framed canvas in the back corner of the storage room, where he had hidden several other originals he had copied.

He took his forged copy of the Courbet, from which he had already removed the modern-day stretchers and positioned the original's stretcher bars on the rear of the canvas, adjusting the position several times. He withdrew a copper tack from the dish, folded the canvas along the side of the stretcher, and inserted the tack, securing the cloth to the bar. He repeated the process until twenty-three tacks were in place. Finally, he flipped the painting over and examined every detail.

Satisfied with the front of the canvas, he now needed to mature the reverse side to create the illusion of age. Mixing paint thinner with umber-colored paint in a small jar, he produced a dirty stain. The mixture resembled the liquid that resulted from cleaning his brushes. Émile tested the stain on a small piece of canvas by rubbing a tiny amount with a rag, then tilted the sample to the light and wiped it with a clean cloth. He nodded. It looked good. He took the forged Courbet, dipped a piece of cloth into the watery mixture, wrung it tightly, and ran the stain across the back of the painting. The process took only minutes but added a hundred years to a canvas that had appeared clean and new moments earlier.

Émile set the painting aside and placed the original's antique frame on the worktable. Then he laid his Courbet face down on top of it. Since he was using the original stretcher bars, his forgery fit perfectly. One by one, he secured the original fasteners that had held the original painting to the intricately carved gold frame. *Almost done*, he thought.

Mori coughed. Émile immediately flipped the frame over and began to examine the painting. His father's cough signaled that someone was approaching his desk. From Mori's position, anyone could see into the storage room.

One of the guards stepped up to the desk.

"What is it?" Mori asked, looking up.

The soldier handed him a stack of forms secured with a large clip. "Just today's delivery papers," the man said before he returned to the front of the gallery to stand by the door.

Mori glanced at Émile. Their eyes met.

Émile stepped back to admire his handiwork. *It's good*, he thought. He set the framed forgery on the floor and placed the *Madonna*, which he was supposed to be repairing, on the easel. He turned to his father and smiled.

Mori attempted a smile, but the edges of his mouth failed to perform. Émile knew why. Jacob was still missing, and Goering intended to show the forged Da Vinci sketch to Bertolt.

43

Jacob was nearly through the window's frame, his body balancing at the waist on the ledge. Half prisoner, half free man.

Before he could scoot the rest of his body to freedom, two massive hands seized his legs and yanked him backward into the stench of the toilets. He crashed onto the sinks and then to the filthy stone floor, rolling to his back.

Stunned, Jacob felt a boot in his gut and looked up directly into the eyes of his abuser. A lanky, fair-haired officer loomed above him, then delivered a swift kick to his ribs, and another to his already injured leg.

"Filthy Jew! This is because of your father."

Jacob raised his arm in self-defense just seconds before all went blank.

44

Monday, July 20, 1942

Émile rounded the corner from Rue Royale onto Rue Saint-Honoré. He prayed his father would find a way out of Paris, but knew they would never leave without Jacob.

There had been no word from Goering, and Émile secretly felt it was his fault that his brother had been taken. He had been thinking about it nonstop, scrambling to come up with another plan to find Jacob. All of this occupied his mind and weighed heavy on his heart.

Émile startled and noticed the absence of the guards. They usually waited in front of the gallery for him to unlock the shop. As he neared he saw that the door was ajar. Had there been a break-in?

He peered inside, catching sight of two silhouettes; the guards were already there. The air smelled stale, but there was another odor. He had smelled it before, but he couldn't place it. Sweet, sticky, overbearing. Where did he know that scent from? He advanced into the gallery and saw light coming from the storage room, then heard a shuffling and scraping noise. Émile flinched. Paintings were being moved.

"Hello?" Émile said, inching toward the storage room, heart racing. Who was there? Had someone discovered the forgeries in the back corner?

Colonel Bertolt appeared at the doorway of the storage room.

Émile froze. Bertolt's hair tonic. He recalled its noxious odor from a visit the man had made to the gallery a few weeks earlier. The heat intensified the rancid scent.

"Why is the *Madonna* taking so long?" demanded the whipcord-thin German.

Émile stared at him for a moment. His lips parted in silence, fear gripping his body.

Bertolt snooped around the storage area, peeking through stacked paintings along the walls. He tipped paintings forward, inspecting the ones behind. His motions appeared random. Was he just killing time and being provocative?

"Well?" Bertolt shouted.

"Excuse me, sir, excuse me." Émile took a deep breath and lied, "My father asked me to repair another work which was a smaller task. I stopped repairing the *Madonna* to do that."

"What other work?"

"A Renoir; there was a chip in the paint and he didn't want to keep it here too long, for lack of space, I presume."

"Where is it?"

"I think it was returned to the Jeu de Paume yesterday when the soldiers made a delivery."

Bertolt's face showed no emotion. He glared at Émile, his piercing blue eyes burning into him.

"Would you like me to find the paperwork for you, sir?"

Bertolt moved past Émile, pushing him to the side. "Where's your father?" he demanded.

"I'm sure he'll be here shortly. He was quite tired last evening."

"I want the *Madonna* returned."

"It should only be a few days."

"Why? It looks finished."

"It is." Émile felt short of breath. "But the paint isn't dry enough yet to seal."

Bertolt stormed to the gallery door, grumbling under his

breath a barely audible profanity about Jews. He turned and glared at Émile. "I want to speak to your father. I'm told he handed over quite a treasure to Commandant Goering." There was no mistaking the hatred in his icy stare. "Your family won't always have his protection, you know." He spat out the words, "Filthy Jews," then turned and slammed the door behind him.

45

Mori sat at the dining room table finishing a piece of baguette. Ruth sat across from him looking grim.

He ruminated on the completed forgeries, which were piling up at the back of the storage room, along with the rolled originals. He worried that someone might find them and he was eager to get them out of the gallery.

Before the Germans arrived, breakfast was a joy. The conversation usually included Émile's continued praise from the École and Jacob's work ethic. Ruth oversaw the meal loving nothing more than doting on her family. Now in addition to the goings on at the gallery, he was concerned about Ruth. Her spirit was eroding. She had not been herself since Jacob's abduction.

She passed him the platter of bread, butter, and jam.

"Thank you, no," Mori said. "I've had my fill. Mon cherie, you should really eat something."

She shook her head, "I'm not hungry." Morning sunlight streamed directly through the open dining room windows, casting enormous shadows of the wood-framed chairs on the papered walls. "They look like iron bars," Ruth said, staring impassively at the shadows. "Like the fence at the corner house."

The air was still and thick. By noon the temperature and humidity would make the dining room intolerable, even on the cooler first floor. The kitchen, where the maid was scrubbing pots, was even worse.

He didn't know how to reassure her, nothing he said seemed to help. Was the Da Vinci sketch an ill-conceived plan? Had he just made things worse?

Ruth rose and retrieved the coffee pot from the sideboard. She refilled his cup.

"Thank you," he said, though he had had enough.

"Have you a plan yet?" she asked, the same question she had been asking daily.

"Actually . . . I had an idea this morning." Mori straightened. He hadn't intended to share it until he had thought it through a bit more, but perhaps it would help her to hear it. "I think it would probably be best if we leave by water. The Seine is the best choice. Our car is too small for all of us, and there are road blocks everywhere." He lifted the sugar bowl and placed it in front of his plate. "We're here." Then he placed a cube of sugar several inches from the bowl. "We need to move north to Rouen—here."

"Why Rouen?" Ruth looked doubtful, but Mori thought he saw a flicker of life returning to her eyes.

"The Germans are east. War is all around us. It's best we move north. From Rouen, we travel to the coast by land." He positioned another sugar cube. "Here. And then we take a boat to England."

"England is at war, too," Ruth said.

"I know, but the Nazis haven't conquered it."

Ruth studied the scene. "Do you think the Seine is safe?"

"It makes the most sense. A small boat, at night."

Ruth frowned and tapped her fingers on the damask table cloth. "I'm not leaving without Jacob."

Mori unhooked his wire-rimmed glasses from his ears and placed them on the table. He took a deep breath. "I've done all I can do, you know that. If there is any way possible to find him, Goering can. I just don't know if he will."

Ruth's eyes filled with tears. She had been crying off and on for the last few days.

Mori reached across the table and took her hand. "No one's giving up hope. It's only been a few days. I'm sure Goering will intercede."

The phone in the hallway rang, and Mori jumped up, Ruth close behind him. *Jacob?* Mori thought. But Émile's voice came through the receiver. He sounded upset. "What's wrong, Émile?"

"Papa, Colonel Bertolt was at the gallery."

Mori's grip tightened on the phone. "When?"

"He just left."

"What did he want?"

"The *Madonna*."

Mori checked his pocket watch. "I'll be there soon."

Ruth squeezed Mori's arm. "What is it? Is Émile all right?"

Mori nodded to Ruth. "Émile is fine." With his heart racing, he hung up the phone. "Bertolt, he was at the gallery."

"Is that unusual?"

"Yes. He usually sends for me."

Before Mori could retrieve his hat and coat, a loud thump sounded from the front of the house. Mori and Ruth looked at each other in confusion. Two blows seemed to have crashed against the glass at the front doors. Mori moved toward the front entrance to investigate the sound.

"No," Ruth whispered, grabbing his sleeve. She studied the lace-covered glass.

"It's alright. I'm just going to peek out." He approached the front door, pulled the lace curtain aside a fraction of an inch, and peered out. No one was there. Then he looked down. "Ruth! Quick!" Mori shouted as he swung open the door.

Jacob's twisted body lay sprawled on the porch.

"Call the doctor," Mori bellowed.

Ruth shrieked and ran to the open door. She crouched down and touched her son's cheek.

"Get the doctor," Mori shouted.

"Yes, yes!" She hurried to the phone.

Mori knelt beside his son. "I'm going to lift you," he said. "What did they do to you?"

Jacob looked up at his father. His lips were swollen, his face covered in dried blood. "I'm alright," he whispered. "Just bruised . . ."

Mori braced himself, scooped up his son, and walked into the house. He kicked the door shut behind him.

Ruth hurried toward them. "The doctor's on the way."

Mori cradled his firstborn and carried him upstairs. "You're safe now," he said, his eyes welling with tears. Mori nudged open the door to Jacob's bedroom. Ruth followed behind them.

Jacob touched his father's shoulder. "Put me down, I think I can walk." His voice sounded hoarse. Mori gently lowered him to a standing position. His supporting arm kept Jacob upright. With Mori's assistance, Jacob hobbled to his bed, turned, and sat on the edge. "Water," Jacob said.

Ruth filled a glass from the cold water tap in the bathroom. She handed it to Mori. "Here," he said, holding the glass to Jacob's swollen and cracked lips. "Slowly."

Jacob took the glass and drank every drop.

Ruth sat beside Jacob, gently holding his hand. Tears streamed down her face. "I can't believe you're home."

Jacob handed the water glass to Ruth. "More," he said, his voice weak.

After he had finished he sucked in a deep breath and color began returning to his face.

Mori felt a rush of gratitude for Émile's talent. The forged Da Vinci had worked. Although Jacob had been brutalized, he was home and he would survive.

"This may hurt a little," Ruth said returning from the bathroom with a damp cloth in her hand. She placed the towel against a cut on Jacob's face. He flinched. "I'm sorry," she said.

His face was scratched and swollen. Superficial scabs had formed over his cheeks and forehead. One of his nostrils was blocked with dry blood, causing him to breathe noisily.

Ruth washed Jacob as best she could. "I need to take your shirt off," she said.

Jacob unbuttoned his torn and filthy shirt. He slowly moved his shoulder, allowing the sleeve to fall. Ruth's eyes opened wide. "Oh Jacob," she whispered. His chest was covered with black and blue marks.

"Maman, I'm fine, just sore. Papa, did Émile get the painting from the dust bin."

"Yes, the Manet." Mori nodded. "Yes, he got it."

"We must let Émile know Jacob's home," Ruth said.

"Yes," Mori agreed. "He's vulnerable. Bertolt is suspicious, and that poses a threat to us all."

"Where did they take you?" Ruth asked.

"The Vélodrome."

She shook her head. "What's there?"

"Jews, thousands of Jews. Men, women, families."

Ruth looked at her husband, her expression accusatory.

"I know, I know. We have to get out of Paris." he said. "But one thing at a time." He turned his attention back to Jacob.

"How did you get here?" he asked.

"I don't remember too much. I tried to climb out of a window in the toilet, but I was grabbed. I hit my head on something, and a Nazi beat me. I don't recall much after that."

Ruth brought her fist to her heart, and Mori set a comforting hand on her shoulder.

"I believe I was put into a truck . . . and then ended up on the porch," Jacob said.

Ruth touched her son's arm—gingerly, as though he might crumble. "Do you think anything is broken?"

"I don't think so."

"Ah, looks like everyone came to greet me," Jacob said,

nodding toward a mouse making its way along the baseboard.

Ruth shooed the creature away. "Mori, I've asked you to set out poison."

"I'll take care of it," Mori said. He turned his attention back to Jacob. "You need to rest and get your strength back."

A muffled groan escaped Jacob when he tried to shift his position on the bed.

"The doctor will be here soon," Ruth said.

"I'm fine, Maman, just tired."

Mori looked at Ruth and nodded toward the door, indicating he wanted to speak privately to her.

"I'll be back in a moment," she said to Jacob who had lowered himself to a reclining position.

Outside the room, Mori told Ruth he had to get back to the gallery. "I need to check on Émile."

"Do you think something has happened to him?" Ruth said.

"No, I think he's fine. I just want to double-check." Truth was, he *was* worried about him. The forgeries Émile had painted were still in the gallery, some not yet mounted in frames, and with all of the turmoil in the past couple of days, they still hadn't created a secure plan for hiding the originals. Had Bertolt seen anything fishy on his surprise visit? What if he sent someone else to search the place? There could be trouble. He and Ruth walked to the landing at the top of the staircase. Ruth's expression radiated fear. She brought his hands to her lips and kissed them. Her lips were trembling. "Please, Mori," she said. "We've had enough. It's time."

Mori nodded and kissed his wife's cheek. He had three people he had to keep safe, four including Alena. He turned to go, when a loud knock sounded at the front door.

"No, don't answer it," Ruth said.

"It's probably the doctor." Mori headed down the stairs, made his way to the lace-covered glass door, and peered through the curtain. He turned to look up at his wife, his face ashen.

Ruth froze, her hand over her mouth.

Mori took a steadying breath and slowly opened the door. On the porch stood a tall, blond German soldier, certainly no more than eighteen years of age.

"Rothstein?" the young man asked.

"I am Mori Rothstein." The reply was said with quiet dignity.

The soldier extended his hand, presented Mori with an envelope, turned, and walked down the front steps.

46

Reichsmarschall Goering
Requests the presence of
Mr. and Mrs. Mori Rothstein
For an Art Reception
Saturday, July Twenty-Fifth
Eight O'clock
Hotel Ritz

47

It wouldn't be long before Bertolt saw the Da Vinci. Mori's only hope was that the colonel would inspect the master sketch within its frame. With no glass separating Émile's work from Bertolt's keen eye, Mori didn't know whether or not the piece would fool him. Mori's checklist of needs kept growing. The forged paintings needed to be finished and moved to a safe place. But, what he needed most was an escape route, a boat, and a destination city along the Seine.

Mori left the house for the gallery mid-morning and hailed a taxi on the Champs. The temperature would surely soar later in the day, but for the moment Paris was lovely. Gray clouds were forming above, creating a blanket over Sacré Coeur. Though completely surrounded by war, the city was relatively unchanged.

The ride took less than ten minutes. The taxi stopped behind the parked transport truck in front of the gallery. Deeply grateful to have Jacob home and safe, Mori now turned his attention to keeping the forgeries well-hidden until they could be dropped into the stream of paintings returning to the Jeu de Paume.

With Goering's invitation in hand, Mori walked past the two guards sitting in their truck and entered the gallery. "Émile," he called.

His son appeared at the storage room door, and Mori sighed a breath of relief to see his face.

"Where have you been?" Émile said.

Mori walked quickly to the storage room. "Jacob's home."

Émile grasped his father's arms, and heaved a sigh of relief. "Such good news. When? How?"

"About an hour ago."

"Is he alright?"

"He was beaten badly, but he doesn't seem to have any broken bones. The doctor was on his way when I left. Your Maman is with him. She'll call once he's been examined."

"I'll finish here and go home."

"No, I need you to keep working. I think we're running out of time." Mori showed him Goering's invitation.

"Why would he invite you?"

"I don't know, but if I had to guess, it probably has something to do with unveiling the Da Vinci."

Émile stood in silence, staring at the ecru invitation and rereading its handwritten, decorative script. He looked at his father. "You have to go."

"Obviously," Mori said. "I hate the thought of socializing with the enemy."

"Has Maman seen it?"

"Yes."

"Alena and I will stay with Jacob."

The expression on Émile's face said he understood what was on the line. If Bertolt recognized the forgery, the whole family would be on their way to some unknown, and ungodly, destination.

48

Saturday, July 25, 1942

Mori and Ruth arrived by taxi in front of the Ritz Hotel shortly after eight. An afternoon rain had calmed the sweltering heat and cleansed the air of the persistent humidity that had plagued Paris for the past week. Although the sky shone a bright blue, Mori walked beneath a cloud of doom. All he could think about was the Da Vinci and Bertolt. He hoped to get through the evening without being executed.

"You look beautiful," Mori said, taking Ruth's arm as he assisted her out of the car.

"Thank you. I hope what I'm wearing is appropriate." For the occasion she'd had her hair professionally coiffed and had chosen a pale pink satin Charles James dinner gown with black trim, along with a matching jacket. Affixed to her lapel, a green tourmaline and amethyst brooch. "Do you remember buying this for me?" she asked.

Mori smiled. It had been during a holiday in America in the spring of 1938. He had crafted the sale of Frans Hals's *Portrait of a Builder* to the Metropolitan Museum of Art. Leaving the museum, he'd taken Ruth shopping on Fifth Avenue, using part of the hefty commission he'd earned earlier that day.

"Of course I remember," he said. He wished this evening were as triumphant an occasion as that day had been.

Ruth smiled, but not her signature joyful grin. She was

nervous, and he understood why.

This evening was for show. It was for Goering to display yet another piece of stolen Jewish artwork. As Mori looked up at the swastika-emblazoned hotel, his mind swirled with questions: Why was Goering keeping him so close? And why would he now include Ruth? Would Bertolt discover the ruse? Would a party turn into a death sentence—making Mori an example of what happens to a traitor? He adjusted the jacket of his tuxedo, attempted to draw in a deep breath, and followed Ruth through the hotel entrance.

The appearance of the lobby was greatly improved since his last visit a few days earlier. The carpets had been shampooed, and the crystal chandeliers wiped clean. Chairs and tables were decoratively set in the same fashion they had been prior to the war. A string quartet played folk songs by Johannes Brahms as waiters passed silver trays stacked with assorted canapés. Other staff freely poured champagne for guests dressed in their finest evening wear. Bejeweled women, French and German, clad in lace and beaded gowns floated through the hotel, oblivious to the war outside.

The only sign of the true state of affairs was the German soldiers who stood guard throughout the space and the red Nazi flags with the fear inspiring swastika that covered the elaborate stonework of the lobby's walls.

"Rothstein." Mori turned. Seated with several officers, Goering launched himself from a gilt chair. The German commandant wore a pastel blue satin uniform decorated with numerous jeweled medals.

Mori shook the man's fleshy hand. "I'm pleased to see you, sir." Mori was never quite sure what title Goering should receive as he'd heard several during his visits to the Jeu de Paume. Mori lowered his voice. "Thank you for Jacob. We're truly grateful." Mori bowed slightly. "May I present my wife, Ruth."

"It's my sincere pleasure, Madame." He kissed her hand. "I

didn't know your wife was so attractive."

Mori shifted uncomfortably.

Ruth's high cheek bones colored. "You're too kind. My husband has spoken so highly of you," she said, not flinching at her lie.

Mori glanced around him, trying to keep tabs on their surroundings, scanning for anything unusual. Why would a high-level German officer draw attention to his Jewish guests? Nothing appeared odd aside from Goering's attire. Even his shoes had been covered in blue satin that matched his uniform, and they sported the Nazi symbol. Mori had not expected such flamboyant attire from the officer. This was a complex man with many facets, and here was yet another. Mori had mostly seen a man with refined taste and artistic acumen, the gentle side of an extremely violent person.

"Did you see how I've displayed it?" Goering said, smiling and gesturing to the Da Vinci across the lobby. The small sketch was gently lit from two lamps, one on each side of the framed masterpiece. Goering's newest treasure was front and center for more than a hundred guests to admire.

Even from here, Mori could see the Florentine girl's lovely face glowing in the warm light. Each careful stroke, every shadow brought her to life. "It's the work of a great master," Mori said, having chosen his words carefully. In his mind, he envisioned Émile.

"It's fantastic," Goering said, slapping Mori on the shoulder. "Have a drink, Rothstein, enjoy yourself. You're among the chosen."

Mori's breath caught in his throat for a moment, thrown as he was by Goering's odd choice of words. "Thank you, sir," he said, watching the man's face for a sign of irony, but seeing none. Again he glanced around the room. How could a man so determined to destroy the Jews be so comfortable inviting two of them into his inner circle?

"You come with me," Goering said to Ruth. He slipped his arm through hers and led her across the lobby. Mori followed at a distance. The commandant guided her around to the front of a grand overstuffed sofa near the Da Vinci, and gazed at her as she settled into the cushions. Then the big man sank down into the sofa beside her. "It's a treasure," Mori heard him say of the framed sketch.

"It's lovely, delicate, and mysterious," Ruth remarked.

"You know your art, Mrs. Rothstein."

Ruth was leaning ever so slightly away from the big man. Mori knew she could hold her own. She was smart and agile in any social situation. But she'd been so undone over Jacob's arrest, he worried about her. Nearby, Mori watched the two. Goering seemed out of place dressed as a dandy. The flamboyance and decorations suggested something unusual in the man's makeup. And, he seemed to be flirting with Ruth.

"Your dress is such a beautiful color," Goering said. "It's obvious you share your husband's good taste."

Ruth turned her head away and blushed.

A waiter offered Mori a glass of champagne.

He took the glass and forced a smile. "Thank you."

Although he and Ruth had dined at the Ritz numerous times before the war, tonight he felt out of place. Lone Jews in a desert of Nazis.

He felt a hand on his shoulder. A soft voice said, "You look very handsome tonight." The woman circled around to face him.

Mori forced another smile. "Hello, Coco."

The slender, dark-haired designer wore a beaded, black chiffon, floor-length dress that belted at the waist; at her neck, a small white camellia, and several strands of long, hanging pearls. Her hair was simple and neatly styled beneath a beaded hat with a knit veil. Although well into her fifties, she stood with prefect posture, exuding elegance and refinement.

"It looks like Hermann's taken a liking to Ruth," she said. "Are you jealous?"

Mori didn't smile. At the moment, jealousy was the farthest thing from his mind. Coco slid her arm through his. "Come on, I'll buy you a drink," she said.

He held up his champagne glass, glancing over her shoulder at Ruth, who was still sitting next to Goering.

"Hmm," she said.

"You probably need something stronger. Do you like whiskey?"

Mori had sold several paintings to the well-known couturier over the years for "Bel Respiro," her home in the Paris suburb of Garches. Their friendship was based purely on business. In return, Mori asked Ruth to patronize the House of Chanel.

"I saw the drawing. Hermann's been boasting of it to everyone," Coco said.

Mori grimaced. The last thing he wanted was publicity about the sketch. "I'm so pleased he's happy with it."

"Happy? He's overjoyed."

Coco stood at the center of a cloud of perfume. Mori recognized it as her own brand, Chanel No. 5, the same one Ruth occasionally used, although he knew his wife preferred Arpège.

"What brings you to this party?" Mori asked.

"Hermann spends a lot of time at the Ritz, and I'm here at the Ritz. We met, we've had a few drinks," she said, shrugging her shoulders. "He likes nice clothes," she laughed. "I like nice clothes. We get along. Besides, we're under the same roof, best to be friends." She pulled a cigarette out of her silk clutch, and Mori lit it for her.

He hid his distaste for the woman and her politics. He turned, looking for Ruth, and spotted Bertolt just inside the entrance to the hotel. Mori swallowed hard.

Coco followed his gaze. "Oh, let's hear what the expert has

to say about Hermann's cherished masterpiece."

For a moment Mori was frozen. He had forgotten how to breathe.

Coco took Mori's arm, leading him in Bertolt's direction. She wobbled slightly on her feet, appearing to have had one glass too many to drink. "What happens when two art connoisseurs discuss the same piece?" she asked.

Mori said nothing, reluctantly allowing the woman to lead him to the man he loathed, the man he now feared.

Bertolt and his assistant were heading directly toward the Da Vinci sketch. Coco intercepted them steps away from the piece.

"Rothstein," Bertolt said dryly.

"Mori," Coco interrupted, "have you met Colonel Bertolt's assistant, Lieutenant Weimhoff?"

"Yes." Mori shook the man's hand, then turned to Bertolt, his breath shallow. "Good evening, Colonel."

"This is quite a treasure," Bertolt said, arching his eyebrow just as Errol Flynn might have in one of his swashbuckler films. Was he sending Mori a signal? Could he tell the sketch was a fake? "Where did you ever find it?"

"It was left with me a few years ago," Mori said, working to keep his voice even.

"Was anything else left with you?"

"No. To be honest, I'd forgotten about it until I opened a book where I had placed it."

"You forgot about it?" Bertolt said, raising his eyebrow again. "Whose was it?"

"Paul Betone."

"I know the name," Bertolt said smugly.

Mori wasn't a violent man, but in this moment he felt he could kill Bertolt with his bare hands. Of course he knew the name. Several of Betone's paintings had been delivered to Mori from the Jeu de Paume. *The Expulsion of Hagar*, now secreted

194

away at the rear of the gallery's storage room, had passed through Bertolt's hands.

"You knew the man well?" Bertolt asked.

Mori froze. Bertolt had used the past tense with Paul's name. "Yes, I *know* him well. He's a longtime friend."

Coco blew a plume of smoke between the two men. "What do you think of it?" she asked Bertolt.

The colonel stepped closer to the Da Vinci and bent over to inspect it. He stood like that for a long moment. Finally he looked up at Mori, then back at the sketch. "It's very unusual," he said. "I was astonished to learn of its existence."

"Don't all great artists make sketches?" Coco asked.

"Yes, most do," Mori said.

"True," Bertolt said, straightening. He settled his gaze directly on Mori. "But I have never heard of a sketch for the *Mona Lisa*." He seemed to be studying Mori's face as closely as he had studied the drawing.

Mori's stomach churned and tightened. He could feel moisture accumulating on his skin. "Paul inherited it from his father," he lied.

"Lucky man," Bertolt said.

Was he being sarcastic? This was the same man Bertolt had just spoken of in the past tense.

"I'll take the piece tomorrow," Bertolt said, "and ship it to Carinhall."

Mori was familiar with the name. He'd seen it several times on documents from the Jeu de Paume. Carinhall was Goering's country home in Germany.

"He won't be keeping it here in Paris for his enjoyment?" Mori said.

"His enjoyment," Bertolt snorted, "is his home in the mother country."

"Well, I'm sure he enjoys many cities," Coco said. "Come on, boys, let's enjoy the evening. This is a party, and it's getting too serious in here."

"Of course," Bertolt said to Coco. Then he turned to Mori. "You won't mind if I take a closer look at this gem outside of its frame before I ship it, will you?"

49

Sunday, July 26, 1942

"Bertolt worries me," Mori said at breakfast the next morning.

Émile sipped his café au lait. "I feel the same way, especially since I found him rifling through the storage room at the gallery."

Ruth entered from the kitchen and set a platter of strawberries on the table. She left for a moment and returned with a basket of warm, sliced baguette. There was butter and strawberry confit too. She'd paid triple for them on the black market.

Jacob entered and limped to his chair, hooked his cane over the back of it, and sat.

"How are you feeling?" his mother asked.

"Better, a few sore spots, but I'm alright. I need a new cane."

Ruth walked to his chair, put her hands on his shoulders, leaned down and kissed his cheek.

Once the attention was off of Jacob, Émile leaned toward his brother and whispered, "I know it's been less than a week since you returned. Are you up to helping me after breakfast?"

Jacob nodded. "Sure."

"I heard that. Don't you think you should rest?" Ruth said, a worried expression crossing her face.

"Maman, I'm not a cripple."

"Yes, you are!" Émile grinned.

Jacob was the first to laugh. The rest of them chuckled along with him, the moment of levity a welcome change.

"What can I help with?" Jacob said.

Émile glanced at his mother. He didn't want to cause her any additional worry. "Just a little something," he said to Jacob. "Nothing that will be too taxing. I'll show you after breakfast."

When the two brothers had finished at the table, Jacob took his cane and limped behind Émile, passed through the laundry room and into the garage.

Émile leaned against the Citroen. "We've got to get the paintings out of the gallery," he said.

"How do you plan to do that?"

"In a trash can."

Émile pointed to a corner of the garage toward a stack of branches he'd placed on the cement floor.

"Building a fire?" Jacob quipped.

"No, schmuck, I'm building a fence."

"Ha!" Jacob laughed. "You?"

"I mean it," Émile said, bending over the branches.

Jacob watched as Émile grabbed a piece of beige yarn and began tying the sticks together, side by side, allowing the small pieces of wood a modicum of flex.

"If the branches are tied too closely together," Émile said, "I won't be able to bend the finished fence into a cylinder."

Jacob pointed to the metal trash bin on wheels. "Where did you get that garbage can?"

Émile relayed the story about finding the trash trolley in the park on the night Jacob was arrested, and then walking right in front of the Nazis disguised as a street cleaner. "We can put the paintings in here." Émile patted the trash can. "We'll have to make sure they're well hidden. I'm going to line the inside perimeter of the can with the branches. From the outside it will look like garden waste. Then with the center area empty, I can fit rolled paintings side by side. I think it should hold about six to eight canvases when it's finished. Once they're in place, I'll cover the top with a cloth and dump leaves over them. If anyone looks in the can, they'll just see dead leaves."

"I'm impressed." Jacob smiled. "So the Germans believed you were a real street cleaner?"

"That's the part you're impressed by?" Émile chuckled, but his stomach was in knots. "I've been a nervous wreck hashing out this plan. How's your leg?" he asked.

"OK, why?"

"Can you walk a distance?"

"I don't know." Jacob shrugged. "Probably. Why?"

"We need your help to walk the paintings from the gallery to the place where we're going to hide them."

Jacob didn't say anything, and Émile thought he saw fear flash in his brother's eyes. Émile was terrified his brother might be taken again, this time for good. If that happened, he would never be able to live with himself.

"I thought about doing it myself," Émile said, "but that would be problematic. My face is recognizable to the gallery guards. And they're used to seeing me there on a regular schedule."

"Yes, all right," Jacob said.

"If I took the time to move them," Émile said, "not only would that disrupt the production of other works, but the guards might become suspicious of a long absence."

"I said all right." Jacob grabbed his brother's arm. "I'll do it. I *want* to do it."

Émile hugged his brother. "You have to promise me to be careful."

"Who's the older brother, me or you?" Jacob gave Émile a friendly shove.

"We can't tell Maman what you'll be doing," Émile said. "It's bad enough Papa will know. He feels responsible for you having been arrested. I can tell."

Jacob nodded, his expression solemn.

"We'll wait a week or so, until you've had some time to heal," Émile said. "This will have to be done in daylight to draw the least amount of attention. We'll disguise you as a garbage collector. They aren't usually out at night." Then he explained how he would follow by taxi and help secure the paintings into their hiding place at the other end of Jacob's journey. "You'll have to walk back home with the empty trash can. We'll need to use it again."

"It's a brilliant plan," Jacob said. "And I'll be fine."

"Oh, and let your beard grow," Émile said. "For your disguise."

Jacob nodded. "Where are you going to hide them?"

"Parc Monceau."

50

Wednesday, August 12, 1942

Mori stepped outside his front door with the morning copy of *Le Petit Parisien* tucked under his arm, the early morning air already as hot as Albert's oven. He looked out over Avenue François wondering how this would all end. His nerves were on edge. He kicked at a leaf that had settled on the landing during the night, and prepared to launch himself into his day.

Ruth, still dressed in her robe, opened the door and stepped outside beside him. She placed her hand on his shoulder. "Please be careful," she said softly.

"This could all go wrong." He exhaled a long breath. "Bertolt's going to inspect the Da Vinci. Probably soon. It's been more than two weeks since Goering's party." He did not share his fear of being caught with his wife.

Ruth squeezed his arm. Her touch caused his heart to ache. She'd been through so much, and all along she had urged him to get them to safety. She had had the foresight, and he had foolishly refused to act.

They grasped hands and he leaned into her. With his cheek against hers he whispered, "We need to prepare to leave." He stepped back and saw hope and fear play tug-of-war in her gaze. "I'm going to go to the river and scout around for a boat. The major towns will be a problem, but we will get as close to the Atlantic as we can, then we can move north by land and find a fishing boat on the coast to help us cross the channel."

"All right, Mori." Ruth clutched his hand tightly.

"Pack a few things," he whispered. "Only necessities, nothing more." The only other things we'll take are the paintings. We need to be ready to go as soon as I can find a way out of here."

"Please be careful," she said. "I can't lose any one of you."

"I will." He pressed a kiss to her hand letting his lips linger there longer than usual. Then he turned and descended the front steps.

Mori made his way toward Avenue Montaigne. His usual route to the gallery required a right turn. Today, however, he turned left and headed for the Seine.

51

Émile and Jacob stood in the garage examining the tied branch barrier lining the perimeter of the trash can. During the two weeks that had passed, Jacob had regained his strength. His beard had grown scruffy. They stood back to admire their handiwork.

"There's something wrong," Émile said. He broke some of the branches, creating an irregular pattern in their heights. He tucked a few of the broken pieces crosswise into the tight weave of sticks. "Better," he said.

Jacob leaned on his cane. "You think this will work?"

"It has to," Émile said. "I can't think of any other way to move them."

"It's a long walk to Parc Monceau from the gallery."

"Are you sure you're up to it?"

Jacob nodded. "I'll take my time. I'll make it work."

"You can wear those clothes." Émile pointed to a pile of soiled clothing on top of some stacked boxes. "It's what I wore the night you were taken."

Jacob unfolded the pants and shirt, dried dirt falling to the floor. He made a face.

"I know this seems strange. You're Mr. Perfect-Dresser." Émile patted Jacob's cheek. "Your beard looks good." He glanced at Jacob's hands. They were clean, his nails groomed. "Wipe some dirt on your face and hands, especially under your fingernails. We have to keep you safe."

"I'll be the most authentic looking trash collector you ever saw," Jacob said.

Émile picked up a straw hat his mother wore while tending to her flower garden. He pulled at the brim, bending and tearing it in an irregular pattern. "Here." He handed it to Jacob. "Smear some dirt on that, too. It'll protect you from the sun and hide your face."

"You think of everything."

"There can be no mistakes." Émile's voice was firm, almost paternal.

Jacob used both of his hands to grab hold of the handle on the trash can and rolled it several feet. "This will give me the same support as my cane, so I won't need it."

"Perfect," Émile said. "And your limp shouldn't draw attention. It just adds to the character. You'll need to walk it to the gallery first.

"Move along the far side of the Champs. Stop along the way to pick up trash—just enough to make your disguise appear real. There won't be very much room for garbage after the canvases are inside. Once you pick up the paintings, follow the directions. I'll be at the pyramid when you get there." Émile handed his brother a map he'd created. The two reviewed the route from the gallery to the pyramid in Parc Monceau. Émile detailed every step of the journey, indicating where German soldiers stationed themselves, instructing his brother to avoid the streets where potential problems could take place.

"I'll be looking for you," Jacob said.

Émile knew he was putting his sibling and best friend in danger. "Jacob, this is risky. Don't deviate from the route and keep your head down. If you're discovered, they'll kill you."

"I understand. I'll be fine." But he was nervous.

Émile worried it was too soon after his brother's ordeal. He wished he didn't have to send Jacob on this dangerous mission, but they had no other options.

Émile gave his brother's arm a squeeze, and for a moment he didn't want to let go. "Be safe, Jacob."

52

É mile left the house a few minutes after Jacob. Once beside his worktable at the gallery, he realized how bone tired he was. In almost three days he'd had little sleep and no time to see Alena. Getting the rest of the forgeries framed, and hiding the rolled originals were of utmost importance. His family's responsibility to their patrons depended on it. The completed canvases were accumulating at the rear of the cramped space, barely fitting in their temporary hiding places behind stacks of framed paintings. Thank heaven there were only a few works left to copy.

Propped on Émile's side-by-side easels were canvases that before long would be identical—one, Monet's *Afternoon Tea at Argenteuil*; the other, a soon-to-be completed forgery of the nineteenth-century masterpiece. Émile mixed cobalt blue with soft pink on his pallet then applied paint to the copy with quick strokes.

Mori, who had been sitting behind his desk, stepped into the doorway separating the gallery from the storage room. He inclined his head in the direction of the soldiers who stood at their usual post inside the gallery at the front door.

Émile nodded to his father, acknowledging the position of the guards. They had become skilled at communicating without words.

Mori stood for a moment and watched his son.

Émile applied thin coats of paint to a canvas that he'd

previously layered with gesso—a shortcut to imitating Monet's texture. A sharp pain in his gut sent his hand to his abdomen.

"What's wrong?" Mori said.

"Nothing . . . stomach cramp. It's the stress. I just want to finish the rest of the paintings and get them moved."

Mori clasped Émile's shoulder. "I'm so sorry."

"Papa, none of us could have imagined" . . . his voice trailed off. He straightened and kept painting.

Mori leaned in beside his son. "Where did you learn this?"

"I don't know, I just did."

"When will it be finished?" Mori motioned toward the front door.

"It'll be pretty quick. I use only a thin layer of oil."

Émile moved some paint around the canvas with his fingertips. "Jacob should be here soon. I've got eight canvases rolled in the dust bin out back."

"How will you know once he's arrived?" Mori grimaced—just slightly, but Émile had seen it. He knew his father felt as bad as he did about sending Jacob out again on a dangerous mission.

"We planned it last night," Émile said. "When Jacob arrives in the courtyard behind the gallery, he'll transfer the canvases from the dust bin into his rolling trash can. Then he'll knock on the door two times." Émile took note of Mori's anguished expression. "Papa, we've been through this over and over, there's no other way to get everything out of here. We need Jacob."

"I know. I'm just nervous."

Émile turned quickly, knocking into a portrait. "I can barely move back here," he said.

Émile gazed at Monet's painting—the table set for afternoon tea, the soft tones of pale greens mixed with gentle hues of pinks and fuchsia. He could feel the cool of the distant Mediterranean, kissed by hillsides washed in bright sunlight.

Although this wasn't the first Impressionist work he'd copied, it was his favorite.

"Beautiful, isn't it?" Mori said.

Émile nodded, saddened by how distant this scene was from what their own lives had become. There was no time to stop and enjoy the beauty that surrounded them. He missed school. He missed his friends. He missed the lectures, even the professors who droned on and on. He missed the ability to create rather than copy. Most of all, he missed the constant encouragement mixed with the not-so-subtle criticism from men who had devoted their lives to educating young talent. But what broke his heart was the scarcity of time for Alena these days.

Émile studied every brushstroke on the surface of the Monet. He made quick, simple adjustments to his copy. A gentle splash of dusty yellow above a faraway cloud. A stroke of teal under a wave.

Finally, it was finished. Émile took a small brush, dipped it into a mixture of paint thinner and sienna paint, and placed the artist's signature on the canvas. He stepped back to compare the two works. They were identical.

Émile removed the original from its frame and secured the still damp copy temporarily in its place. He removed the stretchers from the original, rolling and securing the canvas with cotton ties. He handed it to his father who tucked it behind a framed portrait of a 17th century French nobleman at the rear of the storage room.

Émile and Mori gazed into the gallery.

The pathway from the front door to the storage room had widened considerably. A week earlier, they had each separately noticed that a delivery of new paintings had been skipped. It was the first day that had happened. Neither had said anything to the other. But when the same thing repeated the following day, Émile had spoken up. "Papa, we can't pretend it's not happening."

With pickups still occurring almost daily, and no new deliveries, the stacks of paintings in the gallery were thinning out. With each pickup, it was as though they were watching their own life force draining.

Mori turned back to Émile. "You'll need to hurry, son. How soon can you finish completely?"

"There are only two paintings left to copy. I don't know, a few days."

"You have to make another copy of *The Expulsion of Hagar!*"

"Why can't we use the one I did for school."

"No," Mori said sharply, his voice hushed. "You need to make another." His jaw was set. "That was a gift from you to me. I will keep it till the day I die."

Émile was moved by his father's statement, but he also felt the pressure double. "Then I'll need more time."

"Then you must hurry."

There were two small knocks on the back door of the storage room, and both men startled, even though they were expecting it.

A moment later, they heard the gallery's front door open. The silhouette of a man was framed in the doorway.

"I need to speak to you, Rothstein."

Bertolt stood at the front of the gallery, a nasty smile on his face.

53

Mori headed toward his desk in the gallery, not so much looking at Bertolt as feeling his presence. Mori's moist shirt clung to his body but he chose to keep on his suit jacket. A flimsy shield of armor.

The colonel made his way through the widening maze of paintings, brushing his hand along the tops of the frames as he walked the path toward Mori. He looked in the direction of the storage room. "Your son is still here? I expected him to be finished by now with the few repairs you mentioned to Commandant Goering."

"He is finished. He's just doing some cleanup and checking, tightening a few canvases that were loose in their frames," Mori lied.

Bertolt raised an eyebrow at Mori before sitting on the small wooden chair across the desk from him. He crossed his arms over his chest. "I have some concerns about the drawing."

Mori heard Émile in the storage room and wished his son was safe at home. He knew what Bertolt meant but he played dumb. "There are so many drawings that have been in the gallery," he said as casually as possible. "Which one are you referring to?"

Bertolt twisted in his chair and crossed his legs.

Mori saw the man's jaw clench.

"The Da Vinci," Bertolt said, his expression radiating hatred.

"What concerns you?" Mori knew what concerned Bertolt.

The man was privy to the same information as Mori. Bertolt was cunning and calculating. And he was smart.

"Provenance," Bertolt said.

Mori could feel tiny droplets of sweat forming at his hairline. "I don't have much information about the piece," he said.

"Not *much?* Well, what do you have?" Bertolt's voice rose. "Show it to me."

Mori's mind raced, searching for his next sentence. "I have a letter."

Bertolt raised his eyebrows and extended his hand, waiting to receive the letter that didn't exist.

"When Paul Betone asked me to hold the sketch," Mori said, "He gave me a letter describing the piece and how he had come to have it in his possession. I never researched its history, since I was simply holding the piece." Mori took a breath and tried to slow down. *Steady voice*, he told himself. *Not defensive.* "Although I have limited historical documentation, what I have certainly affirms that the piece is authentic."

Mori had chosen his words carefully. *Authentic.* He could have said original, but *authentic* seemed more scholarly for the conversation, and he thought Bertolt might like being spoken to as a fellow historian rather than an officer. "The letter is at home," Mori said.

"I'd like to see it." Bertolt's tone had calmed a bit.

"Of course, I'll send it over tomorrow."

"No," Bertolt said abruptly. "I'd like to see it today."

"Of course. I'll go home and get it and deliver it to the Jeu de Paume," Mori offered.

"That won't be necessary." Bertolt strode to the door. "I'll stop by your home."

"When?"

The colonel didn't respond. He just kept walking.

"Allow me to give you my address," Mori said, his heart pounding and his mind in a frenzy.

Bertolt turned and faced Mori. "I know where you live, Rothstein."

54

Jacob pushed the camouflaged garbage can beneath a hot midday sun. Sweating under layers of filthy clothing Émile had provided, he followed his brother's directions exactly. At the rate he was able to walk, it would take him less than half an hour to reach Parc Monceau.

The route Émile had mapped out would take Jacob several blocks out of the way, but it also avoided assorted government buildings, as well as the Crillion Hotel, which was packed to the gills with Nazis. Jacob didn't mind the extra distance. The garbage can brought an unforeseen advantage. Leaning on its handle created a perfect support, better in a way than his cane. His limp was still there, but he felt an odd, unexpected freedom.

Several minutes out from the gallery, he turned down a small street.

"You." A voice, male and peevish.

Jacob turned.

"There," an old man pointed to a small pile of dog droppings in front of his gate, shaking his head.

"Excuse me?" Jacob said.

"There." The man hunched a shoulder, holding his small barking poodle. "The shit, pick it up."

As his brother had instructed, Jacob had placed the priceless rolled canvases into the can, and covered the tops of the rolls with a cotton cloth for protection. On top of the cloth, he'd dumped leaves that he'd collected to camouflage the paintings.

Jacob looked at the man.

"What are you waiting for?" the old man barked.

Jacob looked at the shit, then at the can, which held a treasure in art. *Don't draw attention to yourself,* he recalled his brother saying. *Blend in.* Jacob removed a rake and a small shovel from the metal loop on the side of the trash can. He scooped the little pile from the walkway and carefully placed it atop the leaves at the center of the can. His gaze rose to the old man's. Jacob smiled at the chap. The old man blew air from his mouth, put his dog on the ground, and walked up the path to his house.

Continuing on the assigned route, Jacob stopped briefly to rest here and there, all the while turning his head from the stink in the trash which had become overwhelming in the heat of the day. As he rounded a corner onto the final stretch to the park, he spotted a German soldier walking toward him. Heart pounding, he stopped and pulled a tattered broom from the side of the garbage can and began sweeping a small area of leaves and debris. The park was only a block away, but at this moment it might as well have been in another country. He felt exposed and vulnerable. He lifted the swept waste with his hands and tossed it into the can, his breathing labored.

"You missed something." The soldier pointed toward the bushes at the side of the walkway. Some small bits of half smoked cigarettes and an empty package of matches lay inches away.

Jacob moved the can between himself and the soldier. He retrieved the garbage and tossed the small pile into the can, then waved his hands, palms wide open, hoping the stench of the dog's gift would travel in the Nazi's direction.

"Shit!" the soldier shouted.

"Oui, shit. It's all I do all day. Leaves, shit, cigarettes. Then I go to my shit house, with a wife who complains without stop, a baby that cries all night. Better out here!" Jacob waved his arms like a crazy man.

214

The soldier spit at Jacob's feet, flicked his lit cigarette into the can, then turned and walked away.

An ember from the soldier's cigarette sparked on top of the leaf covering. In a panic, Jacob scooped up the dried leaves, and threw them to the ground. He stomped out the nascent blaze.

Trembling, he leaned against the trash can to steady himself, and waited for the soldier to turn the corner. He'd lost precious minutes, and Émile might already be waiting for him.

Jacob finally entered Parc Monceau and found the pyramid where he was supposed to meet his brother. Émile was nowhere in sight, and it was a quarter of an hour past the time they'd agreed on. Certainly he wouldn't have come and left.

The afternoon sun was now hidden behind neighboring apartment houses lining the street opposite him. Tall Linden trees cast long shadows over the green lawn that lay between the walking paths. Flowers appeared faded in the shadows, their delicate color reminding Jacob of the blooms Émile painted. His brilliant brother. Where was he? Émile was more than an hour late.

Jacob wheeled the trolley at a slow steady pace around the park, stopping to pick up trash here and there, as Émile had instructed. The park was empty but for a few children playing near their mother, but he kept an eye out for soldiers who sometimes gathered there in the afternoon.

When he'd circled back to the pyramid, he pulled out the broom and began sweeping at nothing in particular. As he bent, pretending to gather a small pile of torn paper and dead flowers, he heard footsteps crunching through the leaves behind him.

He righted himself and was relieved to see Émile emerging from behind the trees carrying two large canvas bags.

"Where were you?" Jacob said. "I was worried."

"I got delayed. I'm sorry. Bertolt showed up at the gallery and I couldn't leave." When Émile neared his brother and the trash can, he said, "What's that stink?"

"It's shit, what do you think it is?"

"Where?"

"On top of the paintings, that's where." Jacob briefly recounted his journey.

Émile glanced around them, reached into the can and pinched the corners of the fabric that held the leaves on top of the paintings. In a simple move he brought the four corners together, and lifted the cloth and its contents, dropping it all into a nearby flower bed. "Come on, let's move," he said.

"By the way, what's in the bags?"

"Lime."

Jacob pursed his lips and followed Émile to the pyramid. He hadn't seen the hiding place yet. His brother had been very secretive about it. Émile glanced around, then kneeled beside an undersized door on one side of the stone structure. He pulled out a key, opened the lock, and tugged on the small door's handle.

Jacob was stunned. He'd been to this park many times over the years but had never noticed the pyramid had a door.

"Quickly," Émile said, crawling into the miniature tomb. "Hand them to me, fast."

Jacob pulled the precious cargo from the can and slid two paintings at a time through the opening. A few passes and the deed was complete.

Émile stuck his head out, "Pass me the canvas bags please."

Jacob slid the two sacks to his brother who pulled them into the darkness.

"Alright, now go home," Émile said closing the door from the inside.

The route home would be shorter than the distance from the gallery. Jacob couldn't wait to get there. He wanted to rid himself of these filthy clothes and take a bath. Taking the back alleys, he stayed in character all the way there, stopping to sweep and gather debris along the way.

He smiled. His part of the plan was almost complete, at least for today.

55

Inside the pyramid, Émile turned on a flashlight and unpacked eighteen small boxes from the canvas sacks. He climbed down the ladder to the lower level, carrying one box of lime at a time. He had decided to do this part on his own, having kept the lower chamber a secret from his brother. The fewer who knew about all this, and the less they knew, the better—mostly for their own safety. He hadn't even told Alena he was going to use their tryst spot for this purpose.

Émile carefully opened the boxes, exposing the powdered lime, and placed them around the perimeter of the small space. Lime was the only way to absorb moisture from the air, protecting the masterpieces which had been carefully propped upright in the center of the chamber.

After making sure the paintings were safe from the lime, he climbed up the ladder and closed the trap door in the floor, stomping on it to make sure it was secure. He turned off the flashlight, poked his head out of the pyramid and looked around, then crawled out and stood beside the stone structure. He rested his back against its cool, rough grit, a moment's respite from the day's heat. Jacob had done well. Their father would be proud of him. He would be proud of both of them.

The afternoon sun cast a long shadow of the pyramid onto the nearby lawn. In the stillness of the park, Émile heard the crunch of leaves. He turned, already smiling.

Alena appeared from the opposite side of the pyramid. Her

yellow, floral dress swayed as she moved. Its sheer fabric showed every curve of her silhouette against the afternoon sky.

"You got my message," Émile said in a hushed voice.

"I've missed you," she wrapped her arms around him.

Her touch melted his fatigue. He breathed her in and pulled her to him, his arms holding her close.

"Never let me go," she whispered.

"I won't." He brought his lips to hers for a long, warm kiss then took her hand and led her to the pyramid's small door. "Come on." He didn't feel they were safe out in the open for long and he feared his proximity to her put her in danger, especially so close to the hidden treasure.

Once inside the pyramid, they were in a world of their own. All else fell away—the war, the danger, even the paintings tucked safely beneath their feet. Émile turned on the flashlight and grabbed the blanket they'd left from their last rendezvous, and spread it over the dirt floor.

They sat together on the soft wool. He took her face in his hands. "You know I love you," Émile said.

Alena sighed. "I'm scared, for you, for us."

With danger all around them, and the race against time to finish the paintings, he offered her the only goodness that was left. "I'm going to keep you safe."

Alena relaxed into his arms. "If we make it through this—" she let her voice trail off into the darkness of the tomb around them.

He pulled back and searched her face in the dim light. "My love, we'll make it through this. We'll be together."

He kissed her with urgency and her passion sparked. They disappeared into each other's embrace, the outside world fading away. For a moment in time, in their private island in the middle of the war, they grasped and moaned and all but consumed each other, as though they were making love for the last time.

Afterward they lay exhausted, their bodies moist in the

stifling heat of the pyramid.

Émile turned on his side, propped up on his elbow. He caressed her damp skin and kissed her shoulder.

"It won't always be like this," Émile said, "Making love inside this tomb. Freezing in the winter and sweltering in summer."

"I won't be able to come here soon." Alena rolled onto her side to face Émile.

He felt a shock run through him. "Why not?"

She drew closer, her lips almost touching. Alena whispered, "Because soon I won't fit through the opening. I'm pregnant."

56

Moments after Bertolt left the gallery, Mori grabbed his copy of *Le Petit Parisien,* and walked out the front door. Neither soldier on duty paid much attention as he strode past them. Bertolt intended to come to his home to inspect documents that didn't exist. That now represented the most serious obstacle to Mori and his family escaping Paris.

Mori crossed the street in the direction of Albert's café. Would Albert be able to help? The man had secured passage for his wife and children to England. Mori wanted to know how, and why had Albert not been able to leave himself? He must have been devastated to watch his family depart. Mori couldn't imagine the horror of being separated from Ruth and the boys.

All of Mori's influential contacts, clients, and suppliers had either gone missing or had left Paris months earlier. He had no one else to turn to. He and Albert had been friendly neighbors on the street for years, and yet they'd never been particularly close. They came from different walks of life, and dealt in different businesses. Now he needed Albert's help, and this time it was a bigger favor than the use of his oven.

Mori glanced through the paned café window. He saw Albert seated in the back at a small round table, but he couldn't see with whom. Albert was talking and laughing. Mori stepped to the left a bit, and the others came into view, two men in Nazi uniforms.

Mori's heart raced, and he stepped out of sight. Albert looked to be on friendly terms with the Germans. Too friendly. Could Albert be a sympathizer? Was he in some way working with the Nazis? Was that how he had secured safety for his family? How could that be, Mori thought. The man's a Jew.

Was his friend now his enemy? Every possible scenario of evil and fear flew through Mori's mind.

He shook his head as if to magically expel the paranoia of his thoughts, and something did, in fact, shake loose—a new thought: *I myself have been working with the Nazis. Albert knows it. Yet he has continued to trust me.*

Mori took a deep breath and straightened his jacket, then entered the café. He approached the bar. His eyes darted from the waitress behind the counter to the other patrons, and then to Albert and the Germans.

"Bonjour," the young woman said.

"Café au lait, please."

Mori felt a hand on his shoulder. He startled.

"Relax," Albert said.

Mori watched the two soldiers leave the restaurant.

"I didn't want to disturb you," Mori said.

"Disturb me?"

"It appeared you were enjoying a few laughs with your friends." He was careful not to sound sarcastic. He had come to distrust everyone. The pressure of this occupation had gotten to him, the pressure of working for the enemy.

"My friends?" Albert smirked. "Are you crazy? They come here all the time. What am I going to do, throw them out? Business is terrible. I need to work. They come in, they're friendly, they ask me to sit and drink with them. We laugh, they pay the bill. Then they leave, and I wish them dead, every time."

"It just looked . . ." Mori shrugged.

"What? You thought I'd joined the other side? Do you know me? I've watched them come and go from your gallery for months. You told me you had a complicated arrangement with the Nazis. I understood. You asked me to use my ovens. I never doubted."

A wave of shame flooded through Mori. "I'm sorry," he said. "I should never have questioned you." He dropped his gaze, unable to look Albert in the eye.

"It's okay," Albert slapped Mori's shoulder in a gesture of friendship. "We're all under pressure. I can't imagine having my family here to worry about."

Mori looked up then, his eyes welling. "It's destroying me."

"Is there any way I can help?"

Mori was moved by Albert's kindness, even after he'd openly doubted him. "If I can't trust you Albert, I can't trust anyone." Mori whispered, "I'm in trouble. I need to get my family and myself out right away."

"It's impossible. There are no papers to be had. I've tried."

Mori's head throbbed, and he found it difficult to breathe, as though all the air had been sucked out of the café. He leaned closer to Albert. "I think they're going to kill me, and my family too."

Mori and Albert stared at each other in silence for a moment.

"I'm looking for a small boat," Mori said.

"What, the Seine? That's ridiculous. It won't work." Albert shook his head. "There are soldiers all along the river. The only boats that come and go are fishermen. They all tell me that the German soldiers constantly board their boats for inspection and then steal fish for themselves. Even if you travel up the river, the major ports will be a problem."

"But the fishermen?" Mori said.

"It's too dangerous, my friend. I would go with you if I thought we could actually get through."

"How do the fishermen do it?"

"They do it. They have papers. They get through the check points."

"Then I need a fishing boat, a large one."

57

Mori hurried home from the café. The anxiety of Bertolt's impending visit weighed on him.

He made his way to the study and sat staring at the typewriter on his desk, glancing frequently out toward the street. There was no telling when the colonel would arrive. Convincing the man of the authenticity of the *Mona Lisa* sketch was paramount. If that went wrong. . . Bah, he couldn't waste time thinking about that now.

He pulled a blank sheet of paper from his desk and inserted it into the typewriter. After a moment though, he changed his mind. He yanked the paper from the machine, wadded it into a ball and tossed it into a small waste bin.

In the absence of Paul Betone's personal stationery, Mori needed something simple, a note the man had jotted in haste on any paper at hand.

Mori slid his chair away from the desk, stood, and crossed the room. He stopped at the bookcase to the left of the fireplace. Beneath the tall shelves stacked with neatly arranged leather-bound books were two cabinet doors. He opened one and removed a dusty box. Across the top written in perfect penmanship was the word *Père*.

Mori made room on his desk and set the box there. He lifted the top and removed several small books and a pen. Then he pulled out a Sotheby's auction catalogue and thumbed through its pages, stopping at a couple of circled items. The first was

Renoir's *Collette*, a painting he had given Ruth, which hung in their dining room. The other was the sketch for Raphael's *Alba Madonna*, which had been painted in 1510, four years before the artist was appointed chief architect of St. Peters. Mori couldn't recall ever having seen the sketch, but he did remember seeing the painting in Washington, DC, when he'd visited America. There was nothing remarkable about the sketch, and he wondered why his late father had circled the description. He set the catalogue aside.

At the bottom of the box he found what he was looking for. Flat, clean, and undisturbed for years, a small stack of cream-colored stationery with the name Meyer Rothstein and the address of the Saint Honoré gallery smartly engraved in black letters. Mori lifted a sheet from the box and held it to the light. A watermark with the name Smythson, London was clearly visible. *Perfect*, he thought. He removed the small stack of paper placing it on his desk, then returned the pen, books, and catalogue to the box. He slid the lid into place and tucked the box into the cabinet.

He shut the door then pulled it back open. *Wait.* He grabbed the box once again and tossed the lid to the side, seizing the catalogue. It had been there, right in front of him. The Raphael sketch. Number 103. He had just read the description, but it hadn't registered until now. At the end of the lengthy narrative was a footnote. "Although this work has been examined by our experts and those of both the National Gallery, London, and the Tate Gallery, London, no formal provenance exists for this piece. It has been held by a private family for several generations."

"Thank you, Papa," Mori said softly. This was proof for Bertolt that some valuable works had no official provenance.

He set the catalogue on his desk and placed the box back into the cabinet. He closed the cupboard doors. He took a sheet of the cream-colored paper and placed it on the leather desktop. He positioned a straight edge tightly beneath his father's engraved monogram and carefully tore off the top edge of the sheet, leaving what he hoped would appear to be a deckle edge. Although the deckle edge was predominantly known to be used in bookmaking, such a border had become popular as a decorative edge on personal notes. He took the small piece with his father's letterhead, folded it, and stuffed it into his pocket.

Mori cranked the newly sized sheet of paper into the roller of the typewriter. It felt as though his father were there with him, looking over his shoulder. He hadn't felt his Papa's presence so strongly in a long while.

With renewed hope, Mori took a breath, ready to create the proof of provenance for this rare sketch by the master Da Vinci.

58

Émile was still absorbing the importance of her announcement. He caressed her bare belly, his mind racing in a combination of joy and fear. "Are you sure?"

She nodded. "I've been feeling queasy and tired for a while. But this week I know."

What a strange time to bring a child into the world. How would they manage? Yet it felt like a sign, a positive omen, an affirmation that life would win out.

"Émile . . ." Alena sounded tentative. "Are you happy?"

Émile sat up. "Happy? I'm so excited, I could burst." He grinned. "This is wonderful news." He kissed her again and again. "You are carrying the future, our future.".

Émile knew what he must do, what he had thought about and wanted to do for so long. "Alena," he said, searching out her eyes in the dim light. "Will you marry me?"

Alena sat up and threw her arms around Émile's shoulders. "I've been waiting all of my life to marry you."

"We should do it soon."

"As soon as you like." Alena drew back suddenly. "I haven't said a thing to my parents."

The excitement of the moment calmed.

Émile loved her with all his heart. His parents loved her. But, there was the difference in their religions. He had no idea if her parents would accept the marriage. As modern as France was, some still frowned on interfaith unions. The Nazis had made it all worse. He was afraid for her to be seen publicly with him. How would they get from hiding in this pyramid to living freely together in such a crazy world?

59

3 January, 1940

Dear Mori,

My grandfather gave this sketch to my
grandmother on the occasion of their
marriage. It had been passed to him by
my great-grandfather, who had received
it from his father. I don't know how
far back it extends in my family before
that. I only know that it has been in my
possession since my parents passed on,
and it is my greatest treasure.

With your agreement, I will entrust this
sketch to you for safekeeping.

Please watch over her, my friend. I will
collect this gem when I return to Paris
once this turbulent world calms.

Yours most sincerely,

Paul

60

Mori cranked the brass handle of the typewriter's roller until the page was released from the machine. He examined the letter, studying each word in hopes that it would pass the careful inspection Bertolt would make of it. He laid the paper on the desk and folded the note in half, allowing the deckle edge to extend slightly beyond the clean-cut bottom. Now the paper appeared to be a folded note rather than a sheet of stationery.

Please let this work, Mori thought. The letter, together with the Sotheby's catalogue entry—if needed—might just convince Bertolt of the sketch's authenticity.

He took the fountain pen from its marble holder and held it firmly. His hand was trembling. Bertolt was smart. He knew art and the art world. Would this pass his scrutiny? Mori swallowed hard, trying to recall how his friend signed his name. After a moment, he set pen to paper and inscribed "Paul" at the bottom of the page.

He placed the document under a large crystal paperweight, then grabbed the Sotheby's auction catalogue and slid it between assorted other catalogues on a bookcase near the desk. His eye landed on the fountain pen he had used to forge Paul's name. *Best to move that, too*, he thought. He transferred the pen and its stand to the back of a low shelf in a cabinet across the room.

Finally, Mori collapsed into his chair and closed his eyes, though his mind was anything but still. In all his years he had never second-guessed his every move as he did now.

61

Thursday, August 27, 1942

From his desk in the gallery, Mori saw Émile open the rear door of the storage room and place a small rolled canvas into the dust bin, then return to his easel. It had been two weeks, and still Bertolt hadn't come by Mori's home to see the letter of provenance. Mori existed in a constant state of anticipation, wondering if each day was the one the colonel would show up unannounced, demand to see the letter, and pronounce it a fake. The gallery put Mori equally on edge. The inventory of paintings under his care was growing smaller each day. He understood all too well what an empty gallery would mean for him and his family, yet he had not been able to find a boat or any other path of escape. Ruth's constant requests that he find a way to safety didn't help. She was increasingly agitated over the Nazi presence in the neighborhood. She rarely ventured out anymore. Easily startled, she reminded Mori of a trapped animal.

While Mori tried to prolong the process of evaluating paintings, he also urged Émile to work faster on his forgeries. In a world that was completely out of his control, the one thing Mori still could influence was the rescue of masterworks that had once belonged to his clients.

Mori stepped into the doorway to the storeroom. Émile was fast at work on a copy of *The Expulsion of Hagar.* He had been working on it for several days.

Émile studied the masterwork. "Unlike at the Louvre, I can get as close as I want," Émile said. "No museum guards."

Mori's eyes came to rest on one particular spot, the small satchel the young Ishmael carried. In the original, the satchel had no straps. Émile had added three straps to the boy's sack in the copy he had made for the École. It had been his way of making the canvas his own.

This copy of *The Expulsion* would be different. It would match the original exactly.

Émile looked up at his father. He looked as troubled as Mori felt. "This is it," he said. "The last one."

"How much longer will it take?" Mori said.

"A day, maybe two. Much of it's dry, so just a few more touches."

Mori took a step toward his son. "We need to get my paintings out of here, too." He gestured to several stacked nineteenth and twentieth-century masters at the rear of the storage room— Picasso, Van Gogh, Cezanne, Gauguin, Toulouse-Lautrec, Seurat.

"That's a little more difficult," Émile said.

"Why?"

"What will we do with the frames?"

When Émile copied a painting, he placed the copy into the original's frame and stored the rolled original in the park. There were no extra frames to get rid of.

"We can just stack them at the rear," Mori said. "It's not unusual to have empty frames in a gallery."

Émile nodded, and continued his work.

Mori returned to his desk and to his swirl of worry—escape routes, Bertolt, the *Mona Lisa* sketch. He was sure Bertolt had not forgotten his intent to investigate the provenance of the DaVinci. This was his sick way of torturing Mori, delaying his arrival at Mori's home, keeping him in a terrified state of suspense.

Mori looked around the gallery. The walls were bare and bleak, reflecting light from the late afternoon sun. He also smelled traces of brush thinner and oil paint, the familiar scent of the gallery ever since Émile had begun his work. He glanced at the opening to the storage room. Small flecks of paint dotted the floor—a smear of red from an unknown cardinal's robe, a splat of pale blue undoubtedly from a Monet sky. The path through the gallery had widened, with the thinning stacks of paintings now only three or four deep along the walls. His work for Goering was nearing an end—the commandant's protection surely ending with it.

Mori had explored every possible avenue of escape. German guards were stationed at checkpoints along the roads day and night. The Seine, Mori's first choice of travel, would not allow his family safe exodus to the coast, where he hoped to cross the English Channel. German soldiers patrolled the route downstream. Albert had not offered him any alternatives either. He felt trapped and desperate—a failure at protecting his family.

The sound of the front door startled Mori from his dark reverie. One look at the doorway forced him to his feet. "Colonel Bertolt." From the corner of his eye, Mori saw Émile pull the forgery of *The Expulsion* from the easel and slide it behind a stack of paintings against the wall of the storage room.

Bertolt waved his hand to the guards seated near the window, indicating their momentary dismissal. Both soldiers promptly left. The colonel surveyed every area of the gallery, his eyes darting around the space. He walked to a row of paintings stacked carefully against the wall and flipped through them as though through files in a drawer. He paused at a small canvas, then pushed the frames back into place.

"May I help you find something?" Mori asked.

Bertolt continued to another stack of paintings. "No, but I

do want to see the paperwork on the Da Vinci."

And here it was, after weeks of torturous delay.

"Yes, of course," Mori said. "I have it at home." *As I told you*, Mori thought.

Bertolt stepped into the storage room and surveyed the space. Mori followed. Émile gave a nod, cleaning his brushes. The colonel began flipping through the paintings against the storage room wall.

Mori's temples throbbed. This was the stack behind which Émile had hidden *The Expulsion* forgery. The wet copy was the last one, closest to the wall.

Bertolt paused halfway through the stack to gaze at Renoir's *Day at the Beach*—a large portrait of a young girl in a straw hat looking out over the water. He rested his hand on the elaborately carved frame—Mori's client's frame, which earlier in the day had held an original masterpiece. Bertolt casually glanced down at the canvas and then turned to Mori. "I'll have the rest of these picked up in the next few days."

"Of course," Mori said.

Bertolt tilted the paintings back into place in front of the wet canvas. He had stopped short of exposing *The Expulsion*. Mori swallowed hard, his heart still racing.

Bertolt turned to Mori. "Your son is finished here?"

"Almost." Mori barely could find his voice. He exited the storage room, hoping Bertolt would follow. "These canvases are loose in their frames." Mori waved a hand in the general direction of several rows of paintings along the gallery wall. "Émile will be tightening them in the next few days." There was nothing wrong with the canvases. He just needed a little more time.

Bertolt walked to the rows of paintings Mori had indicated and inspected several. "They don't appear to need tightening to me."

"Some of the supports are loose," Mori said, hoping he

sounded calmer than he felt.

Bertolt's brow furrowed.

"Émile mentioned it in passing before he left yesterday," Mori said. "He was in a hurry to see his girlfriend, actually fiancée. You know how children are. They recently announced their plans to marry." Mori grappled for conversation. Why, he wondered, had he shared such personal information with someone he truly loathed? Someone he feared?

"Later this evening," Bertolt said.

Mori tilted his head. "Later?"

"I'll stop by your house to see what you have on the Da Vinci."

Mori could hear the cynicism in Bertolt's voice, and he understood why. There had never been any history of a sketch of the *Mona Lisa*. This would either be the art world's greatest discovery, or the quick demise of the Rothstein family.

"Yes, of course," Mori said.

Bertolt turned and strode out of the gallery.

Mori breathed deeply, as though Bertolt's departure had left more air in the room.

The door opened again, and both soldiers resumed their positions.

Mori knocked on the door frame of the storage room. "I'll see you at home," he said, with a wave to his son. He grabbed his suit jacket from the back of the desk chair and slung it over his arm. He pushed his wire-framed glasses onto the bridge of his nose and departed the gallery, ignoring the guards.

With Bertolt's imminent arrival at his home, Mori had to search every last possible recourse for getting his family out alive—even if it meant revisiting the avenues he'd already explored. He found his mind returning again and again to Albert, who had gotten his wife and children out far later than anyone else Mori knew. Was it possible Albert was as suspicious of him as Mori had been of Albert? The man had seen Nazis coming and going from the gallery for weeks. Would telling him the full story—the details of his dealings with Goering and Bertolt—help in some way? Or would it damn him and his family that much sooner?

Through the window of Albert's café, Mori saw a waiter mopping the tile floors. Mori entered the restaurant, greeted by the aroma of coffee—a familiar and comforting smell. Albert was behind the counter placing cups on the shelf above the coffee machine.

"You work so hard," Mori said.

Albert turned. "Mori!" He gestured to a nearby table. "Sit, coffee?"

"Alright, please."

Albert brought over a cup and set it before Mori. "You look like you're carrying the war on your shoulders."

"It's at my door," Mori said.

Albert blew out a small laugh. "It's at all our doors, my friend."

Mori glanced around the café. He paused until both waiters had walked into the kitchen. "No, it's really at my door." Mori envisioned the Nazis breaking in the doors of his house and taking him and his family away. His time at the gallery was just about at its end, and Bertolt would surely catch on to his ruse. He lowered his voice. "I'm trapped, and I think everything's going to explode in the next few days."

Albert sat down at the table with Mori. "We're all living with the damn Nazis." He put his hand on Mori's shoulder. "They'll leave sooner or later."

Mori leaned forward and, in a hushed voice, said, "I've been cheating the Nazis at the highest level. They're going to catch on to me, soon, very soon. Maybe even tonight."

Albert looked into Mori's eyes "What did you do?"

"I've had no one to talk to. Ruth is so frightened and I'm doing my best to protect the boys." Keeping his voice at a whisper, Mori told Albert about the forgeries, his relationship with Goering and Bertolt, and what he was doing with the originals.

Albert said nothing. He just stared.

Mori then explained the Da Vinci sketch, and why he'd asked Émile to create it. "Bertolt is coming this afternoon or evening to see the letter that proves it's real . . . which is also fabricated."

Albert drew in a deep breath and sat back in his chair. "Do you still have the key to the café?"

Mori had borrowed it to gain nighttime access for Émile to use the bread ovens, though he had never told Albert before this what Émile had been baking up. "Yes, Émile has it."

"You know you can always hide here," Albert said, holding his arms up to the walls of the café.

"Thank you my friend but there are five of us. And the Nazis are in and out of here all the time."

Albert seemed to study Mori's face, then his gaze moved around the café, as though checking every inch of the space, for spies? Interlopers? Traitors? Finally he leaned across the table, his face within inches of Mori's, and in a barely audible whisper he said, "I think I can get you out of France."

Mori wasn't sure he had heard him right. He didn't know what to think. Was this a joke? "You can?" he said. "Why? How? Why not earlier?"

Albert leaned back in his chair again, and the two men stared at each other in silence. Had Mori's ears betrayed him? Had Albert really given him a morsel of hope?

"Why now?" Mori said finally. Albert had known for months that Mori wanted to get his family out of France. Was this some kind of setup? Mori leaned in and whispered, "What do you mean you can get us out of France?"

"It's complicated," Albert said, "and it's dangerous."

"Dangerous?" Mori said. "My family could not be in more danger than we are now."

Albert stood and walked to the doorway of the kitchen. He

glanced in, then returned to the table. "You must not repeat anything I'm about to tell you," Albert whispered. "Not to anyone. Give only the vaguest information to your family."

Mori nodded, taking in the gravity of Albert's tone.

"I have a cousin in Antwerp. She and her friends are part of a resistance group that operates the Comet Line. They help Allied soldiers return to England."

The two café workers returned from the kitchen, and Albert stood and walked toward the bar. He gave a little nod to Mori to follow. Mori brought his cup of coffee with him.

As the workers chatted, they dragged tables and chairs from one side of the restaurant to the other and mopped the exposed floor. Albert wiped down the bar with a damp cloth. "As I was saying," he told Mori, no longer whispering, "business has been slow."

Not missing a beat, Mori said, "For all of us." He eyed Albert's employees, wishing they would leave again. Albert had tossed a thread of hope in his direction, and he clung to it.

When finally the workers returned to the kitchen, Mori pressed Albert for more.

"The details aren't important. Just get yourself and your family ready."

Mori was still absorbing the impact of Albert's news, going over in his head what it would mean to get his family ready. And what of the paintings hidden in the park? "I have things I need to get out of Paris." Mori said.

Albert shook his head. He whispered, "It's you and your family. You can't take anything more than you can carry in one hand." He glanced again around the café. "No bags. No belongings."

"But valuables?" Mori whispered back.

"Money, jewelry, as much as you have. It will be useful to pay off border guards."

"Where will we go? And how soon?"

"I'm not sure yet. There will be very little notice. You'll need to be ready when I tell you."

Mori nodded, his heart racing with hope as well as the fear and uncertainty of not understanding how all of this was going to work.

"You'll need false identity papers," Albert said. "That will be arranged for you. Choose sensible clothing and sturdy shoes. There will be a great deal of walking."

"Where will they take us?" Mori asked.

Albert wiped the bar again and shook his head. "I don't know. It's always different."

"What do you mean different?" Mori said.

"South to any number of towns. Then over the Pyrenees to Spain. From there, Bilbao, Madrid, or Gibraltar. It varies. The final destination is England."

"A long journey," Mori said.

"Yes, and a strenuous one."

Mori thought of Jacob, of his difficulty walking.

"There are many routes," Albert said. "It just depends on safety and timing."

Mori drank in every word his friend was speaking. He rubbed his forehead with both hands, feeling his body begin to relax, the pain he'd felt in his stomach for weeks slowly melting. He knew his friend's offer to be real. It was kind and generous, and he felt ashamed for not trusting him from the start, a trust Albert had now more than earned.

Mori grasped Albert's hands. "I hardly know what to say."

"Once you commit to leaving, we'll take care of everything."

"I understand," Mori said. "Consider this my commitment. We are ready."

Albert looked Mori in the eye and nodded. "Bon."

"I don't know how I can ever repay you, my friend."

"It's what we do, Mori. I'll tell you once I know when we can move you."

Albert took a cardboard box from under the counter and placed several baked items inside. He pushed the box to Mori. "Put some money on the counter and thank me."

Mori followed his instructions, arranged several coins on the bar, and accepted the package. "Thank you my friend."

62

When Mori stepped out of the café he found himself face to face with a magenta sky. Even in the midst of an invading army delivering atrocities upon innocent people, God saw fit to paint the sky into a gorgeous spectacle of art.

He hurried home and ran up the front steps, eager to share the news with Ruth. Finally he had something hopeful to offer his wife—though he also remembered Albert's words, "Give only the vaguest information to your family." He would make her promise to speak of it to no one. He slipped his key into the lock and turned. As the door swung open he heard a scream. It was Ruth. Mori bolted across the entry, through the dining room, and into the kitchen.

Ruth was backed into the corner, her mouth tight, a butter spreader raised in fury.

Mori scanned the room and saw she was alone. "What's wrong, *ma chérie*? What happened? Was someone here?"

"There." Ruth pointed to the bottom of the cooking range. "Six burners, two ovens, and one mouse at home underneath. You said you'd take care of this."

Mori laughed, a wave of relief washing through him. "A mouse problem is welcome news compared to what we've been dealing with the past few weeks. Are you going to kill it with that knife, or spread it on toast?"

Ruth smiled then laughed.

"There hasn't been laughter in this house for a long time,"

Mori said.

"You laugh all you want." Ruth tossed the useless weapon into the sink. "I'm not making supper until you take care of that pest."

Mori traipsed to the basement. He found the mouse poison on a high shelf across from where Ruth stored fruits and vegetables she had canned for the winter months. Row upon row of peaches, plums, and tomatoes lined several shelves in the small room under the kitchen. Mori looked up at the exposed beams and the crawl space under the house, which gave proper ventilation to keep Ruth's jars cool. Still, they had rotted and would not be used after all her efforts.

With the box of poison in hand, Mori headed back up the wooden stairs to the kitchen. "Alright," he said.

Ruth handed Mori a porcelain saucer with a chip on the rim. Delicate pink flowers intertwined with pale green leaves around the outer edge. So lovely for such a deadly mission.

Mori poured a small amount of the lethal powder onto the center of the plate, then knelt down and stretched out on his side in front of the range. He pushed the saucer to the rear wall, using the handle of a long cooking spoon to tuck the bait neatly into the corner.

He rose to his feet. "All done."

Ruth took the spoon and threw it into the sink. She wrapped her arms around Mori's neck and brought her lips to his, then hugged him tightly. "You're my hero, you know. You saved me from the monster."

Mori drank in Ruth's touch. She had been so distraught lately, the only closeness they'd shared were his efforts to comfort her. "I love you so much," Mori said.

"I know." She kissed his cheek. "I love you, too."

Over Ruth's shoulder, Mori caught sight of the clock on the stove. His smile vanished. He hated to end their intimacy with his next news, but he needed to prepare her. "I think Bertolt's coming here this evening. He wants to see the provenance on the Da Vinci sketch."

Ruth stepped back, alarm visible on her face.

"I know. I'll have to do my best to convince him of its authenticity." Mori watched her face.

"This is a dangerous path," Ruth said.

"All we need to do is survive a little longer. Come here. I spoke to Albert today." He sat Ruth down at the small table next to the kitchen window. He shared the news from his visit with Albert, requesting that she speak of it to no one outside their family.

Ruth clutched his hand. "Is this real?" she said. "How? Who will get us out?" Hope glinted in her eyes.

"Let's talk about this later. We need to be ready as soon as possible."

"Like that, we leave?" She gazed around the kitchen, which was filled with cherished items handed down across generations—her mother's jelly molds hanging on the wall, her grandmother's tea service gleaming on a small shelf by the window.

"There won't be time to pack. We'll hide what we can," Mori said, thinking of all that Ruth would have to sacrifice. "My work is all but finished for Goering. The Nazis don't need me anymore, and when they catch on . . ."

"If they catch on," Ruth said, touching his arm.

"Ruth . . ." Mori took her hand in his. "It's just a matter of time. All I can do is hope we stay ahead of them."

63

Mori peered out the library window, his heart hammering. Bertolt was heading up the front steps two at a time. His silhouette appeared black against the glow from the street lamp, only the swastika on his arm catching the light.

When a firm knock sounded at the door, Mori motioned to Ruth.

She nodded, then slowly walked across the entry hall, straightening her skirt. She arrived at the glass panels, took a breath, and smoothed her hair.

Mori had asked her to answer the door as a sign of warmth and friendship, even though he felt neither for Bertolt. His goal was to convince the colonel that the Da Vinci was genuine, and he needed all the help he could get. Bertolt may not have had Mori's experience in the field, but he was well educated and an exceptional art scholar.

Ruth peeked through the lace curtains.

"I'm Colonel Bertolt to see Mr. Rothstein," he said loudly from the other side of the door.

Mori hurried back to his desk; that's where he would sit to greet the colonel.

Opening the front door, Ruth said, "Good evening. Won't you please come in, Colonel Bertolt."

The lanky soldier entered and rubbed his leather-gloved hands together.

"Are you chilled?" Ruth asked.

He grumbled a response.

"My husband is expecting you. Please." She led him to the library and knocked on the open double doors.

"Colonel Bertolt." Mori stood, trying to appear relaxed. He motioned to a nearby chair, as if he were welcoming a friend.

Bertolt strode by Ruth and sank stiffly into a green leather chair that made a whooshing sound as he descended.

He adjusted his jacket on his lean frame. Each highly polished button and medal on his tailored uniform sparkled in the lamplight.

"I'll fix coffee for you, gentlemen," Ruth said.

"Is there any of your apple cake left?" Mori said.

"Of course," she said, playing her part perfectly.

"Not for me," Bertolt said, his voice icy.

"Oh, Colonel Bertolt," Mori said, conjuring as jovial a tone as he could muster. "It's a cake that will melt in your mouth. It's absolutely heavenly."

Ruth stepped into the hallway and closed the door.

Bertolt looked around the room, studying each painting. "I wasn't informed of your personal collection," he said, his gaze resting on the large Picasso.

Mori knew that the Germans had burned an assortment of modern master paintings, including a Picasso, only a few weeks earlier.

"And yours. I saw you save a Van Gogh the other day. Not the usual preference of the Führer," Mori said, intending to stall, but instead sounding provocative.

Bertolt pursed his lips, jaw clenched, and exhaled sharply.

"I'm sorry," Mori said, "I meant no disrespect." He lifted the Da Vinci sketch from his desk.

"I thought Commandant Goering had it," Bertolt said.

"He asked that it be reframed. He wanted something more elaborate. I had Émile do it."

Bertolt stared at Mori. "Let's see it," he said, wasting no

time. Staring first at the framed sketch, then directly at Mori, Bertolt said flatly, "Where's the letter?"

"It's here." Mori rummaged methodically through his drawers. "I just looked at it a few days ago." Where was Ruth with the coffee and cake? Refreshments always eased tensions. Mori glanced at the door, then back at his desk. "Ah, here it is," he said, "right under my nose." He lifted a large crystal paperweight and removed a folded note. "I knew it was here."

Bertolt reached for the letter, but as Mori leaned across the desk to hand it to him, a pain shot from his shoulder to the back of his head, causing him to wince.

"Something wrong?" Bertolt said.

"Nothing," Mori said as casually as possible. "Just a kink in my neck." The tension was grabbing at him from all sides.

Mori watched Bertolt examine the document. He was looking at it too closely, and for too long. Finally he glared up, his mouth twisted into a frown. "This doesn't create a provenance for the drawing."

64

Ruth put a kettle of water on the stove and turned the gas handle. A flame rose beneath the pot. This was the first time she had met Colonel Bertolt face to face, and she could feel in her bones the depth of cruelty in the man. Mori wasn't going to sell the soldier on the sketch's authenticity. He wasn't going to sell him on anything. From the sideboard she removed the last of her apple cake. She cut it into bite-size pieces and arranged them neatly on a porcelain plate adorned with flowers and birds.

Her hands were shaking. Ever since Jacob had been abducted, she had been aware of how easily she trembled. Every day it seemed another person was rounded up. Jacob had been returned to them, but two of her friends had since gone missing. Now, finally, there was hope for her family to escape. She would have to leave everything behind, but it was a small price for her family's safety. She glanced around the kitchen. She would miss her modern appliances, her dishwashing machine, her Frigidaire shipped from America.

Ruth set two cups and saucers on a silver tray, along with the cake, then scooped several heaping spoonfuls of ground coffee into a metal filter. Waiting for the water to boil, she ducked out of the kitchen and slipped through the dining room to see if she could overhear the men's conversation. She had barely reached the entry hall when she heard shouts.

"That doesn't make it an original." Bertolt sounded angry.

Ruth froze.

"It's not unusual for objects such as the sketch to go without recorded history." Mori's voice was firm.

"I beg your pardon," Bertolt said, his voice dripping sarcasm. "Yes, it is unusual."

Ruth retreated. *Keep your calm, she thought.* It was just as she'd feared. The man wasn't falling for Mori's ruse. What was to keep him from running right out of here and exposing her husband to Goering? The thought sent shivers up her spine.

The kettle whistled. She turned off the gas and used a kitchen towel as a hot-pad to grip the handle. Perspiration dotted her upper lip. She set the filter containing the coffee grounds over an open pot and carefully poured the bubbling water over them. A moment later, a trickle of dark liquid seeped into the pot. She studied it. There must be something she could do to help her husband, her family.

Ruth poured the coffee into a silver pot Mori's parents had given them as a wedding gift. She checked the finished tray—coffee, sugar, milk, cups and saucers, spoons, and cake. From a drawer she removed two lace napkins with the initial "R" embroidered at the corner. This might be the last time she would use this coffee and tea service. All of this would have to stay behind. "Only what you can carry in one hand," Mori had told her. That was if they were lucky and Bertolt did not betray them to Goering.

As she carried the tray into the hall, she heard Bertolt's thick German accent. "I think Commandant Goering will not be pleased."

Ruth stopped in her tracks nearly dropping the tray. This was not good. She returned to the kitchen, her mind reeling. They were so close to escaping from France, finally a light at the end of the tunnel. She would not let this man steal that light. She knew what she had to do.

She hurried to the basement door and ran down the steps.

The small red box was missing from the high shelf across from her preserves. Where had Mori left it? She ran back up the stairs and glanced around the kitchen. Her eyes traveled to the floor then landed on the stove.

She knelt down, and bent forward to look under the massive steel structure. She didn't see the box, but there was the small plate, in the corner. She grabbed a cooking spoon then lay on the floor, reaching for the dish with the utensil. The spoon was too short. *"Merde."* She rose to her knees, and reached up, snatching a long soup ladle. She tried again, this time hooking the ladle over the small plate. She slid it out from under the oven.

Once on her feet, she didn't hesitate. She opened the lid of the silver coffee pot, tipped the dish and poured the powder into the brew. She gave it a good stir.

Ruth straightened her dress and smoothed her hair. She tried to draw in a deep breath, but there didn't seem to be any room at all to breathe. She lifted the tray and hurried through the hallway. She stood for a moment outside the open library doors.

"A letter alone isn't proof of anything," she heard Bertolt say. "It simply shows that Mr. Betone had possession of the piece."

Ruth entered. She set the tray on the table near the sofa. "Here we go," she said. Mori stood at the book shelf across the room. *Stay there*, she thought. *Don't move, Mori.* She turned to Colonel Bertolt. "Milk and sugar?"

Bertolt looked up from the document he was reading. "Thank you, nothing for me."

Ruth felt a trickle of perspiration slide down the center of her back. *Steady yourself*, she thought.

"Nonsense," she said. "You'll love my apple cake."

Working to keep her hand steady, Ruth poured two cups of coffee. She placed one in front of Bertolt, and left the other on the tray. She handed Bertolt a napkin and then offered him the plate of cake. "My grandmother taught me to make this recipe."

"You're very kind," Bertolt said, his tone softening.

Ruth sat on the sofa and clenched the fabric of her skirt.

Bertolt lifted a cube of apple cake and popped it into his mouth. "Mmm, it's delicious," he murmured.

Ruth smiled.

"Where is it?" Mori mused, flipping through some books in front of the shelves.

Ruth held out the sugar. "Milk, sugar?" she urged Bertolt. "You'll want something to wash that down with." She smiled and helped herself to a small piece of cake, though she had no appetite at all.

Bertolt removed two sugar cubes from the bowl and dropped them into his cup. He added a splash of milk and then a quick stir. He lifted the cup to his lips.

"Here it is," Mori said. Ruth tensed. Bertolt put the cup down. He hadn't yet taken a sip.

Mori had pulled a Sotheby's catalogue from the shelf and was flipping through its pages. Ruth's jaw clenched.

"What is it?" Bertolt asked.

"It's the catalogue I was telling you about," Mori said.

No, Ruth thought. *Stay there*. But Mori was headed back toward them. She inhaled sharply. "Another piece of cake?" She offered the plate to Bertolt.

"Thank you." He tossed another chunk into his mouth. Bertolt lifted his cup and finally sipped. Ruth held her breath.

Mori handed the catalogue to Bertolt, the page open to a picture of a Raphael sketch.

"What's in this coffee?" Bertolt said.

Ruth stopped breathing. Her mouth went dry. "It's just coffee," she managed to get out.

Bertolt looked directly at Ruth. "It's delicious. There's a flavor, I can't make it out, but the taste is most pleasant."

She exhaled slowly and offered a weak smile.

Mori sat beside Ruth on the sofa and put a piece of cake into his mouth. If he were to lean forward he could reach the cup of coffee on the tray. Her gaze settled on her husband's hand. She resisted the urge to grab it. *Not now, in front of the colonel. It wouldn't be appropriate.*

"Not every painting, or sketch for that matter, has provenance," Mori said. "If the piece hasn't sold or been loaned in a long period of time, it might disappear from public knowledge."

"Hmm," Bertolt said. "I'm not so sure about that." He lifted the cup to his lips again and drank. "It really does taste like you have a special ingredient, Mrs. Rothstein."

Ruth refilled Bertolt's cup.

65

Mori felt the tone of the room had calmed since Ruth's arrival with the coffee. He sank back into his chair, but he stayed vigilant.

"Let me see that letter again," Bertolt said.

Mori picked up the note from where Bertolt had thrown it in anger, and handed it back to him. "I had the same concern as you," Mori said. He leaned forward and lifted the cup Ruth had left on the tray for him.

Ruth made a small sound. He glanced at her.

Her face appeared ashen.

Mori set down the cup and leaned toward Bertolt. "It really is just a letter, however, in it, Betone references family."

Bertolt flipped the paper over a few times, inspecting each side.

"If a work falls from family member to family member, generation to generation, there very likely would not be a tangible provenance," Mori said. He leaned forward again to reach for his coffee, but Ruth rose in the same moment and walked between him and the coffee service, bumping the tray and splashing coffee from the cup onto the linen napkin. Irritated, Mori looked up at her. What was she trying to do? Didn't she understand this was a crucial moment?

"Oh my," Ruth said, lifting the tray. "Look what a mess I've made."

Bertolt removed a handkerchief from his pocket and wiped

his brow. Droplets of perspiration had formed along his hairline.

Ruth set the tray on Mori's desk, then refilled Bertolt's cup. "Another piece of cake?" she asked, her smile brittle.

"No, no more." Bertolt's face was now covered in a sheen of sweat. He pulled at his collar. "I'll take this with me," he said, waving the forged letter. He rose to his feet but seemed unsteady, swaying for a moment in place. He looked almost confused.

"Can I get you something else?" Ruth asked. "Some water?"

Mori rose. Was the man unwell?

The colonel took a few steps toward the library door, gait awkward. He grabbed for the handle and missed. "I'm not sure, I . . ."

"Let me help you," Mori said.

Bertolt staggered out of the library, but before he could reach the glass front doors, he stumbled and came down hard on one knee. He attempted to rise, but the colonel's lanky frame seemed to crumble, and he toppled backward, his head crashing onto the stone floor.

66

After a walk in Jardin du Luxembourg, Émile led Alena through the back gate into the Rothsteins' courtyard. Would his parents, with all their concerns, be happy for him? He and Alena had chosen a date only a week away. It wasn't much notice but the wedding would be simple.

He unlocked the back door to the house and they crossed the laundry room that held Ruth's Bendix washing machine from America. Émile planned to give Alena such luxuries with the proceeds from his paintings. He would create a beautiful home for her and their child.

As they entered the dining room, Émile heard a scuffle toward the front of the house. Then shouting. It was his father's voice: "What were you thinking?"

Hurrying into the foyer, he saw his father gripping his mother's arm.

"What's going on?" Émile looked down, and an audible gasp escaped from his mouth. A man in a Nazi uniform lay sprawled on the floor, face drained of blood, piercing blue eyes vacant of life. "Colonel Bertolt."

Alena came from behind Émile and gasped.

Émile pulled her to him, trying to shield her from the sight. "Maman? Papa?" he said. "What happened?"

Mori released Ruth, who stood frozen at the center of the entry hall.

She appeared to be in shock.

"Maman?" Émile said. He couldn't fathom what might have happened here.

"I didn't know what else to do," Ruth said, looking at Émile.

"What happened?" Émile said again, but no one answered his question.

Alena trembled next to Émile, her hand over her mouth. Émile held her tightly to him, his heart careening inside his chest. "Someone tell me what's going on," he demanded, staring at the figure on the floor.

"Your mother did a very brave thing," Mori said, then relayed the details of the demise of the man who had terrorized him.

"I've never seen a dead man," Émile said.

By the time Jacob arrived, the rest of them were sitting in the dining room. Jacob limped in from the kitchen, cane in hand. Unbuttoning his tweed jacket, he balanced a cigarette between his lips. "What's going on? Why are you all sitting in the dark?" The only light in the room came from a tiny lamp on the sideboard.

"You tell him," Mori said to Ruth. "Émile, come with me." Mori pushed up from the table.

Émile kissed Alena's cheek. "I'll be back, chérie."

A chill ran through Émile as he walked with his father into the darkened entryway. It was usually lit by a chandelier and double-stemmed wall sconces. Mori had turned them off in favor of a small lamp on the side table in the curve of the staircase. Émile understood, less attention to the house from the street was best.

Bertolt lay motionless on the stone floor, a puddle of blood pooled beneath his head from the fall.

"We need to get rid of the body," Mori said.

Jacob appeared in the entry. He studied the bloodless face and looked like he might be sick. He steadied himself against a chair and breathed heavily.

Mori put his arm around his son's shoulders. "I know," he

said. "It's a shock."

"It's him," Jacob said. "The soldier who beat me up at the Vélodrome." He inhaled a deep breath. "I'll never forget those blue eyes."

"Fucking bastard." Mori bent down and closed Bertolt's eyelids. He turned to Jacob. "He's dead. He can't hurt you ever again." Mori embraced him.

Émile watched the anger seething in his father's face, even though the perpetrator had now paid for his crime. This was the man who had regularly berated his father and terrorized his family. Now, in an instant, all that was done. Just like that. But could the man, in his death, bring them the same threat?

"What are we going to do with him?" Émile said.

Mori blew out a breath. "I don't know, but we need to figure it out quickly. We don't have much time. The housekeeper will be here early tomorrow morning."

"We need to get him out of here and clean up this mess." Émile said.

Jacob, appearing to have recovered from his shock, said, "Where do you think we should put him?"

"He needs to disappear," Émile said, surprising himself with his blunt tone.

"Get some wood," Mori said. "We'll make a fire in the library."

67

Émile, wet with perspiration, rolled the trash can Jacob had used for transporting the paintings, over the stone tiles in the hallway. The wheels hitting the grout lines were the only sound in the house. When he reached the foyer, Mori and Jacob were standing over Bertolt's body. Ruth was sitting on a chair across the room, her hands cupping her face.

"Are you alright?" Mori asked Émile.

"Of course I'm not alright." Émile said, his tone harsh.

Mori laid a hand on Émile's shoulder. "Calm yourself."

"I'm sorry," Émile said. He hadn't meant to speak disrespectfully to his father, but disposing of a dead man his mother had killed was beyond anything he had ever imagined doing. He removed the twig surround he had created for the trash can to hide the paintings.

"Come on," Mori said, "Let's get this done. Jacob, help us get him out of his clothes. We'll burn them in the fireplace in the library."

Jacob sneered. "What's that smell?"

"He pissed himself," his father said.

The three men began to strip Bertolt's corpse, throwing his clothes into a pile near the wall. Moving the body left blood smears on the floor. "Ruth, get a towel and wrap it around his head," Mori said.

When all that remained on the body was the undershorts, they all paused. "There's no power without the trappings of a

Nazi officer," Mori said. "He's just another thug."

Émile stared at the man's ribs showing along the sides of his chest. "And skinny at that." Émile looked up at Mori and registered a mix of emotions on his father's face—relief and anxiety. His nemesis was dead, but they had to get the body out of there as quickly as possible. Even in his death the man could bring them down if he was found anywhere near them.

"Those too," Mori said, pointing to the undershorts.

Jacob slid the boxers free of Bertolt's body.

The man was completely exposed, no uniform, no medals, no guns. Nothing to protect him or make him powerful, nothing to inspire fear. Just pale flesh.

"Boys, take the medals off his coat," Mori said.

"Yes, they won't burn," Émile said removing the three cluster oak leaves pinned to each side of Bertolt's gray jacket collar. He tossed them next to the silver German Cross he tore from the officer's breast pocket.

Mori grabbed hold of Bertolt's legs, and Émile his arms.

"Alright," Émile said, looking at his father.

They hoisted Bertolt's folded body, both of them huffing and sweating, and managed finally to stuff the corpse into the garbage can. The body protruded from the top of the container, and one of the arms hung out to the side. Émile bent the limb backward, forcing it to a lower position, and cringed when he heard the snap of cartilage.

He then took the cylindrical twig surround and maneuvered it around the body, tucking the bottom third of it into the can. The tied sticks extended higher than before, but it would suffice.

Mori, Émile, and Jacob stood shoulder to shoulder, looking at the lifeless form of Mori's arch enemy, now no better than yesterday's trash.

"I don't know what I would have done without you both," Mori said. "We're all together, and we're all safe."

Émile heaved a deep breath. "For now, anyway."

68

Leaving the challenge of disposing of Bertolt's body to his sons, Mori headed into the library and closed the door. He walked from table to table, turning off each light. With just the glow of a small lamp, he fumbled through the top drawer of his desk and pulled out his address book. He was soaked in perspiration. He wiped his brow with a handkerchief, flipped through the pages until he found the one he wanted.

Mori ran his fingers down the page and stopped halfway at the entry he sought. He tapped the name. "That's it," he said softly.

He glanced at the clock above the mantle. Just after eleven. With trembling hands he dialed the phone.

A click sounded on the other end of the call, and then a familiar voice. "Hello."

There was a crackling echo through the receiver. Was someone listening? If the number he was calling was a party line—a shared phone service for multiple users—there was no way to tell who else might be on the phone.

"Albert, is that you?" Mori whispered.

"Yes."

"It's Mori." When he heard Albert sigh he said, "I'm sorry, I know it's late."

"It's alright. What's the matter?"

"Can you come over?"

"Now?" Albert asked. "It's after eleven."

"I know." Mori hesitated, choosing his words carefully. "I'd like to show you something."

After a long moment, Albert exhaled. "Alright, I'll be there soon."

69

Émile stood beside Jacob in the hallway, staring at Bertolt's body protruding from the trash can.

"He hardly fits," Jacob said.

Standing back, Émile examined the trash trolley from several angles. "It doesn't have to be perfect. It just needs to be good enough to move him."

"Émile, his arm is hanging out."

"It's okay. Get me some heavy twine from the garage. We'll tie him in."

Alena and Ruth entered from the kitchen. Ruth carried a stack of rags and a bucket of soapy water, Alena, a broom.

Alena swept up the dried twigs that had scattered on the floor from the trash can. "I'll put these in the fireplace."

"No," Émile said. "I'll need them for repairs to the trash can."

Jacob returned and handed Émile a spool of green silk ribbon. "This is all I could find."

"Gift wrapping?" Émile hesitated then said, "It'll work fine." He wound the ribbon around Bertolt's hand, then tied it tightly to the man's naked torso. "That should hold."

Jacob gazed at Émile's handiwork.

"Staring at him won't make him disappear," Émile said. "Go light a fire in the library. We need to burn the clothes and rags."

"We should use the incinerator outside," Jacob said.

"No, it's too late. No one burns trash this time of night.

262

Chimney smoke won't draw attention."

Alena picked up Bertolt's uniform and scrunched her nose in disgust. She followed Jacob to the library.

In the entry hall, Ruth knelt on the stone tiles and submerged a rag into the bucket of sudsy water, then set to scrubbing the blood-stained stone. Émile had never seen his mother scrub a floor before, nor do any type of house cleaning, other than tidying up after dinner.

He knelt beside her, dipped his hands into the soapy water and wiped them on his pants. Then he wrapped his arm around her shoulder. She turned to him and buried her head against his chest. "I'm sorry, I'm so sorry."

"Maman, you saved us."

"He was a bad man," Ruth said. "He hurt Jacob."

Émile stood, drew his shoulders upward, then circled them back, trying to relieve the tension. He picked up the twigs Alena had swept into a pile. "Jacob," he called out to the next room.

Jacob emerged from the library and stared at his hunched-over mother. He glanced from her to Émile. "Should I help Maman first?" He seemed nervous and unfocused, uncomfortable in Bertolt's presence, even in death.

"I'm fine," Ruth said. "Help your brother." She did not look up from the blood-stained rag in her hands.

Émile set to work on the trash bin. "We'll do the same thing we did with the paintings," he said to his brother. He worked the broken twigs into the branch barrier, tucking the ends down around the body. "We'll put the leaves on top to hide him."

Mori returned to the entry hall. He gazed at the Van Gogh paintings in the upper gallery, then into the library. He put his hand on Émile's shoulder and whispered, "When you're done with this, there's something else I'll need you to do."

70

Friday, August 28, 1942

É mile pushed the garage door open just wide enough so they'd be able to slide out the trash can containing Bertolt's body. "Wait here," he whispered to Jacob. He slipped into the moonlit courtyard, careful to stay in the shadows of the towering elms that hugged the garage. The night was not really cold, yet he felt a chill run up his spine. He scanned the area then glanced up at the windows of the neighbor's house, which looked directly onto the Rothstein's gravel courtyard. Peering eyes were the last thing they needed tonight. When he was satisfied all was clear, he peered back into the garage and gave his brother a nod.

Jacob, dressed in the filthy clothing he'd used for transporting canvases to the park, rolled the trash container out of the garage, but came to a dead stop when the trolley's wheels became bogged down in the gravel. He'd gotten less than a meter into the courtyard.

"It's too heavy," Jacob said.

Émile helped him drag the can back into the garage, dead leaves falling in its wake, like Hansel and Gretel's bread crumbs, then closed the door.

Jacob shook his head. "What now?"

"Just a minute," Émile said. "I have an idea."

Émile rummaged through dirty shelves and boxes, tossing

the unwanted containers on the floor. He wiped his hands on his pants, then looked up. "Merde!" There it was in plain sight.

He climbed onto the hood of the family's Citroen, then stepped up to the car's roof. Reaching with both hands, he swatted at a coil of rope lying across the rafters, until it came crashing down. He jumped from the auto and grinned. "Okay, we're in business."

Émile fashioned a loop of rope around the bottom of the metal can, securing it to the axel. He brought up the two ends and wrapped them tightly around his wrist. "Alright," he said, "let's try again."

Émile pushed the garage door open, and then pulled the heavy can forward on its lead. With Jacob guiding the load from the rear, he slowly dragged it across the courtyard, the wheels grinding through the gravel, fearing the awful noise in the dead of night would wake the neighbors. The boys paused when they reached the gate and scanned their surroundings. No lights turned on. No movement.

Once they managed to move the trolley out of the gravel and through the courtyard's entry gates, pulling the trash can became easier, and the wheels made only a quiet rumble over the cobblestones.

They turned left onto Rue François. The Pont des Invalides, the lowest bridge in Paris, was only a couple of blocks away. There, they would toss the body into the river. Émile looked over his shoulder every two seconds, his stomach in knots. He prayed they could make it to the bridge without encountering soldiers.

They stopped to rest for a moment, and Émile removed the rope from the can. "Better to push it now."

Jacob took over, pushing the trolley like a proper street cleaner. When the two reached the corner of Rue François and Rue Bayard, they turned right.

"Just another block," Émile said.

Jacob paused and rubbed his leg.

"Are you alright?"

"It's a little sore. I'll be fine."

The brothers walked toward the river, but moments later Émile stopped in his tracks. "Wait," he whispered.

"What?"

"Shh." Émile held up his hand. "Nazis." He nodded toward the end of the street. No soldiers were visible, but in the absence of the rumble of the trash trolley, the sound of soldiers' boots rose into the night, punctuated by the bark of an indecipherable command.

"We have to backtrack," Émile whispered.

The brothers maneuvered the trash can in the opposite direction. They saw men in uniform marching along the quay at the end of the street— just where they had been heading.

"Now, what?" Jacob asked.

"Let me think." Émile looked up through the quaking leaves of the trees overhead. Small flecks of silvery luminescent sky shone through the dark shadows, blinking like a million eyes. What had seemed like a simple plan was history. Leave the house, go to the river, dump the body, and get home. It wouldn't be that simple. They would have to go around the obstacle. An alternate route to the river would be longer, but hopefully without disturbance.

Bertolt's body, along with the weight of the branches, leaves, and trolley, proved a heavy load to push. Jacob seemed to be straining.

"Let me take over for a while," Émile said.

"I'm fine. The handle actually helps support me."

The quiet rumble of the trolley eclipsed the sound of the nearing footsteps, until they heard, "Halt!" from behind. The brothers jumped slightly.

The two froze under the shadow of a large tree. Jacob pulled a rake from the can and began to clean a small area on the

walkway, ignoring the order. Émile followed his brother's lead.
"Halt!"

Heart pounding, Émile glanced at his brother. They stared
at each other wide-eyed in the dark, as they swept and raked in
the shadows. Jacob turned first, then Émile, to see two soldiers,
walking briskly toward them. "Where do you go this time of
night?" the taller of two soldiers demanded.

"We go nowhere," Jacob said, hunching over his rake. "We
clean up crap." He looked the two uniformed men up and down.
"It's what we do every night: leaves, spit, cigarettes, shit." Jacob
flailed his arm out, gesturing to all the dirt in the city.

Émile watched his brother nervously. *What was he doing?* His
open disrespect for the soldiers was a dangerous ploy. Yet Jacob
was truly convincing in his act. If Émile hadn't known him,
he would believe he was part of the uneducated working class.
His choice of words, his brusque way of speaking, the way he
moved—a street cleaner through and through.

"Peasant," the soldier said.

Jacob looked up from his hunched position.

The man scowled and kicked. Jacob dodged the blow. The
man returned with a solid connection to the trash can, knocking
the heavy barrel to the ground with a clanging thud.

"Pick up your trash and get back to work."

Émile looked at Jacob in horror. From the corner of his eye,
he saw the fingers of Bertolt's twisted hand extending from the
container.

"Yes, sir." Émile stepped forward, blocking the soldier's
view of the can. He lowered his head in subservience.

One soldier spat on Jacob and bumped Émile's shoulder
before moving on with his compatriot.

When the soldiers were several paces down the street, Émile
whispered, "Quick, help me here," and he knelt beside the
fallen can.

Jacob bent to his good knee. He grabbed the rim of the

container and began to lift. "Oh!" he said, and lurched back from the dead man's hand hanging out of the can.

"Yes, hurry," Émile whispered. "I was worried they would notice."

Émile and Jacob hoisted the battered container to an upright position.

"Wait for a moment," Émile said. "Those two haven't gotten far."

Jacob took a broom and stepped in front of his brother, blocking the view, should the soldiers look back. He swept at invisible debris on the walkway.

Behind Jacob, Émile secured Bertolt's hand, hiding all signs of the corpse. Then he grabbed a rake and joined his brother, waiting for the Germans to disappear.

71

A sharp knock sounded on the front door. Ruth and Alena looked up from scrubbing the stained floor.

Mori hurried across the entry and peered through the lace curtain. "It's him." He opened the door. Albert stood on the porch, looking past Mori at the women on their knees.

"Come in," Mori said, quickly closing the door after Albert. "Thank you for coming at such an inconvenient hour."

Albert peeled off his jacket. "What happened?"

"That's what I need to see you about," Mori said. He motioned for Albert to follow him into the library. The two men sat on the sofa and Mori took a deep breath. "My friend, if you can get us out of Paris, I need you to arrange our escape as soon as possible.

Albert sat and listened while Mori explained the events of the evening. "So you see, we're not safe here anymore." Mori took a crystal bottle from the coffee table and poured himself a glass of whiskey. "Nerves." He threw back the shot. "Drink?" Mori held out the bottle.

Albert waved him off. He had listened expressionless, neither judgment nor condemnation on his face. Now he rose and walked to the window. "There might be a slight delay," he said, peering past the sheer material to the street below.

"What kind of delay?"

"There's a lot of detail in moving someone. That takes time, and you're not just one person, you're a family."

"We don't have time. My wife—" Mori still hadn't fully digested the fact of what had just happened in his home. "We just killed a Nazi."

"It's nothing we can't handle. It just might take a little longer than desired. May I?" Albert said, pointing to a tablet of writing paper on Mori's desk.

"Of course, and Alena, my son's fiancée has to come with us."

Albert took a pen and scratched a few lines, then passed the pad to Mori. "Memorize this address. Then destroy it."

Their escape route and the date remained uncertain, but hope filled Mori's heart despite the fear lodged in his chest.

Albert rose from his chair. "I need to go."

Mori walked Albert out of the library into the foyer. Ruth and Alena were not in sight, but the floor was spotless. At the front door, Albert said, "I'll work on this immediately. Prepare your family to leave on a moment's notice. You'll take only what you can carry in your pockets. Cash and jewelry will help during your travels."

Mori nodded.

"When you receive my call, immediately walk your family to that address. No taxis. Draw no attention to yourselves along the way. No large possessions. Do you understand?"

"Yes," Mori said, a wave of gratitude washing through him, his eyes stinging with unexpected tears.

William Ian Grubman

72

É mile helped Jacob push the cart along the sidewalk, its wheels bumping and clicking over the paving stones. "We can't use the Pont des Invalides, it's rife with soldiers," Émile said.

"Alright, then the Pont de l'Alma." Jacob said. "It's not much further.

The roadway in front of them appeared quiet. "Not the best choice," Émile said, "the Nazis use the l'Alma as a meeting place for prostitutes."

"How do you know that?"

"Never mind. All we have left is the Pont Alexandre. It's further away, but it's our best bet. This way," Émile said, nodding toward their only option.

Both brothers scanned their surroundings with every step. The boys approached the bridge with caution. Émile saw no traffic ahead of them over the water. They were alone, not a Nazi in sight. Once they were a few meters on Pont Alexandre, they were more vulnerable with no buildings or trees to hide them from view. It was the only way.

They pushed their heavy load onto the dark bridge, the jostling and bumping growing louder over the rounded cobblestones. Émile wished he could silence the noise. He motioned to Jacob. They stopped and slowly tipped the trash container on its side. Their feet slid on the damp stones. Émile pulled at the folded, stiff arms that protruded from the metal

271

trash can until Bertolt was lying on the ground. In the darkness he was nothing more than a shadow cast by the moon. A short stone balustrade was all that separated the cold soldier from his final resting place.

Émile untied the ribbon that had held Bertolt's arm to his torso and flung it into the water. "Quickly," he said, tilting his head toward the stone columns. "Let's get him over."

The two grasped Bertolt's limbs.

"Okay," Émile whispered. "On three. One, two . . ." A piercing sound punctuated the air. A soldier's whistle. The brothers looked at each other as they heaved Bertolt's body over the balustrade and into the Seine.

Émile glanced from side to side, searching for the source of the alarm. All remained still—possibly an event on a neighboring street. He gathered the soldier's medals from his pocket and threw them after the corpse. Then he tossed the scattered twigs and leaves into the trolley. "Let's go." As Jacob swept any remnants into the river, Émile said, "Hurry."

The brothers moved quickly with the trolley off the bridge and back onto the city streets. As they neared the corner of Rue François and Bayard, they could hear Nazi soldiers running up the street, lots of them, their boots ringing out on the cobblestones, shouting German taunts.

"Stop," Émile said, breathlessly, extending his arm. He motioned his brother into a narrow, dark recess between two houses. There was little foliage available for cover, and he hoped the dark crevice was enough to keep them hidden. "We'll stay here." he whispered, "just until they've passed."

From the right came the sound of more running boots, closer this time. The brothers faced each other, each with their back to a wall. Émile could hear Jacob's labored breathing. He put his hand over his brother's mouth and his own finger to his lips—both of them silent in their dark alcove.

Half a dozen soldiers passed within a few feet of them.

73

After Albert had slipped out the front door, Mori glanced at his watch. It was past two in the morning. Where were his sons? He had expected them back by now, and he prayed they had not met with any trouble. Pulling loose his tie, he turned to see Ruth and Alena holding hands in the dim light of the stairwell. "We're leaving Paris," he said.

Alena gasped. Ruth put her arm around her shoulder. "When?" Ruth said softly.

"I'm not sure, but soon."

Ruth looked around, eyes darting over the walls and back toward the kitchen.

"Don't," Mori said. "Stop looking. We can't take anything." He saw tears well in her eyes.

"As long as we are all safe, that's the only thing that matters," she said.

Mori went to her and took her in his arms. She pressed her face into his shoulder and began to cry. Mori drew Alena into their hug. "I'm so sorry for the danger we've put you in." He peered into her tear stained face. "You'll come with us?" he asked her.

Alena nodded. "Of course."

A sound came from the kitchen, and all three turned with a start.

The door swung open, and Jacob and Émile, filthier than Mori had ever seen them, lumbered into the entry hall.

Alena ran to Émile and threw her arms around him.

"You're both safe," Ruth said, hugging her sons.

Mori clasped both boys by the shoulders. "It's done?"

Émile said, "Yes, Papa." Jacob nodded.

"Thank God you didn't get caught," Ruth said.

Mori sighed. "Everyone come into the kitchen. I need to talk to you." He led the way and motioned them to the table near the window. They might be leaving Paris, but he knew Ruth would never allow the boys, filthy as they were, to sit on her velvet dining room chairs.

They all took a seat.

Mori sank into his chair. "I've been able to secure safe passage to England for all of us," he said. He related his conversation with Albert and told them to prepare to leave. " It could take as long as two weeks or it could be tomorrow morning. We have to be ready to leave on a moment's notice."

They all stared at him in silence. Mori gave them a weak smile. "You don't really think we can steal from the Nazis, murder one of their own, and then expect to be ignored?"

Émile grabbed Alena's hand. "You're coming with us, right?"

Alena nodded.

"Of course, she'll come," Mori said. "She's family now."

Alena feigned a smile, but Mori saw tears were falling again.

Mori looked into each of their faces. "We tell no one with one exception. Alena, you speak to your parents. We take nothing with us," Mori reiterated, "only what you can carry in your pockets or your purses. Everyone wears sturdy shoes and a warm coat." Mori glanced at Émile. "What's left to do at the gallery?"

"Nothing really. We moved the last canvas to the park this afternoon. All the copies are in the original frames. The damp ones are stacked in the rear of the storage room." Émile paused. "I'd like to get my brushes."

Mori knew how much Émile treasured his brushes. The

avenue to his son's career as a painter most likely had just been sealed off. "I'll gather them and bring them to you."

Émile rubbed his wrist. "Papa, I'd like to pick them up myself. I want to make sure I've got everything. Besides, I left my watch there somewhere."

"Alright, fetch your watch and brushes in the morning then get out of the gallery quickly. Alena, you should speak to your mother and father in the morning and plan to stay here."

She nodded.

Mori glanced at the clock over the stove. "It's late. Did you tell your parents you're spending the night here?"

"Yes," she said.

Mori looked slowly around the table at his family. "Nothing happened here tonight," he said sternly, leaving no room for response.

The kitchen was silent.

Mori's gaze turned to Ruth. "When the maid gets here tomorrow, send her away. Tell her someone's ill and you don't want her to catch it." He rose then and said, "Everyone should try to get a little sleep. It'll be daylight soon."

Before Mori left the room, he said, "Émile, Jacob, I have something I need you to take care of first thing in the morning. Where's the trash cart?"

74

The crisp morning air chilled the gallery. The heating system in the building had not yet been fired up for what felt like an early autumn. Wearing his tweed jacket, Mori sat at his desk, carefully gathering notes and ledger pages he didn't want to leave behind—a precious history of the ownership of paintings his sons had hidden. He folded the pages and tucked them into his inside breast pocket.

The gallery door opened and Mori felt a pair of eyes looking at him before he saw the silhouette in the doorway. His stomach lurched, and he jumped to his feet. Although he couldn't make out the details of the shadow blocking the stream of early morning sunlight, there was no mistaking who it was. How long had Goering been standing there?

"You haven't visited me in a while," the commandant said.

"I'm sorry. Colonel Bertolt has been keeping me busy." That was strangely true. "And, after discovering the Da Vinci sketch, I wouldn't know where to begin to find you something as precious as that."

"Is it here?" Goering said.

"No, Colonel Bertolt has it," Mori lied. It was on his desk in his library at home.

Goering adjusted the shoulders of his jacket. He was dressed in full military regalia. Assorted medals hung from colorful ribbons across the torso of his brown uniform. Elaborate decorations bordered his lapels, and various ropes of gold draped across his breast from festooned epaulets. A wide black belt with a brass buckle attempted to cinch his rotund waist.

"You look very official this morning, sir," Mori managed to get out, hoping he didn't sound anxious. Ruth was alone at home, the boys were out, and Bertolt's body was in the Seine.

"I'm receiving visitors this afternoon," Goering said.

It always astonished Mori when Goering spoke to him like a friend rather than as a servant—or a prisoner, which was how he felt. "Would you like to have the Da Vinci to display? I can check with the colonel and have it delivered to you." Another lie.

"No, it's not necessary. I'm sure it's safe." Goering flipped through a few stacks of paintings that lined the gallery's walls, his fingers stopping briefly. "Have you seen him this morning?" he asked.

Was he playing a game? Did he know about Bertolt?

"Not yet. He usually stops by in the afternoon. He's most likely at the Jeu de Paume," Mori lied again.

"No, he's not there," Goering said. "I visited the museum before coming here."

Of course, he's not there, Mori thought. The bastard is at the bottom of the river. "Oh?" Mori said.

"When he shows up, ask him to contact me," Goering said.

"Of course."

Goering walked to the gallery door and turned. "On second thought, I do want the sketch. Bring it to the Ritz this evening."

75

Late that morning, Émile headed to Alena's house. She had gone there earlier to spend some time with her mother and father. When Émile arrived, the plan was to tell her parents about their imminent departure.

Instead of taking his usual route, Émile walked to the intersection of Avenue Montaigne and Avenue George V to purchase flowers for Alena's mother. When he emerged from the shop with a small bouquet of pink roses, the steely sky was beginning to glow with the promise of sun. The parkway along the river was relatively quiet, but for a few elderly women gossiping in a group on the benches.

In the distance he could see two gendarmes astride their rugged mounts. The two Grullo steeds reminded Émile of book ends. They were exactly alike in size and pattern. Beyond the horses, he saw that a crowd had gathered along the river. As he drew closer, he crossed the street to steal a glimpse, joining the fringe of the crowd. "What is it?" he asked a young woman, who cradled an infant in her arms.

"I'm not sure. I think someone jumped," she said. "Maybe a prostitute."

Émile felt a sinking feeling in his stomach, but he couldn't tear himself away. He stood on his toes, yet couldn't see past the people's heads. The only thing he could make out clearly was the Tour Eiffel across the water.

Holding the flowers close to protect them from being

crushed, he pushed his way forward to the low stone wall separating the street from the river, and strained for a better look. Uniformed police lined the Pont de l'Alma and both sides of the Seine, keeping the onlookers at bay. Men's voices shouted from below, and Émile caught a glimpse of soldiers on a barge along the edge of the water.

He glanced around at the faces in the crowd, but it was the stars that caught his attention; some of those gathered had yellow stars sewn to their jackets and shirts. Jews stood out in any crowd. Émile felt a flood of hatred for the Nazis, and yet it was because of a Nazi that he and his family no longer had to wear the humiliating badge.

He decided not to cross the river here, as he had intended. Instead he began to walk along the river's edge. He hadn't gotten far when a gasp rose up from the crowd. He glanced over to see the police at the top of the bridge pulling on thick, taut ropes, hoisting something from the water.

Émile turned to steal a last glimpse. He squinted to get a clearer look.

The body was swollen and grey but there was no mistaking it. It was Bertolt.

76

Mori glanced into the storage room. All that was left were Émile's supplies. He looked through his desk, opening each drawer, making sure he had gathered the most important papers. Satisfied, he slipped his glasses into his breast pocket and stood. Then, for what might be the very last time, he walked out the door of his gallery—his father's gallery—passing both guards on the street. He raised his chin and nodded.

Under the welcoming noon sun, he turned right on Rue Royale and headed directly to the Jeu de Paume. He needed nothing at the museum, but it was crucial that he cover his tracks. Others had to believe Mori knew nothing of Bertolt's absence, and he had promised Goering he would retrieve the sketch from the man, so he intended to make good on that promise. Hopefully this ruse would keep the Nazis away from his family until they could flee Paris.

Passing the guards at the museum had become much easier. The German soldiers standing at the entrance recognized him from his many visits. He nodded, pushing open the double doors. Inside, a young officer sat behind a poorly lit worktable. The museum's overhead lights cast cumbersome shadows on every surface.

"Good day, sir," Mori said.

The man shuffled a few papers and motioned Mori past.

"Colonel Bertolt?" Mori asked.

"He's not here," the man said.

Mori leaned the weight of his body against the table. He was nervous and tired. There had been little sleep the night before.

Another young man appeared, dressed in the traditional brown of the Nazi party. "Can I help you?"

"Good day," Mori said. "Colonel Bertolt has a small framed sketch that I need."

"He's not here."

"Yes, I was just informed of that. So I'm hoping you can be of help."

"I can check the log book." The young man produced a pencil and pad of paper from his pocket. "Who's the artist? Is the piece named?"

"I don't think it will appear in your book. It's a piece Colonel Bertolt received from Commandant Goering."

"Without some information, I don't know where to look," the soldier said, already bored.

"Of course," Mori said. "It's a small sketch of the *Mona Lisa.*"

"Who is the artist?"

Mori formed a fist in his pocket. Could this man, surrounded by the world's greatest paintings, really be this ignorant? Mori took a deep breath. "Da Vinci," he said as calmly as possible.

"Just a moment, please. I'll speak to my superior." The young soldier walked behind a partition. A few minutes later he reemerged. "I'm sorry. I can't find a record of the piece."

"It must be in his office," Mori said. "Perhaps we can look there."

The man hesitated for a moment, but his superior peeked his head out from behind the partition and nodded. "Accompany him to the colonel's office."

"Of course," the soldier said. "Please," and he motioned Mori forward.

The two men entered Bertolt's office. The small, pale green, windowless room was stacked with books, paintings, and assorted papers and folders.

Mori looked over every available surface. After several minutes, he said, "It doesn't appear to be here. Would you please tell Colonel Bertolt that I stopped by?"

77

The bouquet of roses in hand, Émile ran across the gravel courtyard to the entrance of Alena's building, then took the stairs two at a time. He pulled off his sweater moments before arriving at her apartment, out of breath. He flipped the unpolished brass knocker a couple of times against the worn wood before the door opened.

"What took you so long?" Alena said, pulling Émile into the entry hall.

He held up the flowers. "For your mother."

She took the bouquet and kissed him. There were tears in her eyes.

Émile heard sobs from the kitchen. "You told them."

Alena nodded.

"I thought we were going to do it together," he said.

"We were, but I knew there was never going to be a good time to break the news, so I just sat them down and—"

"I'm sorry I'm late, and I'm sorry I wasn't here with you." Émile bent forward and brought her close. "I saw them pull Bertolt's body from the river," he whispered in her ear.

Alena pulled away, her mouth open in surprise. "When?"

"On my way here."

"What now?"

"I don't know, but I'm sure someone will be coming around to ask questions."

"Where did they find him?"

"Pont de l'Alma."

Alena stood motionless.

"Don't worry. There's no reason anyone would suspect us."

"But there will be questions, like you said. The Nazis aren't going to just let this pass. They'll come to see your father. He worked with Bertolt."

Émile considered her statement. "Papa's at the gallery," he said. "If they come around, he'll know what to say." He looked into the kitchen. Alena's mother stood at the stove, wiping at her cheeks with a handkerchief. "Where's your father?"

"He had to go back to work," she said.

Alena's mother was stirring something in a large blackened pot. She turned and caught sight of Émile and put down the spoon. She came to him, put her head on his shoulder and sobbed.

"You know how much I love her," he said.

She didn't answer. She was losing her daughter.

"I promise I'll take care of her."

She sagged against him, sobbing harder. "She's all we have."

"I know," he said, tears welling in his eyes too. "I'll guard her with my life."

Alena's mother pulled back to look at him. "I love you both, and I'll pray to God every night for your safety."

"Thank you," he said, and he meant it.

"When will you leave?"

"I don't know. Tonight? Tomorrow?"

"You'll write? You'll have Alena write too?"

"Yes, of course," Émile said. "Once we're safe."

Before Alena's mother let go of Émile, she held his cheeks and kissed his forehead. Then she pulled a worn blue plaid hankie from her pocket to wipe her eyes. "You'll eat before you leave."

Émile turned to Alena. "We should go," he mouthed.

Alena shrugged. "Of course we'll eat."

Émile hoped lunch would end quickly, but more than two hours passed before he could pull Alena away.

Before they left, Alena hugged her mother tightly. The two women cried together. When, finally, mother and daughter seemed emptied of their tears, Alena took Émile's arm and they headed to the front door, Alena's mother following.

"I'll pray for you, too," Émile said before they left. "I promise."

78

Mori exited the Jeu de Paume and buttoned his suit jacket.
Darting between cars and taxis, he crossed the Place de
la Concorde and headed home along the path bordering the
Champs-Élysees.

He patted the bulge of ledger pages in his breast pocket. He
needed to get the others from his desk at home. These were
the only existing ownership documents of the paintings lying
beneath the pyramid in Parc Monceau.

The afternoon sun on his back offered some much needed
comfort. He took a deep breath and proceeded alongside a
canopy of horse chestnut trees whose leaves were turning the
golden color of wheat. In a month or two a strong wind would
scatter them in every direction, leaving twisted branches to
gather snow and ice from winter storms.

He took a left on Avenue Montaigne and glanced over his
shoulder. When he turned again, onto Rue François, he peered
behind him, scanning his surroundings with an eye out for Nazi
soldiers, gendarmes, or even a lone individual who might be
following him. His nerves had been frayed since the ordeal with
Bertolt. He was eager to get home in anticipation of Albert's
call, and he hoped his whole family had assembled back at the
house by now.

Mori entered the residence through the motor court rather
than the front door. That gave him the advantage to casually
look around before shutting the gate behind him. A few

moments later, he stepped into the kitchen. Ruth was pouring water through a tea strainer. She lifted her gaze, a look of relief on her face, and set down the kettle. "I'm glad you're back home." She held up a cup. "Do you want some?"

He nodded, "Thank you. Where are the boys?"

"Émile went to Alena's parents' apartment." Ruth took a second tea cup from the shelf. "And Jacob's making yet another trip to the park."

"I know you hate Jacob making these missions with such valuable paintings in his possession, but I have confidence in him. He's proven himself adept at blending in to the city surroundings."

"Well, he's already made several trips to the park and has remained completely unnoticed," Ruth said.

She handed Mori a cup and saucer and set a plate of biscuits on the table. She slid a sugar bowl and spoon toward him. "Will you sit a moment?"

"I have to get some papers from the library. I'll take this with me," he said, raising the cup with one hand.

"Wait," Ruth said. "How long do you think it will be?" She looked around the kitchen and gave a helpless shrug. "How long before we leave?"

He set the cup on the table and took her in his arms. "I don't know. We'll have to wait for the call."

"It's the waiting, the not knowing," she said. "It's making me crazy."

"I know. Our lives are about to be upended, and what might replace it, well, I just don't know." Mori glanced around him. "This house is where we brought Jacob when he was born. Then Émile." His eyes stung, but he refused the tears. He needed to be strong for her now. For the whole family. He bent and gently kissed Ruth's lips.

She held him tightly. "We'll come back," she said. It was more a question than a statement.

"Yes." He nodded, but he wondered if the house would still be there when they returned. With his world crumbling, he could still hope. "I'll be in the library."

"I'll join you in a minute," Ruth said.

In the library, Mori set his tea cup on the desk and began the task of gathering as many important papers as he thought he could tuck into his pockets. When he was done, he went through them again and narrowed his selection. He'd had no idea how much documentation he had accumulated over the years—a testament to the number of master artworks that had passed through his hands, and his father's.

Next he crossed the room and knelt before two carved cabinet doors at the foot of a tall bookshelf. Before he could open them, he heard Ruth walk into the library behind him— her small, soft steps immediately recognizable, so different from his grown boys' blustery movements. He knew every sound this house made. It held a lifetime of stories within its walls.

"I wish the boys would get back," she said.

"Me too," he replied, sitting back on his heels and turning to his wife. "My stomach's in knots. It won't be long before the Nazis realize Bertolt's missing. On top of all that, Goering expects the Da Vinci in the next few hours."

Mori returned his attention to the cabinet. He grabbed the two bronze knobs and swung the doors open to reveal a large steel Mosler safe. He rotated the dial three turns to the right, two to the left, another to the right. Then a click and the lock released. He pulled the steel handle downward and tugged.

"This and your jewels will be our security for the journey," Mori said.

On two shelves were neatly bundled stacks of 500 Franc bank notes, and 100 Pound British Sterling notes.

"Ruth, help me with this."

Mori began passing the neatly bundled stacks of cash to his wife, and she placed them on top of the desk.

"Thank heaven for the clients who paid me in cash," Mori said. "If not for them we'd be penniless. There's about 250,000 in Francs and around 200,000 British Pounds. This cash is our saving grace. With the Nazis in control of the banks, our money's as good as gone."

When the safe was empty he stood and looked over the spoils of his success. The collected stacks looked small on the large desk top. Was this it? Was this what his life had amounted to? Some stacks of cash? Without the promise of work that fulfilled him, a home he loved, a life made in a beautiful city with his family, the money seemed striped of significance.

"We need to hide all of this," Mori said.

"How will we carry all of it?" she said.

"There are five of us. We'll have to do it. We'll fill our pockets and your biggest handbag," Mori said. "Hopefully this will cover bribes, food and God knows what else." Mori kept his voice calm for Ruth's sake, but his body was a tangle of nerves, and the tension gnawed at his shoulders and gut. Where were the boys? The sun had already passed the front of the house, and Albert could call at any moment.

If he had gotten his family to safety months earlier, they could have prepared, sold some of their things and safeguarded others. But he had been blind to all the signs surrounding them—either blind or stubborn. Now they would have to simply walk out the door with virtually nothing, not even an assurance that they could come back to what was theirs. Done and over with—an entire life.

Mori heard boots on the cobblestones outside and slowly approached the window. Four German soldiers were walking past the front of the house in the fading light. He felt a stab of concern, but they didn't appear to be looking at his home. Merely passing by.

79

Arm in arm, Émile and Alena crossed Quai du Louvre and headed to the Tuileries in the direction of Émile's home where the family was to gather and wait for Albert's call. They walked in silence, his arm around her shoulder. Her body felt tense, rigid, as though it had become a dam that held back a reservoir of grief. He didn't know when she would see her parents again. He could only imagine her sadness.

Just inside the Tuileries, they stopped beside the winged statue of History, and Alena leaned against the pedestal.

"Are you alright?" Émile asked, worrying the stress was too much for her.

Alena wrapped her arms around his waist. Their eyes met for a moment before she buried her head in the crook of his neck and wept again, her body shaking out the sobs. He held her tightly, wishing he could make her feel better.

"I'm sorry," she said.

"You don't need to apologize. I know it hurts." He stroked her temple, brushing her hair from her eyes with his fingers. "But there's no other way. We have to leave. We're not safe here."

"I know." Alena drew a handkerchief from her purse and dabbed her eyes and nose. She pulled at her collar. "I hate this coat. The wool itches and this color brown looks terrible on me".

He smiled. "You look fine. It may not make a fashion

statement, but the coat will keep you warm." He hugged her and then as they walked he said, "When we get to my home, take one of my cashmere scarves. It'll stop the wool from scratching your neck."

In her purse she carried photographs of her parents and a rosary she'd received at her First Communion. Tears slid down her cheeks. "I don't know if I'll ever see them again," she said.

"I know, my love. I'm sorry." Émile gently laid his hand on the small of her back. He wanted to get them home so they could be ready when the call came.

They had only walked a short distance when Émile stopped short. "Merde!" he said. "I forgot my watch, my brushes. I meant to go to the gallery for them."

"That's OK, we'll go now. It's not far out of the way."

It wasn't on the route to the Rothstein house, but a short detour wouldn't pose a problem.

"Come on." Alena pulled at his arm, offering a tight, crooked smile. He knew her too well not to see the pain behind it.

They hurried to the gallery, their heels clicking on the sidewalk.

"I can't stop thinking about the sight of Bertolt's body being hauled out of the river," Émile said as they walked.

"Well, you need to stop thinking about it. We both need to stop thinking about it."

He gazed at her for a moment. She had stepped into his usual role, the guide and protector. "You're right," he said.

"Come on, let's get your things and get back to your house."

"I love you," he said.

"I love you, too," she replied. "And this one loves you as well." She rubbed her belly.

At Rue de Rivoli they saw German soldiers— more soldiers than usual—and yet the people on the street didn't even seem to notice. Had Parisians really become that habituated to the Nazi presence? Émile and Alena did not have that luxury. They could no longer afford to ignore the Germans. Instead of going straight, as they'd intended, they turned right and went a block out of their way.

"I won't be long at the gallery," he said. "Just long enough to get my watch, tie up my brushes, and take a quick glance around. Then we'll go to my house."

He smiled at her, but his head throbbed. When had the world become so complicated? It wasn't that long ago that his life had been simple and calm. Joyful even. There had been art for art's sake, parties, late nights at local bars, and constant debate over the great masters and their works. Where had all that gone? How could everything turn upside down overnight on account of a few men who told others what to do? Now, whenever he left the house, he was constantly glancing over his shoulder. His and Alena's future was uncertain. Not to mention their child's.

Once they reached the corner of Rue Royale and Rue du Faubourg Saint-Honoré, it was only fifty meters to the gallery, but things did not look normal. Instead of the usual single German transport truck in front of the gallery, there were several along the street. He pulled at Alena's arm. "Wait!"

They retreated to a recess against a building— the very same spot he had stood to witness his brother being beaten and thrown into a police truck. A wave of guilt and shame flooded through him, and he felt sick to his stomach.

"What is it?" Alena said.

"Shhh." He put a finger to his lips and nodded in the direction of the gallery, rigid with fear.

"What are they doing?" she whispered.

Several soldiers gathered around two of the transport trucks, which were parked directly in front of the gallery's display window. An officer came out of the gallery's door, looking troubled.

Émile squinted but didn't recognize the dark-haired man who appeared to be in charge.

One of the guards pointed to the officer's uniform. The officer looked down. He seemed to be smoothing out his jacket, but then he extended his hand and wiped it on the building. On the stonework the man had left a streak of blue.

"Oh God, it's paint," Émile whispered. "He knows."

When the officer turned, Émile could see the blue smear along the bottom of his brown jacket. The man yelled orders to the guards in German.

Émile's breath went shallow, and Alena pulled him more deeply into the shadowy recess.

"I've got to call home," he whispered. "They'll come for my father."

Alena gripped Émile's arm, her fingers digging into his muscles.

"Be calm," he whispered. "Don't make eye contact with anyone."

He and Alena slowly walked past the gallery. From the opposite side of the street they observed the activity which had caused onlookers to stop and stare. They continued to Albert's café, being careful not to look directly at the scene. They passed by unnoticed.

Émile stopped at Albert's door and pushed it open, keeping Alena close. They walked to the end of the bar.

Albert stood behind the counter, wiping wet wine glasses and looking out over the café.

Émile glanced around to see if it was clear to speak.

"Quite a gathering across the street," Albert said calmly.

"Yes, we—" Émile began, but Albert interrupted him and handed him a glass of wine. "I think this is one you'll like." Albert poured a second glass for Alena. "It's full-bodied and has many subtle flavors."

Émile was confused and turned to Alena. She too had a quizzical look on her face. A door slammed, and Émile glanced toward the rear of the restaurant, where a German soldier had just exited the toilet. Émile closed his eyes and released a breath. He could feel Alena gripping his hand.

"You try that on and let me know what you think," Albert said, nodding to the wine.

The soldier waved to Albert.

"Thank you for coming, sir," Albert called out. His gaze followed the soldier out the door, and when it closed, he turned to Émile and nodded. Quietly he said, "Now you can speak, Émile."

"We're in trouble," Émile whispered.

"Yes, I can see."

Through the window Émile saw paintings being removed from the gallery. Frame upon frame were being loaded into trucks. The *Madonna* that had been on and off his easel for months was leaning against the tire of a transport truck. He looked but couldn't see the repair.

He heard the muffled shouting of the officer in the street. "Achtung," he was screaming at a soldier. "Be careful!" The soldier was carrying none other than *The Expulsion of Hagar*. A smile would have surfaced on Émile's lips had he not been so frightened. The original Hagar was secured beneath the pyramid in Parc Monceau. The painting the soldier carried was Émile's second forgery.

Émile tore his eyes from the scene and looked at Albert, waiting for him to tell them what to do. Something, anything.

80

Mori and Ruth sat in silence on the library sofa as the light faded, the room lit only by the fire Mori had built against the chill of the approaching evening. He felt a profound sadness over what had become of his cooperation with Goering.

The phone rang, and Mori looked at Ruth. What if it was Albert? The boys had not yet returned. They couldn't leave without them. It rang again and Mori reached for it.

"Hello?" he said. There was a moment's pause, with static on the line.

"Papa." He heard Émile whisper.

"Are you OK?" Mori said. "Where are you?"

Ruth tugged at her husband's arm. "Émile? Jacob?"

"Papa, I'm with Albert. You and Maman have to leave now."

"But Jacob's not here yet."

"Alena and I will find him," Émile said. "Go now. Go to . . . where you were told."

"Alright," Mori said. "Be safe." He replaced the black handset and looked at Ruth, his heart racing. "Get your coat."

"Now?" she said. "But the boys . . . Where are they?"

"That was Émile. He'll find Jacob."

"Alena?"

"She's with Émile. No more questions. We have to go now."

Ruth nodded. She put on her coat and closed her bag.

"Hurry, they're on the way," he said, grabbing his coat. He knew how fast the Germans could move across the city.

"Who's on the way?"

"The Nazis."

Ruth took her purse and rushed into the darkened entry hall. Mori followed behind her. Through the tightly gathered lace curtains on the front door, Mori spotted the silhouettes of approaching soldiers.

81

Albert guided Émile and Alena through the kitchen to the rear of the café where the lingering aroma of baked breads and pastries reminded Émile he hadn't eaten since breakfast. The three of them scooted past the abandoned baking area which would bustle once again in the wee hours of the next morning. They stepped into the service alley." Moments earlier Albert had confirmed that they knew where to go for safety. Now Albert held Émile by the shoulders and peered into his face. "Find your brother. You know the rest. God will have to guide you now," he said before he sent them off into the dusky light.

Somewhere between the gallery and the park Jacob was pushing the trash trolley, unaware of the danger his family faced. Émile would try the park first, taking the route his brother traveled. He and Alena followed the alley to Rue Royale, turned left, and set out for Parc Monceau.

82

Mori grabbed Ruth's arm. "Shh," he said in the dim light, pulling her away from the front door and back down the hall in the opposite direction. They heard movement on the front porch as they quietly raced through the dining room and into the kitchen.

Mori peered through the kitchen window to the street a half-flight below. One transport truck was parked at the curb near the front of the house. The gate to the motor court was unguarded. He opened a drawer near the sink and withdrew a large kitchen knife. "This way," he whispered.

Ruth's eyes were wide with terror. He tugged her arm. "Come on," he said quietly.

"I'm scared."

"I am too. Just follow me. Hurry."

He guided Ruth through the laundry room and out the back door. They slowed down in the motor court to keep their feet as silent as possible as they crossed the gravel yard. When they reached the large gate, Mori pushed the smaller door in the gate open a crack and peered out. The street light cast a soft glow at the front of the house, but the entrance to the motor court stood in shadow.

"I'm going to open the gate," he whispered. "We walk out quietly and go left. But we must walk slowly, casually, so as not to draw attention."

Trembling, Ruth hung onto Mori's arm.

He quietly opened the gate. In the darkness, he and Ruth stepped onto Rue François and turned left, heading away from the house. Slowly, arm in arm, they walked toward the river, steering clear of the circles of light from the street lamps.

They were a safe distance from the house when the sound of tires screeching triggered a reflex, and from the shadows Mori turned to look behind him. A long, white convertible Mercedes Benz pulled up in front of their house, followed by a transport vehicle. The driver hopped out and walked quickly around the car. Soldiers poured out of the truck. When the driver opened the rear passenger door, Goering exploded into the street, yelling, "Move. Out of my way!"

He stomped up the stairs to the front door. "Kick it in!" he commanded.

83

Through the dark streets, Émile and Alena traced the route Jacob followed to and from the pyramid in Parc Monceau. This route had been Émile's design. He had chosen quiet neighborhood streets that didn't normally attract soldiers.

So far they had not come upon Jacob.

Émile wished he could break into a run, not stopping until he found his brother. He had lost Jacob once. He could not allow that to happen again. For Alena, however, he kept their pace to a brisk walk.

"Come on," he said, lightly grasping her arm. "This way. He takes the side streets past Avenue Matignon."

They snaked through residential neighborhoods on narrow streets, seeing little automobile traffic and fewer pedestrians. Warm light glowed in the windows of the houses as families no doubt sat together for supper or parents put small children to bed. He thought of his own parents, and his breath caught in his throat. He prayed they had left the house in time and gotten themselves to safety. His entire family was in danger. He clung more tightly to Alena's hand.

As they moved along the route, Émile kept a careful watch for police and soldiers. *Just get Jacob to safety.* He repeated this thought over and over as they crossed Boulevard Haussmann, then took a right on Hoche.

Straight ahead of them was the park, less than a block away. Alena tugged at Émile's sleeve and stopped just a moment.

She bent down, removed her shoe, and tipped it over. Two tiny stones fell to the sidewalk. "That's going to feel a lot better."

They crossed to Avenue Van Dyck. The entrance to the park loomed in front of them.

"He's got to be in there," Émile said.

"How do you know?"

"We haven't passed him and he never strays from the route."

The canopy of trees glowed in the light from the street lamps, shades of yellow and gold triumphing over the pale green fading with the season. It dawned on Émile that nothing changed here. The park didn't care whether the continent was at war or the city was occupied. Leaves still grew and died, grass turned from green to brown and then green again, flowers bloomed spring after spring, war or not. Somehow this offered him a speck of solace, even in the face of the dread that filled his belly.

They charged along the pathways inside the park. Émile searched the darkened landscape for Jacob and his trash bin, but he spotted neither.

Even at the pyramid, they didn't see Jacob. They walked to the backside of the pointed structure. There was no sign of him there either and no sign of his trolley.

"I'm worried," Émile said.

Alena gripped his hand. "What are we going to do? Where else might he go?"

"I don't know," he said.

Émile shrugged his shoulders. He didn't want to say it, but he agreed with Alena. The natural thought was that Jacob had gone back to the family's home. Perhaps he had traveled faster than usual, eager to rejoin the rest of them as they waited for Albert's call. He could be anywhere between here and their house.

Émile swallowed hard. If they went to the house, they were risking their lives. If they didn't, Jacob might arrive there alone, with no one to help him.

"I have to go back to the house," Émile said. He refused to do nothing this time. He would not lose his brother again.

Alena's eyes were wide with fright. "No."

"*Ma chérie*, I'll be fine. I want you to go to safety. Do you remember the address?"

Before he could convince her to let go of his arm, they heard a small scraping sound from the front of the pyramid. They hurried quietly around the structure, and Émile spotted the small metal door. It had been closed moments earlier, but now it was open. Then he saw the best thing he had seen in days, Jacob's head peeking out of the opening, then retracting back inside.

Émile ran to the door of the pyramid and opened it.

"Jacob, you scared me half to death," he said.

Jacob peered up at him. "I scared you?" He scooted out of the opening on his hands and knees then stood. "You two just about made me piss my pants."

"I thought I'd lost you again," Émile said, grabbing his brother and giving him a bear hug.

"Why are you even here?" Jacob said. "You weren't supposed to meet me." His expression darkened. "Is everything okay? Papa, Maman?"

"Everyone's okay . . . We believe everyone's okay. Long story. We'll tell you when we get there."

Émile watched his brother lock the door on the pyramid with the new bronze-finish padlock he'd bought earlier that week. It was sturdier than the previous one, though still not a guarantee that someone couldn't break it if determined.

"Is everything safe?" Émile asked, nodding toward the pyramid.

"Of course," Jacob replied. He exuded a self-confidence Émile hadn't seen much in his brother.

"You were able to get down the ladder alright?"

"Yes."

"Good. We have to get out of here now. Where's the trash can?"

Jacob pointed to the wooded area behind the pyramid. I hid it when I went inside."

"We need to get rid of it. We can't leave it here," Émile said.

"We'll dump it in an alley along the way," Jacob said.

"Same route home?" Jacob said.

"We're not going home," Émile said. "I'll explain everything." He headed into the bushes and returned with the trash trolley. "I don't suppose your cane is in here?"

"It's tucked inside," Jacob said.

"You can always lean on me, too," Émile put his hand on his brother's shoulder.

84

Goering stepped back as a spray of glass shards flew into the darkened foyer of Mori Rothstein's house. The soldier who had sent his rifle butt through the front door reached in and turned the knob.

"I never should have trusted that God damn Jew," Goering grumbled as he pushed his way past the soldiers into the grand mansion. Three other soldiers followed behind him, one with the Gestapo SS patch on his lapel. Glass crunched beneath their leather boots. "Get a light on," the commandant shouted. He stood in darkness while his underlings fumbled with torches in search of a light switch. "Hurry up!"

A moment later the entry was illuminated. Wall sconces with tiny silk shades cast their warm glow on the walls.

Goering's mouth fell open. The soldiers stood in silence.

On the walls hung magnificent hand-carved, gilded frames—each with its painting missing. Goering had only been to the house once, but he never forgot a work of art. He had seen the Rubens, the Renoirs, the Fragonard angels. All gone. He glanced up to the second floor gallery that overlooked the entry hall. Six Van Gogh farm scenes, gone.

Goering gazed at the walls of the entry hall in disbelief. Empty frames everywhere. Even Rodin's terracotta bust of *A Young Woman* was missing from a marble pedestal in the corner, where it had sat opposite the front door. He strode to the library, lit only by the soft glow from the embers in the fireplace. "Bastard!" he yelled.

A soldier came up beside him.

"Get the lights!" Goering spat.

The young man located the switch. Instantly the room was illuminated by a chandelier and lamps. At both ends of the room, large frames hung empty. The Picasso and the Fragonard, gone. Smaller frames were also vacant. "I trusted that fucking traitor," Goering said. Then he spotted the safe, its door wide open. "God dammit!"

He stormed back through the entry hall to the dining room, where he remembered having seen a lovely Renoir of a young woman. "Lights!" he yelled, and a soldier fumbled for a wall switch.

When the room was illuminated, Goering stopped in his tracks. Not only was the Renoir gone, but something else hung in its place.

"Huh!" he grunted—almost a laugh.

It was the framed Da Vinci sketch of the *Mona Lisa*.

Goering walked toward the drawing of the famous face. He gently lifted it from the wall and admired the graceful strokes. He touched the glass. "Magnificent," he said quietly.

His chest flushed hot. Flooded with rage, he lifted the sketch above his head and smashed it to the floor, sending fragments of glass flying.

"Bring me that fucking Jew," he hollered. "Now!"

85

Hand in hand, Mori and Ruth walked through residential neighborhoods, crossing familiar boulevards and shopping streets. A sliver of an early moon appeared on the horizon. Gas lamps lined the curbs, creating circles of light on the cobblestones. Mori and Ruth kept to the shadows. Over and over in his mind, Mori repeated the address Albert had given him. Was he recalling it correctly? Had he twisted the numbers mistakenly?

Even though the evening air was cool, Mori began to perspire. He squeezed Ruth's hand. "Are you alright?" he asked in a hushed voice.

Ruth stopped and put her hands on her knees, out of breath. Mori led her into the leafy shadows of a large honey locust, keeping watch while Ruth caught her breath.

"I'm concerned about the boys," she said.

"They'll be fine," Mori answered her. "I have faith in them." After a moment, he took Ruth's hand. "We must go. We're not safe on the streets."

He had seen how quickly the Nazis could cover territory. Soon soldiers would be combing the neighborhoods surrounding the Rothstein home in search of them. Their only hope was the address Albert had given them.

They pushed on. Mori wondered how safe the secret location would be? Would the Germans know about these people who harbored "the enemy?" At this point Mori and his family had no choice. It was the only option left for them. One thing was certain. They would be on their way out of Paris shortly, either via a safe route or in the rear of a German transport truck.

Shortly after eight, they arrived at 57 Rue le Peletier. Mori looked up at the nondescript stone house a kilometer from the Opera. "This is it," he said, taking a deep breath. He glanced into the surrounding darkness up and down the street. All was quiet. He wrapped his arm around Ruth's shoulder and hugged her close. She glanced up at him, stood on her toes and kissed his cheek.

Mori put his hand on the small of her back and guided her up the five steps that would hopefully lead them to safety.

He knocked.

A moment later the door opened a crack. "Yes?" a woman's voice asked.

"My name is Mori Rothstein, and . . . ."

The woman opened the door wider and said in an urgent tone, "Come inside, quickly now."

Until Mori exhaled, he hadn't realized he was holding his breath.

"Thank you so much," Ruth said as she entered.

The woman led them to a sparsely furnished room, dimly lit by two candles flickering in a little dining alcove. At a small dining table set with a steaming pot of tea and a plate of biscuits sat Jacob, Émile, and Alena.

EPILOGUE

Tuesday, May 18, 1999 - New York City

I walked from my home in the eighties to my office on Park Avenue at Fifty-Fifth Street this morning. It's a beautiful day, and I arrived at the fifteenth floor refreshed and happy to be alive.

The small brass plaque on Suite 1502 reads Porter Roth. That's it, nothing else. Anyone passing would have no idea of the treasures locked behind my doors. But that's the art business. It's all referral.

After my secretary, Priscilla, said "Good morning," she added, "Lou Nelson's waiting in the conference room."

"She's never come here before. What does she want?" I dropped four auction catalogues on her French-style desk.

Priscilla shrugged. "She's in the conference room, so ask her." My secretary is all sass, but she's smart as a whip and stellar at her job, so I cut her some slack on her demeanor.

I took a quick look around the gallery before I headed to the conference room. I never tire of admiring the works that pass through my showroom, all masters and all in impeccable condition—currently two Monets, a Renoir, several Caillebottes, Pissarro's *Flags*, a Degas ballerina, and Rembrandt's *Bust of an Old Woman*. I still haven't found a buyer for the Rembrandt, though two museum directors' are panting for the piece. One of them just needs to up the ante a bit. A fifty plus million dollar sale will deliver me a nice commission. Too bad the piece will most likely wind up in China.

Like my grandfather's gallery in Paris, the walls in the showroom are covered in burgundy velvet. My father, Émile, taught me that it shows off artwork best. To be honest, I don't know if I agree, but old habits die hard, even across generations. The walls in my private office are covered in burgundy, too. That's where the jewels of my collection hang. They include Fragonard's *Le Parasol de Mademoiselle Céleste* and Picasso's oil sketch for *Saltimbanques*, both gifts from my dad. Grandpa received the Picasso as a gift from the artist in the thirties. Neither piece is for sale. They'll be passed on to my children.

The conference room sits at the rear of the gallery. It's a glass-enclosed space, and with the flip of a switch, all four walls become opaque for privacy. The rear wall views the painting vault. Paintings not on display in the gallery hang on movable partitions that glide along steel tracks. This gives me the freedom to move paintings in front of clients without them having to budge from the conference room. I sometimes wonder what Grandpa Mori would say if he could see this space.

I pushed open the glass door, balancing a cup of coffee. "Hi, Lou."

She stood beside a black swivel chair on wheels. Her white gabardine pantsuit, accented with gold jewelry, was obviously tailored for her. It hugged her trim and tall figure perfectly. Her silver-blue eyes have always reminded me of the color the Impressionists used for skies.

"Good morning, Porter," she said, tossing her blond-streaked hair.

"Coffee?"

She held up her hand and shook her head.

"I don't think you've ever been to the gallery. This is a first," I said. "I thought you never left the museum."

She laughed.

"What brings you out on this beautiful day?" My guess was that she wanted to chat about the Rembrandt.

"Art," she says. "What else?"

"Okay," I say, chuckling. I slide into a chair across the table from her.

"The museum owns the Maji triptych," she says. "Well, two of the panels, anyway."

I raise an eyebrow. Not what I expected. "Yes, I'm familiar with them," I say. The panels depict the Gospel of Matthew's three wise men.

"The third has surfaced, and it would be wonderful for the museum to have all of them."

Fuck me. I paused for a moment, a bit speechless, but I was curious to find out where this was going. "So why are you telling me this?"

"I'm hoping you'll consider using your influence with one of your clients . . . to make the purchase for the museum's permanent collection." She pulled a large manila envelope from her briefcase and said, "Here," sliding it across the glass conference table.

"Why don't you tell me what's inside to save us time."

"Photos, testing results, carbon dating information, provenance, you name it. The piece is Greek, dates to at least the second century BC, and it's in pristine condition for its age."

"And you've inspected the piece?"

"I have."

"And it's the absolute mate of the two in the museum's collection?"

"It is," she said.

She was lying. The piece was a forgery and she knew it. I waited a moment, hoping some trace of doubt would appear on her face, but there was none. "Where is the piece now?"

"Here in New York."

"Who owns it?"

"Porter, you know I can't give you that kind of information. It's confidential. I will tell you it's a Middle Eastern investor."

"So, why me? I've already agreed to loan the museum a large collection early next year—not to mention the extended loan of *The Expulsion of Hagar.*"

She fidgeted with a button on her jacket.

"Has Jeffrey signed off on this?"

"Yes. He's initialed all of the reports, as well as signed the authentication letter."

Another lie. *How could she be so stupid?*

"And all those reports and signatures are in this packet?"

"Everything," she said.

"You haven't mentioned the price."

"I don't know, most likely in the four to six million dollar range."

"That's a big range, Lou."

"As I said, I don't know."

"What about commissions?" I asked. "Have you built in a commission for yourself?"

"I have."

And there it was. It was not a direct museum buy. She was soaking the museum for a commission. She had just blown it. I gazed at her, allowing my eyes to rest directly on hers. "Let me give this some thought," I said, staring right at her.

Lou stood. She cleared her throat and walked around the table toward me, her hand extended. "This could be something spectacular for the museum," she said.

I stood and shook her hand. "On another note," I said guiding her out of the conference room, "I've got a couple of transparencies in my office for Jeffrey. Would you mind?"

"Not at all, I'm on my way back to the Met from here."

Lou followed me past Pricilla's desk to the double doors that led to my office. I'm a gentleman. I stepped aside, allowing her to enter before me.

She took two steps before she let out a tiny gasp and stopped short.

"I'll just scoot by you," I said, strolling to my desk. I sat down, fumbled through some papers, then looked up at her.

"Porter," she said, but she seemed to have lost her words.

"Oh, do you like it?" I nodded toward the Maji Panel hanging over the sofa. "It dates to approximately two centuries BC."

Lou stood speechless, eyes glued to the panel.

"Jeffrey's always known where the third panel was," I said. "He's never shown any interest in it."

Lou sank into a side chair as though her body weighed a thousand pounds. She buried her face in the palm of her hand. "I'm guessing I'll be terminated immediately."

"Why? Because you just tried to swindle the biggest art dealer in New York, or because the biggest art dealer in New York is personal friends with the director of the Met, who just happens to be your boss?"

"Porter—" she began.

I held up my hand. "Save it, Lou. I think for now we can keep this conversation between the two of us."

She reached for the manila envelope with her documentation.

"No," I said. "I think I'll keep that. This could come in handy."

I slid the packet with Jeffrey Bell's forged signature on the falsified documents into the center drawer of my desk.

"I'm so sorry, Porter. I hope this won't alter your decision regarding the upcoming exhibition you're sponsoring?"

I'm not stupid. I knew I needed the Met as much as they needed me. The museum brings prestige to my gallery. I had no intention of burning any bridges. "My commitment is sound," I said. Momentarily I glance up at *The Expulsion of Hagar* that hangs on the wall across from my desk. It's the copy my father painted as his acceptance to the École de Beaux Arts as a young man. The original is tucked safely away in the storage room.

Lou sighed. She looked so small sitting there in my office, a child in trouble.

"But, rather than the Met hanging the show," I said, "I'd like to do it myself."

She raised her eyebrows. "That's highly unusual."

I gave her the most disingenuous smile I could muster. "I'm sure you can make that work," I said.

She stood, defeated. "Of course, whatever you wish."

She walked to the door then turned back toward me. "This probably isn't the right time, but the insurance company will want to inspect *The Expulsion of Hagar* since it's going to be on permanent display.

"You're correct. It's not the right time. And it's only being loaned. I paused for a moment and took a deep breath. "The insurance company can come here anytime they want to see the painting."

I tilted my head, indicating she should leave.

Saturday, January 22, 2000

Claire and I walk up the steps to the Metropolitan Museum like we own the place. Perhaps for this evening we do. Earlier today there was a dusting of snow from skies that resembled smeared charcoal, but that has now given way to a blanket of stars. What could be more fitting than a heavenly occurrence on this special evening?

I hear the rustle of Claire's gown as we walk—layer upon layer of blue tulle under the most beautiful shade of cobalt silk. The draping of diamonds and sapphires at her throat is nothing less than regal.

"What time is Dad getting here?" I ask.

"I told the driver to pick him up at eight. He'll come through the service entrance. The front steps are too difficult for him." Claire says.

"You think of everything."

She's radiant tonight. I love her so much. I squeeze her hand. "Are you ready, Mrs. Roth?"

Claire flashes me a million dollar smile and fluffs her full skirt before we walk through the entrance doors.

In the large stone rotunda, guests are gathered for cocktails and hors d'oeuvres. The party will remain outside the exhibition hall until nine o'clock, when the collection will be unveiled. At the far end, a large band is playing music from The Great American Song Book, favorites of Claire's—Cole Porter, Gershwin, both George and Ira.

We spot our children, Mathew and Emily, the moment we walk through the doors. Halfway across the hall, we exchange long hugs and kisses. They're both in college in other cities, so their presence tonight is a wonderful treat for a pair of empty nesters.

"Congratulations, Pop," Mathew says. Emily tells me she's proud of me. That's something I would normally be saying to her. I adore having them near me.

It's an evening of smiles. Mine's so wide, it hurts.

"I've got some schmoozing to do here. You guys have fun. We'll catch up at home later."

Claire and I meander through a sea of well-wishers, stopping for the occasional photo. Jeffrey Bell, the director of the Met, is in his glory. A crowd surrounds him like he's royalty. I wave from across the foyer. He throws a wide smile back in my direction.

Then I see Lou Nelson. She stands at the far corner of the room, as far as one could possibly get from the entrance, and from Jeffrey, her boss. Nothing happens here without her knowledge. She vets everything that comes and goes from the institution. Lou's taste and understanding of art are impeccable. Less impeccable are her ethics.

From across the room Lou spots me, shoots me a tentative smile, and returns to her chat with a couple of board members. She will, however, be aware of my presence and location in the room the entire evening. I'm curious to see how long it takes for her to approach me, and how quickly she makes her escape afterward.

When the band begins playing "Night and Day," Claire leans in and squeezes my arm. "There's your dad," she says.

"I'll go get him," I say and kiss Claire on the cheek. "See you in a few minutes."

My father is all smiles.

Dad doesn't get out much these days. Walking is a bit difficult for him and his eyes are beginning to fail.

"Are you hungry?" I ask him.

"No, I'm fine," he says. "You have guests, go socialize."

At nine o'clock an announcement invites the guests into the Roth exhibition. Claire and I hold hands while carrying stemmed wine glasses as we walk the long hall toward the gallery. Above the arched stone entrance, large polished brass lettering reads, *The Roth Collection.* I've got to admit, it's a bit of a thrill. If my father hadn't changed our name from Rothstein to Roth when we arrived in this country, the lettering would have been a lot smaller and certainly less impressive. Our friends, museum patrons, clients, and guests file into the large, dramatic art gallery with its burgundy walls— my selection, of course.

Large, dimly lit crystal chandeliers glow in the upper area of the gallery. Spotlights are positioned on forty-eight master paintings that include works by Renoir, Monet, Pissarro, Caravaggio, Rembrandt, Goya, Hals, Vermeer, and Titian.

With trays of champagne glasses, waiters stand at attention at both ends of the space.

"May I have your attention, please?" Jeffrey Bell says from a podium at the far end of the chamber.

The buzz in the room quiets.

"It's my honor and delight to welcome you to the Met this evening," Jeffrey says. "We are graced by your presence at the openingof this monumental showcase of painting at its finest. Because of the generosity of Porter Roth, we're able to share a collection that has rarely been seen by the public and certainly not ever in one place at the same time.

"Now it's my pleasure and privilege to introduce my friend, Porter Roth."

I walk to the podium. People clap and cheer, which sends heat up into my face. I'm sure my cheeks are crimson.

I stand in front of a burgundy velvet drape that hides the gem of this collection and raise my hands to quiet everyone down so I can be heard.

"I'm a little nervous this evening," I say. That's not a lie. I can feel a swirl of butterflies taking flight in my stomach. I breathe in deeply, "I have made it my life's work to bring fine art to as many people as possible. As you know, Claire and I sponsor education programs in our city in the hope of inspiring young talent to either take up the brush, or to educate future generations about the world's history through painting and sculpture."

My mouth is dry. I pause and wish I had a glass of water. I can't believe I've gotten this far without tripping over my tongue.

"The collection you're enjoying this evening will remain here for the next two years for the people of New York and its visitors to experience."

I can see Claire nodding to me from across the room. She has no idea of what's coming next. I suck in a deep breath.

"May I share a story with you?" I say to the crowd. I see nods in the audience. "My grandparents, parents and my uncle fled Paris during World War II. At that time, my father was a student at the École des Beaux-Arts, one of the most prestigious art academies in the world, and he won many awards for his work. He dreamed of becoming a great artist but that dream ended when Hitler invaded France."

My father sits near the front, his eyes on me.

"During those tumultuous years, my grandfather promised to guard Caravaggio's *The Expulsion of Hagar* for his friend Paul Betone. In addition to that painting, my grandfather, with the expert help of my father Émile, who is here tonight, saved a number of paintings stolen by the Germans from Jews living in Paris."

Another round of applause. I hold up a hand until the crowd quiets and I can continue.

"We were some of the lucky ones. Our family survived the

hardships of the occupation. Many didn't."

"If I may, I would like to honor my father this evening for saving Caravaggio's masterwork, by loaning it to the museum indefinitely. It will hang here safely . . . until Mr. Betone claims it. After the war my father searched for the man, but failed to locate him or any of his relatives. Surely he must have perished. Still, the painting is not mine to donate, only to keep safe."

I pull gently at a gold silk cord, releasing the burgundy velvet drape in front of the painting. The fabric falls silently in folds on the parquet floor.

First there is silence, which is followed by an eruption of applause and cheering. My heart is singing as I wait a long moment for the noise to dissipate.

"I'm grateful to share this evening with all of you and with my father." He waves to me and smiles. I motion to him. "Dad, come join me. If it were not for you, this masterpiece wouldn't be here tonight."

This once-vibrant man, now eighty six, moves forward slowly.

"Dad, let me help you," Claire says. She takes his arm. I step forward, "No, let me." I lean in so no one else can hear me. "Congratulations," I whisper. "You're famous now."

He looks at me with an expression that says, what are you talking about? He hasn't noticed the surprise I have for him. But, he will.

He walks forward and stands within inches of *The Expulsion*.

Holding onto his cane with one hand, he unbuttons his tuxedo jacket, and removes his reading glasses from the inside breast pocket. He slips the tortoise shell frames onto the bridge of his nose and tips his head forward. He draws closer still to the canvas. He squints. His index finger dances in the air for a moment and rests in front of the satchel Hagar's son, Ishmael, carries.

"The straps," he whispers.

The three extra straps Émile had painted when he'd copied the masterpiece as an acceptance project for the École des Beaux-Arts are there in front of him.

Dad turns, appearing weak and searches for a nearby chair. He sits, his head cocked to one side, a questioning expression on his face. I nod and kneel in front of him.

My father clasps my hands and gives me a conspiratorial smile. His eyes well with tears and he begins to weep.

… To Be Continued

ACKNOWLEDGEMENT

My warmest thanks for ongoing and invaluable support, as well as advice, to Lou Nelson who shared her gift of writing and guided my words to paper; Tony Tetro for revealing his secrets of master painting; Laura Taylor for her assurance that I was on the right track; Nomi Isak whose counseling helped bring my characters to life; Kristin Lindstrom whose direction tied my manuscript into its final form; and to my sister Judy Whitmore, who badgered, pestered, nagged, and most of all encouraged me to bring my story to fruition.

28152634R00202

Made in the USA
Lexington, KY
11 January 2019